03/22

W9-BCZ-714

# Remember Me Gone

# Remember Me Gone

BY **STACY STOKES**

VIKING

VIKING
An imprint of Penguin Random House LLC, New York

First published in the United States of America by Viking,
an imprint of Penguin Random House LLC, 2022

Copyright © 2022 by Stacy Stokes

Visit us online at penguinrandomhouse.com.

Library of Congress Cataloging-in-Publication Data is available.

Manufactured in Canada

ISBN 9780593327661 (Hardcover)

1 3 5 7 9 10 8 6 4 2

ISBN 9780593524169 (International Edition)

1 3 5 7 9 10 8 6 4 2

FRI

Edited by Liza Kaplan
Design by Ellice M. Lee
Text set in Bell MT Pro

*For my mother, always*

*People come from everywhere to forget.*

I set down the pitcher of water I'm holding and step off the porch. A cloud of dust kicks up behind a rust-colored station wagon making its way up our drive. It slides next to the other cars lined up on our front yard. The large woman hunched behind the steering wheel looks no different from the rest of the folks who make the pilgrimage here: tired from a long drive, heavy with unwanted memories, and badly in need of a pee.

I squint against the glare of the sun to get a better look at the license plate. Vivi told me and Mama not to hold our breath— Hawaii and Alaska are too far, even for the most memory-burdened people. But I think one day someone from every single state will show up, ready to bury whatever it is that called them to make the long drive to Tumble Tree, Texas.

"Oklahoma," I say when I finally read the plate.

We stopped counting the Oklahomas years ago, once the tick marks filled up an entire page of my notebook. Oklahoma's a decent hike from Tumble Tree—seven hundred and twenty-nine miles, to be exact—but it's not far enough to earn another page in my notebook. Not by a long shot. Hell, I'd take a Louisiana or even a Kentucky over *Oklahoma*. Mama used to say that Oklahoma was about as exciting as Tumble Tree, and there's nothing here but dirt, dust, and dusty dirt. I touch the ring on my right hand—the promise ring Dad gave Mama when she first came to Tumble Tree—and picture her rolling her eyes at the plate.

The woman kicks open her car door and slowly pushes herself out, straining against the seat like it's got hands. A few candy wrappers and an empty bag of Cheetos spill out with her onto the gravel. I can tell by her wrinkled nose that the Memory House isn't what she expected. That, or maybe she didn't think it would already be north of ninety degrees this early in the day.

"Lucy!"

I jump. Vivi's standing on the sagging front porch, left hand perched on the hips of a too-snug blue dress, looking at me like it's my fault it's squeezing her too hard. Sometimes I think the only reason she has such a tiny waist is because she jams her fists into her sides all the time. She likes to brag to people in town about being Dad's *administrative assistant*, but that title would only be accurate if it meant that her sole purpose was to assist my dad in administrating *me*. Not that I can blame her for bragging about her job—it beats the heck out of working at the mines with the rest of the folks in town.

I make a show of trudging up the steps, not caring that the swarm of people waiting to meet with Dad are all watching.

Vivi nods to the pitcher of water sweating on the porch where I left it. "What exactly is it that you're doing, Lucy? These poor people are hot and thirsty. Where are your manners? Are you waiting for me to do your chores for you now?" She motions to the cast covering her right arm, like I'm not fully aware that it's broken. Like she hasn't been waving it at me all summer.

"I was gonna get to it in just a second."

What I want to ask, though, is why I'm still being forced to play waitress when it's supposed to be the first day of my apprenticeship. Shouldn't I be doing something more important, like observing Dad work or clearing my head for the afternoon? But I know better than to backtalk this early in the day. It puts Vivi in a foul temper, and there's nothing worse than a foul-tempered Vivi.

The Oklahoma woman finally reaches the house and lets out a long huff of air, like the short walk took the wind right out of her. Her cheeks flare pink in the heat. I move aside so she can finish climbing the steps. Her eyes scan the cluster of people sweating on the porch and she pauses, looking for a minute like she might bolt.

Vivi breaks her glare with me long enough to give the woman one of her sticky-sweet smiles.

"Welcome! I assume you're here to see Mr. Miller?"

The woman nods, eyes resting on the paint-chipped sign hanging above the paint-chipped front door: MR. MILLER'S HOUSE OF UNWANTED MEMORIES.

**3**

Repaint the house: that's one of the first things I'm gonna have fixed once I start bringing in money around here.

"Well, you've come to the right place. If you don't mind waiting"—Vivi motions toward the cluster of people that disappears with the wraparound porch—"we'll be by shortly to take down your information." Her eyes snap back to mine. "And Lucy here will come by with something cold to drink. Please, make yourself at home. There are folding chairs along the side of the house if you'd prefer to sit."

"Thank you, ma'am." The Oklahoma woman looks down at her feet, then back up at us. "Is there, uh, a restroom I can use?"

"Of course." Vivi smiles again, then nods her head at me so I know that it's my job to show the woman where it is. As if I needed reminding.

"This way," I say with a sigh.

The woman follows me to the back of the house and I point to the small white clapboard building Dad erected a few years back. It looks one sneeze away from toppling over, but it's clean. I know because I'm the one who cleaned it.

"Don't worry," I say when the woman hesitates. "It's an eyesore, but it's nice inside. It has a fan so it's not so stuffy."

She nods but stays rooted in place.

"Ma'am, is everything all right?"

She looks at me, eyebrows pinched and mouth curved down, and I swear I can see the sadness pressing her into the dirt. Her shoulders curl and her face droops under the weight of it. She has the look of a person who lost someone important. I know that look as well as I know the feeling of standing on my own two legs. Plus, we get a lot of those around here.

"Does it hurt?" she finally asks, purse clutched tight to her chest like a shield. "When Mr. Miller takes the memories away?"

"No, ma'am," I say, even though I can't say that I know what it feels like firsthand. But I know the way people look afterward, and there's not a trace of pain on their faces. "It's . . . peaceful. People always leave here looking happy. I promise, you'll feel much better afterward. Like a weight you didn't realize you'd been carrying's been lifted."

I want to tell her that what my dad does is beautiful. I want to tell her that people go home looking like they might just float straight up to the clouds, as if the burdens they brought with them were anvils that my dad snipped away, one by one. I want to tell her how I'm gonna be just like Dad, but instead I smile at her and nod toward the bathroom because she looks like she's about to burst.

"My name's Lucy, if you need anything," I add. Then I turn and make my way back toward the house, resisting the urge to run.

Because as soon as I finish my chores, I'm going to take my first memory.

I press my ear against the door to Dad's workroom, listening for the rumble of voices on the other side. Sometimes it takes a few hours for him to clear one person's burdens. Other times it's a matter of minutes. Dad says some memories are so deeply buried that you've got to keep tugging at all the roots and pieces before they'll break free. Others flow right into his head, like water to a sponge.

All I hear is quiet.

I wait a few more seconds. When I'm sure no one else is inside, I twist the handle and step into the small room. Dad's in his usual spot behind a large wooden desk, the remnants of a sandwich laid out before him. Next to his chair there's a half-torn cardboard box holding a plastic globe, a Tupperware full of cookies, and what looks like a ceramic garden gnome—most likely his last patient's way of skirting full payment. Next to that is another box filled with the empty jars he'll use to transfer the memories. Dad's pay-what-you-can approach is the reason our house looks like something that should be bulldozed. It doesn't matter how many times I tell him to toughen up, all it takes is a pair of sad eyes and a sob story and he's willing to cut the price in half, like discounts and junk are gonna fix the front porch. What in the world are we supposed to do with a garden gnome?

I clear my throat.

When he looks up, the crease between his eyebrows deepens.

"Something wrong, Lucy?"

"It's Thursday. After lunch. Remember?"

I feel a familiar pinch in my chest at dad's expression. His eyebrow crease becomes a canyon.

"You forgot." I don't add *again*, even though I'm thinking it. I just sit down on the peeling leather chair in front of his desk and set my notebook on my lap, pen at the ready. He's not getting rid of me this time. "That's okay. What matters is that I'm here, it's Thursday, and you promised."

"Oh." His eyes dart around the room, avoiding my face. "Look, I'm not sure that . . . it's just . . . today's just not . . . tomorrow might be bett—"

"You *promised*."

He sucks in a breath like he's planning to say something else, but I don't let him.

"What would Mama say if she knew you were going back on your word?"

If I want to get technical about it, he already broke his word by putting me off for as long as he has. I turned sixteen over a week ago. But he slumps back in his chair, defeat clouding his dark eyes, so I don't press. He's probably thinking of Mama and the way she used to dance around the Memory House like it was a place to be revered. She thought memory-taking was beautiful. And just like me, she'd probably be shaking her head and clucking her tongue with frustration at the way Dad keeps acting like sixteen's still not old enough. Like I don't know what it's like to deal with sadness. And burdens.

Dad's gaze shifts from the framed picture of Mama on his desk to the window. Just beneath it is the line of people waiting for his help, melting in the afternoon sun. They deserve to be seen quickly instead of waiting for days on end to have their sadness taken away. And with me working the family business, too, we can make that happen faster. They deserve *our* help, not just Dad's.

"Maybe I can try on one of the people outside?" I suggest. "Help the line along? Every week it seems like more and more people show up. You need my help, Dad. You can't keep doing it on your own." My voice is gentle even though I'm dying to scream at him. Even though I'm dying to remind him that I've been pretty darn patient (all things considered), and a promise is a promise.

Dad pinches the soft skin between his eyes and sighs. Then he motions for me to sit on the couch on the opposite wall. Slowly, he makes his way there, and I practically leap over to the couch to sit beside him.

"I know you think it's all glitz and glory, Lucy, but memory-taking wears on you. Even your great-great-great-grandpa knew that when he first started." He motions to the wall behind his desk, where a grainy sepia-toned photograph of Grandpa Miller hangs. In it, he's standing in front of the newly built Memory House, a big smile on his face like he knows he's about to change the lives of thousands of people for the better. It makes my heart feel all fuzzy with pride when I think about carrying on his legacy and the legacy of all the Miller men who followed.

"I know it's not always easy, Dad. People don't come here asking us to take the good stuff away. They give us their sadness. Which means that I'll have to feel their sadness when I take it from them. I get it. I've been watching you do it for as long as I can remember.

But I want to help people. I want to be like you. It's what our family does—we help people."

I think about how heavy Dad sometimes looks after an especially long unburdening, like the weight's been transferred to more than just his shoulders. But isn't it our job to take away their pain, even if it means we have to experience a little of it? And it's not like I don't know what it's like to be sad or what it's like to miss someone so hard that some days I can barely stay upright.

There's another long sigh, but I can see him waning.

I lean forward.

"Please, Dad. I'm ready. I've been ready. I can handle this. I want to help people like you do. It's all I've ever wanted."

*It's what Mama wanted, too,* I think but don't say.

His nod is so subtle I nearly miss it, but it's there. And I'm so excited I'm pretty sure I could light up a Christmas tree if you plugged one into me.

Then he takes a deep breath. "Okay. But best you try it on me the first time."

# 2

"On you?" I ask, unable to mask my disappointment. I'd much rather take a memory from one of the people waiting outside, but I suppose practicing on Dad isn't the worst thing in the world. I don't want to be all giddy and unprofessional in front of a stranger the first time I do it. Or worse, take something I'm not supposed to.

"It's easier that way. It's how I learned—I practiced on my father and he practiced on his father, and so on down the line. It's a family rite of passage. How about you try to make me forget what I had for lunch?" Dad leans forward and whispers conspiratorially. "It was one of Vivi's tuna fish sandwiches. You'd be doing me a favor."

I smile. Vivi's tuna fish tastes more like the tin can it comes out of than something that used to swim in the ocean.

"Okay, sure."

"Good. Now, it's important that you ask them what they *want* to forget—the words matter. We never take a memory without someone wanting us to, understand?"

I nod. I can't imagine anyone ever doing something so awful as taking someone's personal thoughts without permission. But still, I can't shake the grin from my face. Growing up, Dad never let me into his office to watch him work. I feel like I'm finally being let in on the family secret.

Dad scoots closer to me. "Eye contact is the most important part. It's what helps you find the memory, but it's also what helps the memory find *you*. You can't break away until you have a hold of the memory inside your mind."

"Okay. But how will I know when I have the memory? And what if I grab the wrong one?"

"You won't. When it comes to unwanted memories, people aren't that different—their minds are almost always ready to hand over their burdens. Once the memory finds you, you'll feel a sort of catch inside your head. Then you won't really see it so much as feel it, though sometimes you get flashes of the person in that moment or blurry snatches of a visual, kind of like they're showing you a smeary snapshot. It's a little disorienting at first, but you get used to it."

I nod. "How long will it take?"

"Depends. For simple memories, like what I ate for lunch today, maybe just a few seconds. But if someone wants to forget something that happened to them a long time ago, or something they've seen over and over again, or even a person, it can take much longer to pull out all the pieces. But the pieces will come loose. They always do."

He sounds sad when he says the last sentence, and for the first time I notice how tired he looks. Puffy half-moons circle his blood-shot eyes, making me wonder if he's been getting enough sleep. It makes me think of his earlier warning—the toll that memory-taking has on you.

"How will I know when I've got all the pieces?"

He shrugs, eyes trailing toward the window like he can see all the people waiting down below.

"You just know. There are really only three types of memo-ries most people want to get rid of—memories defined by grief, regret, or guilt—and each type of memory has its own feeling and color. When you stop seeing that color, you know the person's been cleared. Plus you can feel the relief when they've finally let go of all the things that've been weighing them down. Especially if it's a guilty memory. Those are the worst, but thankfully they're also usually the easiest to remove." He swallows hard. "It's tough to explain, you just have to experience it."

I try to look like everything he's saying makes total sense, but my mind is racing.

Dad reaches across the table for his glass of water and takes a sip. Outside, someone coughs.

"'Course sometimes people subconsciously hide things, and that's when we get the Echoes. But those are rare. Most people are all too ready to let go of the burdens they've been dragging around."

I nod once, following his gaze to the window. I know all about Echoes because when they arrive I'm usually the first person who has to deal with them. Fortunately, we haven't had an Echo in months. Our website tells everyone to get rid of any significant physical objects or photographs tied to the memories they want to erase before they come here, but people don't always listen. Or sometimes, they think they've gotten rid of everything, but then they'll stumble on a picture or a trinket that will give way to a memory shard, and then they eventually wander back here, looking for something they lost. Only they can't quite remember what it is or why they think they'll find it in Tumble Tree.

"Anyway, we don't need to worry about that for now. You ready to give it a try on me?"

My heart squeezes—from nerves, excitement, or both—and I nod my head yes.

"Take my hands." Dad scooches closer and floats his downturned palms in front of me. They're cold despite the warmth in the room and the blazing sun outside. "Remember, don't break eye contact until you feel the catch."

I nod and look directly into his eyes, brown unlike my own gray ones. I have Mama's eyes. I have her unruly dark hair, too, and I have to shake my head to keep it from falling in my face and obstructing my view.

He blinks once, and when he finally matches my gaze, his pupils are open windows, beckoning me inside.

I don't blink. I don't think. I just close my fingers more tightly around his hands, tip my chin up, and repeat the words he taught me to say.

"Tell me what you want to forget."

For a moment there's nothing. Just the tick of the barely work-ing fan outside and the squeak of the wooden porch slats as people shift their weight impatiently.

Then I feel a tiny catch inside my brain, like a finger snagging on a piece of cloth. And then, as if the cloth is being slid away, an image slowly flickers and takes shape on the center of a stage inside my mind. At first the edges are frayed, tangled, but slowly it becomes more solid, until finally the picture unrolls around me so that I'm no longer staring into my dad's eyes. Instead, I'm staring at two slices of wheat bread with oozing bits of mayonnaise and tuna fish leaking out the sides. Then just as quickly the picture swirls away, smearing into fog, and I have the sensation of falling, chewing, swallowing, and of filling myself up with something I'd rather not be eating. There's a flash of green, bright as a star in the night sky, and the smears turn green, the stage turns green, my thoughts turn green, and I'm struck with a feeling that can only be described as regret.

*Regret is green.*

That's when I realize what's happening: just like Dad said, the memory is swirling past me, tinted by the feeling of regret that he wants me to take away. I can feel everything—from the hunger that made him eat the sandwich in the first place, to the dissatisfac-tion of eating something I'd rather not be eating. It's like listening to a song—notes and chords and rippling waves of sensation that I can't see, but I can feel.

It's incredible.

I blink and something changes. The stage goes dark and then there's another flash of light, only this time it's a deep, dark red.

My body goes cold all over.

A different image takes shape on the stage in my mind, this time of Mama's face. She's looking backward out a rearview mirror, her lips pressed together in a frown.

*Flash.*

Everything inside my head—the stage, the image of my mother—glows a deep and angry red. The air around me turns to ice, and suddenly I'm filled with a horrible, empty sensation that slices straight through me.

Guilt.

It's everywhere—raw, angry, and undeniable.

I let out a little gasp without meaning to, and suddenly it all slips away from me. The red guilt-streaked image of Mama's face morphs into a green regret-tinted snapshot of the tuna fish sandwich, which quavers and shifts into tiny wisps of smoke before disappearing completely.

Then I'm back on the couch, looking at Dad's slack-jawed face.

"Luce?" He pulls his hands free from mine and places them on my shoulders. "Lucy? Are you okay?"

My hands are shaking. A line of sweat slides between my shoulder blades and down my back. My pulse hammers inside of my head. *Red means guilt.*

"I . . . What just happened? Did I do something wrong?"

Dad's face scrunches up in confusion and he shakes his head. "I don't think so. What did you see?"

"I—I saw the sandwich. And everything went green just like you said, and I could feel the regret surrounding the memory you wanted me to take. But then . . ." I swallow, unable to get the rest of the words out.

*But then I saw Mama. She turned red with your guilt.*

Only that doesn't make any sense. Why would Dad feel guilty about Mama?

Dad's nodding, smiling at me. "That's right. That's great, Luce. That's exactly what you should see. Except—" He stops, pinching the crease in his brow the way he always does when he's puzzling something out.

And I realize his blank expression can only mean one thing: It worked! He's trying to figure out what the heck I'm talking about but can't remember eating lunch because I took the memory away from him!

"It's okay, Dad. You're just confused because I—"

"Hang on." He looks at me, hard. "You felt the sensations I would have felt when eating lunch?" His brow creases more deeply at my bobbing head. "Then I shouldn't be able to remember it. If it happened the way you say it happened, then the memory should be gone. It should be yours now. Huh."

"What do you mean, 'huh'? It worked, didn't it?"

He shrugs. "I don't know, Luce. It doesn't always work the first time. But let's try getting rid of it. If you were able to take even a part of the memory, you should be able to get rid of it, too. It's important that you not hold on to any of the burdens people give you for too long."

He presses an empty jar into my hands and explains how to push the memory into it.

"We have to get rid of them," he says, as if I don't already know, "so that the memories don't start weighing us down."

I take the jar from him, place my hands over the open lip, and close my eyes just like he showed me, trying to recall the green-tinted image of his lunch. I will the memory out of my mind and into the empty vessel, picturing the fragments of green and red sliding neatly inside. When I open my eyes, the jar's still empty and Dad's face is folded in a sympathetic frown.

"Don't worry about it, Luce. It was your first time. If you saw everything the way you described it, then you were close. You just must have lost the connection before removing it. We can try again tomorrow. Sometimes it takes a little practice."

My shoulders sag when I realize what he's saying.

"Are you sure?" I ask, even though the empty jar in my hands is proof enough that I didn't take the memory from him.

"I'm sure. I'm sorry, Luce, but I can still see the whole thing in my brain, plain as day. Sharp as a tack, actually. But don't worry about it. It's perfectly normal not to take a memory on your first try. We'll try again tomorrow."

I sigh. "I must have done something wrong." That's the only way to explain Mama's face and the red-tinged guilt I felt inside Dad.

He pats my hand and offers another sympathetic frown. "It took me several tries before I got the hang of it, and your grandpa told me it took your great-grandpa a half dozen or so times. You'll get it just like everyone else in the family has."

"How can you be so sure?" I ask.

Dad gives me a sideways smile. "Because it's in your blood. It's what our family does, Luce. It's what we've always done. You'll be able to do it, too. I'm sure of it. You just need a little practice."

I look down at my fingernails. Dad's right; we've had five generations of memory-takers in the Miller family. There's no real reason to think I might not be able to unburden people, too. Except—except the Millers have always been boys. What if I'm different? What if I can't take memories because I'm not one of the Miller men?

Outside, someone coughs again. The porch fan ticks. The afternoon sun streams in through the open curtains. Despite the heat, I shiver, as though the cold from the red guilt-tinged memory is tiptoeing down my spine. I *have* to take memories. It's what I'm meant to do.

"Don't worry," Dad says again. "We'll give it another shot tomorrow. It will come, you'll see. I promise."

I give a small smile and do my best to shake off the doubts that begin to poke at me.

He's right. I must not have done it correctly, and that's why things looked so strange.

I just need more practice, that's all.

# 3

*My room is a riot of color, the walls covered from baseboard to ceiling* with maps, pictures of cities cut from magazines, pages ripped from travel books, and a few old license plates I found years ago at a flea market near El Paso. On the slanted ceiling, I've pinned up Mama's old map of North America and marked it with about a dozen or so stars peppering the state of Texas—there's one for Tumble Tree, and one for each of the other places I've been. Which isn't really that impressive, since I've never left the state.

Someday the whole map will be filled with stars. Someday I'll visit every single state from every single license plate that's ever parked in my front yard. I'm even gonna see Hawaii and Alaska, regardless of whether or not someone from those states comes to see Dad. Just the way Mama always said we would.

There's a quick knock on my door and then it swings open to reveal Vivi, hand on her hip. She looks overdone as usual—prim updo, bright pink lipstick, and perfectly tailored sheath dress that makes her stick out in Tumble Tree like a polka-dotted zebra. She doesn't even wait for me to tell her to come in before she's across the threshold and staring down at me.

Once upon a time, I wouldn't have minded if Vivi walked into my room without permission. I would have jumped off my bed and followed her downstairs, where Mama would have been waiting at the dining room table with a stack of cards, a notepad, and a gin rummy challenge in her eyes. They'd let me win a round, but Vivi would come out on top. My mama's best friend always came out on top.

Once upon a time, I had a mother. But no matter how hard Vivi tries, she will never be able to replace her.

"I've been looking for you. I thought you were going to take the trash down to the dumpsters after you finished with your father. It's starting to smell. Do you want your dad's guests to think we're pigs? I swear, your head is going to float up to the clouds one of these days."

I keep my eyes pinned to the ceiling, trailing the squiggle of highway that runs from Dallas to San Antonio. We went to San Antonio when I was five, but we never made it as far north as Dallas.

"I'll do it in a minute."

I try to sound tough, but we both know it's easier to do what Vivi asks than to argue with her. When she decides she wants something she's as relentless as a July desert. That's how she ended up working with my father. After my mama died, she kept showing up at our house with casseroles, tuna fish sandwiches, pecan pies from Patty's Pie Pantry, a stack of cards and a promise to let me win one round, a movie for my dad she promised he would love. Until one day she wasn't just dropping off food and promises—she was running the place. And sure, she's good at it. The place would have probably fallen apart if it had all been left to Dad and me. But that doesn't mean Dad needs her here twenty-four seven. And it certainly doesn't mean I want her here, hovering over me every single day like it's part of her job description, too.

"Lucy, please." She taps the toe of her shoes—stilettoes, always—and glares down at me, making it clear that she's not moving until I do. "I could really use your help. Plus, I'm not paying you to lie around all day."

I clench my teeth and finally push myself up from the bed. She's lucky I want a car badly enough to put up with minimum wage and her bossing me around all summer. As soon as I've saved enough to buy one, I'm finally going on a road trip, just the way Mama and I always planned.

"Make sure to refill everyone's water on your way out," she says to my back. "And offer them a snack—there's a fresh tray of cookies in the kitchen."

Outside, I weave my way through the crowd, filling empty glasses. I swear the line's nearly doubled in length since last week. We don't spend much on advertising outside of our website and a few billboards that run along I-10, but it seems like more and more people come every day. Maybe word of mouth has picked up. Or maybe it's just the state of the world these days; maybe people just have more burdens than they used to.

The porch fan has now puttered out completely, so I pull the cord free from the wall and hide it inside the front hallway. As if it's not bad enough that everyone has to stand outside sweating their brains out, I don't want to taunt them with false hope that the fan will kick back on and offer some relief. Vivi will have to get a new one the next time she goes to the Walmart outside of El Paso. Or she'll just make me go since I do most of the errands round here. It's almost enough to make me miss the school year, when Vivi hires a few part-time folks from town to do chores during the week.

The Oklahoma woman nods gratefully when I come by to fill her glass and offer the cookies. She's seated on one of the foldout chairs fanning herself with a torn paperback book.

"You have any idea how much longer it's gonna be?" she asks me, furiously beating the book back and forth in case I didn't get the message that she's hot. "Seems like there's an awful lot of people here waiting."

I glance down the line. There are a little over two dozen people ahead of her. If their burdens are light, she could be in to see Dad toward the end of the day. But one glance at the burly man standing near the front of the line tells me that won't be the case. Loss is etched in the deep lines around his face, the slope of his shoulders, and the heavy way he sags against the porch. His pain runs too deep to be taken care of quickly. It'll probably take Dad the rest of the afternoon and a dozen or so jars to clear just him.

"It's hard to say how long it will take," I lie, remembering Vivi's

number one rule when managing the guests—don't give any spe-
cifics. The guests get all riled up if things end up taking longer
than we say. "We'll spend as long as needed to help someone forget
their burdens, but each person's a little bit different, so we never
really know. Did Vivi give you the information for the Tumble Inn
up the road when you checked in?"

The woman nods, craning her neck. "Yeah, she told me. I just
figured . . . it's so hot out. Maybe I can go inside for a spell?"

"Sorry, ma'am. There's not enough room to fit everyone inside
the house and it's not fair to pick and choose who gets to come in.
But if you want a rest, you can try Patty's Pie Pantry downtown.
It's about a mile and a half up the main road. They make a great
slice of pecan. But if your name gets called while you're gone, we'll
have to move to the next person in line."

"Can't you just call me or something?"

"No, ma'am, sorry. It's a dead zone around here. You have to
go to the next town over to get any kind of signal, and that's a
few miles away. We'll just let the next person go to keep things
moving. But you can have your spot back when you return. Don't
worry—Vivi runs a tight ship."

She holds up her cell phone and squints at the screen. "What
about sending me an email? You got a Wi-Fi password I can use?"

"No, ma'am," I say. If Vivi had taken my advice and posted a
sign like I suggested, I wouldn't have to have this conversation
eighteen thousand times a day, with nearly every single guest.
"Like I said, it's pretty much a dead zone around here. They've got

internet down at the library, but it can be slow. And a few of the shops have Wi-Fi so they can run credit cards and whatnot, but the bandwidth is pretty limited."

She looks at me like she's just stepped into another dimension, which probably isn't too far off the mark. Tumble Tree's far enough out in the boondocks that even the telecom companies don't want to fuss with us. It's why most folks in town don't bother with cell phones, myself included.

Oklahoma huffs, and I move down the line before she can argue with me. I've seen her type before—they start off polite, but if they still haven't been seen by the second afternoon, they're demanding to see my dad and threatening to sue if we don't let them come into the house. Sometimes we have to call in the police, but usually Vivi can talk them down from their tantrums with her soul-sucking glare, a coupon for a free slice of pie at Patty's Pie Pantry, and the promise of a visit with my dad shortly.

Once all the glasses are filled, the plate of cookies is empty, and everyone has been assured that, yes, they will eventually get to see my father, I grab the trash from the back of the house and start hauling it up the road to the dumpster. It's about a quarter mile past our driveway, but on a day like today I might as well be hiking across the border. The sun is a punishment, and I have to stop every few feet to wipe the sweat out of my eyes. Even the prickly pears are perspiring.

Mr. Lewis is down by the mailbox, shoving a stack of envelopes into the rusted metal opening.

"Afternoon, Lucy," he says with a nod. "It sure is a hot one today."

This is what he says to me almost every time he sees me. Though there's not much else going on in Tumble Tree worth talking about other than the ever-present heat, so I can't fault him much. With Mr. Lewis it's either a comment on the weather, an update on his son, Otis, or both. Usually both.

"Yes, sir." I return his nod. "How're things with you?"

"Oh, fine. Just fine. Otis got promoted a few months ago to Tumble Tree Police Chief. Did I tell you that? The mayor himself appointed him. Ain't that something? Sure am proud of that boy."

"Congratulations. That's exciting." I don't add that he told me the exact same thing yesterday. I try not to make a habit of bursting people's bubbles.

"I reckon he'll do a fine job watching out for all of us. He's sure done a fine job taking care of me since he moved back here."

"I bet he has," I say.

"Well, you have a good day, now. Tell your father hi for me, won't you?"

"Sure thing, Mr. Lewis. You have a good day, too."

He climbs into his mail truck, and I keep my distance until the cloud of dirt that follows him down the driveway dies down.

I finally reach the dumpster and toss the retched-smelling bags inside, quick to let the lid slam down so I can back away from the flies that kick up into the air. I'm about to start the long trek back to the house when a ladybug lands on my knuckle and my breath hitches in my throat.

Memories flood in.

*Ladybug, time for bed.*

*Ladybug, the school bus is here.*

*Ladybug, I love you bigger than Texas. Bigger than all the stars in all the sky.*

*Ladybug, one day we'll fly away from here. We'll see the world. We'll leave this place to the dust and the lizards.*

Tiny legs tickle my skin as the ladybug traverses the peaks and valleys of my hand, and I wonder if it feels like it's climbing a mountain range. Maybe my hand is this ladybug's new red star on a map. Maybe she misses her mama, too.

Memories are funny things. The ones we want to keep fade, and the things we want to forget stay with us until my dad takes them away. I wish we could choose.

The ladybug makes it the rest of the way down my palm and across my wrist. I give her a gentle nudge and watch her fly in the direction of the sun, hoping she finds her way to a new adventure. Or maybe her way home.

I twist Mama's old ring, feeling its warmth against my skin, and decide to go to the park a ways up the road instead of heading straight back to the house. There's not much to see there—just a picnic table and a tire swing hanging from a sad excuse for a tree. But Mama used to take me there when I was little. We'd take turns spinning each other on the swing, tipping our heads back until the sky and clouds blurred around us and we were no longer stuck in this dusty desert border town, but twirling somewhere far away from here.

Gravel crunches under my feet as I round the bend that leads to the park. A sharp, high-pitched laugh cuts through the silent afternoon. I stop once the tree comes into view and I realize who the laugh is coming from.

Manuela sits on the tire swing, legs dangling out of a pair of ridiculously short cutoffs. Marco Warman, Vivi's son and the mayor's nephew, stands behind her with one hand perched on each chain. A swarm of ladybugs takes flight in my stomach at the sight of his smile. It looks like a crooked stretch of highway, the left side slightly longer than the right. You'd think between us going to school together and Vivi working at the Memory House that Marco and I would be more familiar, but the only thing familiar about him is the way he and his friends avoid me.

"Don't, Marco!" squeals Manuela in a way that makes it obvious she really wants him to spin her again.

His smile is a wicked thing as he tugs on the chains, tipping Manuela sideways so the tire twirls. She lets her head hang backward, laughing, and her long dark hair grazes the dusty ground. I hate that she's sitting on Mama's seat like she owns it.

I start to turn around before they see me, but it's too late. Marco catches my eye and straightens. His crooked smile falters. Manuela sees me a second later and puts her foot down on the ground to stop the swing from spinning.

"Lucy, hi." She says it as if I'm an old friend she hasn't seen in a while. When she smiles, her lips are a red smear against the blue sky, and it seems so clear why the Marcos and Manuelas of the world never want to hang out with me. She's New Orleans in the spring, flowers exploding like fireworks from windowsills; he's a busy street in New York City, lights flashing from a million directions at once. I'm Tumble Tree. Marfa. Luckenbach. Every small town between here and Oklahoma.

"Hi," I answer, a few beats too late. I'm suddenly aware of how knobby my knees must look sticking out from my shorts. "Sorry, I didn't realize someone was here. I was just taking out the trash."

I realize how silly this sounds a second before Manuela lets out a snort of laughter.

It's not that Manuela is mean—she's just like the other kids at school. They like that the Memory House makes Tumble Tree more than just another town along the empty stretch of highway leading to El Paso—that there's a reason for people to stop instead of pass through. But I know better than to mistake their polite smiles and "how are you"s for friendship. They think I act like I'm too good for them because I'm always talking about leaving Tumble Tree. That, and back in middle school, someone started a rumor that I could snatch things from people's heads without permission and it stuck, so most of them keep a wide berth. Which is fine by me. I'm not planning to stick around in this dust bowl long enough to need any real friends. If anything, they'd just complicate things. Because as soon as I graduate, I'm taking the Memory

House on the road. And maybe one day I'll build my own Memory House some place far from here, like Portland or Nashville. Tumble Tree can tumble away on a dust cloud for all I care.

Except I can't seem to ignore the tiny voice cawing at the back of my head: *What if you can't take memories? What if you're no different from Marco and Manuela and everyone else trapped in this dusty town?*

I swallow back the lump that forms in my throat and try to shake off the thoughts.

"So, how's your summer going?" Marco asks. The way he looks at me, it's like he actually cares about my answer. "You finally get a chance to take away some memories with your dad?"

His tone is not unkind, but my cheeks heat like I've been slapped. Because that's a weird thing to say. Can he see the failure on my face? And how does he even know? I try to remember if I told him about my plans for the summer before school let out. But that doesn't make sense. Why would I talk to Marco Warman? Or more specifically, why would Marco Warman talk to me? Vivi must have told him.

There's another flutter inside my stomach then, and for just a second, I get a flash of me sitting next to Marco at lunch, both of us laughing and leaning toward each other while his hand rests lightly on my knee. Sitting together the way that two people who are more than friends might.

But that's not right. Like everyone else in this wasteland, Marco keeps his distance. Never mind that he might be one of the few people I wouldn't mind standing a little closer to. Which makes me just as idiotic as the girls that cling to him—girls like Manuela. Marco's the kind of boy made for someplace far away from Tumble Tree—San Francisco, maybe. Or Los Angeles. Somewhere with music, lights, and an ocean nearby.

I realize then that they're both staring at me and that I never answered his question. To Marco's credit, he looks more concerned than afraid. But Manuela's stepped backward to put more space between us, like she believes the rumors that I can dig around inside her head from a distance.

I need to leave before I embarrass myself further.

"I should go," I tell them. "I'm supposed to—I need to—I should get back."

Before they can say anything else, I turn on my heel and run back to the house. Maybe this makes me look even weirder, but at least I don't have to look at Marco looking at me anymore.

Because just now he was looking at me like he could see my insides. Like he knows that I dream of highways and maps and faraway places.

He knows.

And that doesn't make any sense at all.

## 4

*When I make it back to the house, Vivi tells me she has to leave early.* Something about an appointment with her brother, the mayor. Which means that when closing time comes around, I'm the one who has to deliver the news to the waiting patients that they have to come back tomorrow.

The Oklahoma woman scowls at me as though we had some kind of agreement. A few people grumble about how long they've been waiting. But most of them shuffle off without much complaint, probably heading to the Tumble Inn, feet dragging behind them with the weight of everything they're hoping to forget. Once they've all gone for the evening, I stack the boxes of jarred burdens on the porch for collection. Dad pays a few folks from town to haul them off each night and bury them in the desert. There must be thousands of unwanted thoughts entombed in the Tumble Tree dirt, hidden there so folks don't accidentally open the jars and release the memories on themselves.

I remove one of the jars and hold it up the light, marveling at the miracle of what my dad does, of what *I'm* going to be doing soon enough. At least I hope. Inside, the memory swirls. It looks like a shimmering fog with a thicker dark cloud at the center, pulsing like heart. The dark part is the sadness, Dad reckons.

It was my great-great-great-grandpa Miller who discovered we could pull memories out of people. Before that, we came from a long line of listeners and empaths. People used to come from miles just to share their feelings with our family, saying they felt better after they'd gotten all their sadness off their chest. But it wasn't until Great-Great-Great-Grandpa Miller moved to Tumble Tree that he started removing the sad memories completely. No one really knows why or how. Maybe it was the desert heat that helped the memories take on a physical form. Or maybe it was Great-Great-Great-Grandpa Miller's own sadness that manifested the gift; Dad said he came here after the Civil War, looking to outrun his own burdens. Either way, the gift was born and the Memory House became our family legacy. Some days I feel like I might burst with pride from thinking about all the people we've helped throughout the years.

I place the jar back in the box and close the lid. Then I sweep the porch, put the folding chairs back against the side of the house, and head off to clean the latrine before going inside for the night.

Dad's already passed out on the couch.

I pull an afghan from the top of the hall closet and slip it over him, then kiss him lightly on the forehead.

"Night, Dad."

His nose twitches, but otherwise he's a motionless lump.

Upstairs, I climb into bed, pulling Mama's scrapbook from its resting spot on my nightstand. Something falls to the floor, and I bend to pick it up.

It's a necklace. I hold it up, watching the light dance off it. It's simple, but pretty—a thin chain with a single gold star charm hanging from the center. Someone must have dropped it while waiting in line and I forgot that I put it up here for safekeeping. Regardless, no one's come looking for it. And even if they do, there's no harm in me wearing it so it doesn't get lost again, right? I clasp it around my neck. There's something comforting about the way the charm rests against the hollow where my collarbones meet—almost like it was meant to be there.

I turn to Mama's road trip scrapbook, flipping through the pages that have gone soft from the millions of times my fingers have turned them. I stop on a photo of Mama standing in front of her old Buick, her arm slung over the shoulders of a woman covered from neck to wrist in tattoos. Underneath the photo her faded scrawl reads *San Francisco, California, Day 32*.

San Francisco is only 1,283 miles from here, but it might as well be on the moon based on Mama's photos and keepsakes from her time there. She has pictures of tattooed arms, pyramid-shaped skyscrapers, graffitied walls, rows of brightly colored Victorian-style houses, and trolley cars chugging up impossible hills. Mama's in all the photos, sometimes standing next to one of the people she met along the way, sometimes by herself, but always with her smile wide and her dark hair loose around her face, looking like something beautiful and untamed.

"There's so much world to see," she used to say. Her lips would curl into a smile. "Someday we'll see it all, Ladybug. We'll leave this place to the dust and the lizards and make a new home for ourselves somewhere."

On day ninety-five of her road trip across the country, Mama passed through Tumble Tree with plans to only stay the night— she wanted to see the Memory House and meet the man who took away people's heartache. But when she met Dad, the one night turned into days and the days turned into weeks. My mama, who never stayed in one place long enough to call it home, fell in love with a man who hadn't been much of anywhere outside of the small town he'd grown up in. And when she found out she was pregnant with me, she set the scrapbook aside. Guess that's what love does to people.

When I was little we used to do mini–road trips around Texas, but never ventured too far away from Tumble Tree. There was always school or business or something that called us back. Until the summer I turned eleven. Dad was going to shut down the Memory House for a whole month and we were going to drive across the country, straight through Texas into Louisiana and then down to Florida, where I'd finally get to see the ocean.

Except Mama died in a car accident before the summer came.

As soon as I get my car, I'll pick up traveling where she left off. I'll drive to San Francisco to see the trolleys and the Victorian houses and the impossible hills. Then I'll head back east and south to New Orleans and keep driving until I hit the Florida beaches, just the way we planned. Dad and I will take the Memory House on the road, leaving Tumble Tree to the dust and the heat and the lizards, and we won't stop until we've seen it all; until the map on my ceiling is filled with red stars and Mama's scrapbook is overflowing with our own pictures, ticket stubs, and matchbook memorabilia.

I can't help but smile as I imagine a life where there's only me, Dad, and a long stretch of highway.


I don't remember falling asleep. But I wake sometime later to the sound of arguing downstairs. At first I think I'm dreaming. Then, as my eyes adjust to the dark, I notice the light reaching through the crack between the floor and my bedroom door.

There's a *shhh*, then something that sounds an awful lot like *you'll wake her up.*

The clock on my nightstand reads 12:37 a.m. Who would be here at this time of night?

I slip out from under the sheet and place my feet on the floorboards, careful not to make anything creak, which is a bit like trying to cross a trampoline without bouncing. But I manage. Then I tiptoe down to the landing so I can hear better.

The downstairs lamp casts a column of light onto the stairs. I slide my head between the slats of the railing and lean out. From there, I can just catch sight of the mayor standing on the porch.

Even though it's the middle of the night, Mayor Warman looks like he's been hard at work—Carhartt hat tipped low over his eyes, cotton button-down with sleeves rolled up to his elbows and sweat rings pooling under each arm. What the mayor is doing laboring at this time of night is beyond me. But the oddest part is that he's still wearing sunglasses even though it's pitch black out. Come to think of it, I don't think I've ever seen the mayor without his sunglasses.

He tugs at his beard. His sun-worn skin reminds me of the lizards that take cover in patches of shade along the highway. He looks like something that was born from the desert—thick-skinned, thirsty, and determined.

A shiver runs down my spine. The mayor's always been perfectly polite to me whenever I've seen him, but still. There's something about him that feels off. I'm just not sure what it is.

He smiles a crooked smile, and for just a second the mayor looks like an older version of his nephew, Marco. "It won't take long." His voice is low and gravelly. "I'll have you home within an hour. Just up to the mines and back. You can ride with me."

"This is the fourth night this week. We agreed to two—this is getting out of hand—"

"Another big order came in. We adapt. Things change."

"Come on, not tonight. I'm not—"

"Charlie, let's not do this. We both know you're going to come with me, because we both know what will happen if you don't. Let's just get on with it."

There's a long pause followed by Dad's heavy sigh. Then the coat closet squeaks open.

"Let me just get my shoes on."

The light clicks off and my father's shadow follows Mayor Warman outside. A few minutes later a truck grumbles to life.

Why would the mayor want my father to come with him to the mines in the middle of the night? And what does he mean, *We both know what will happen if you don't?*

The hairs on my arms rise. The moment feels oddly familiar— all the way down to the scratchy hardwood cutting into my thighs and the cool slats of railing resting against my cheeks.

When I was a kid I used to sit on the landing and listen to the sound of my parents talking when they thought I was asleep. Mama would talk about road trips and leaving Tumble Tree. Dad would make his usual promises to her—once I was older, maybe when school's out, maybe when things were less busy. Sometimes I would listen to the rumble of their voices so long and hard that I would fall asleep with my face still pressed against the wooden slats, barely stirring when one of them finally found me and carried me back to bed.

But this is . . . different. Mama isn't here. And what if Dad is in trouble?

It's a twenty-minute bike ride to the mines. Fifteen if I pedal extra hard. I could follow them and be back before anyone realizes I'm gone. Just long enough to make sure Dad is okay, figure out what would lure him out of the house in the middle of the night, and what in the world could drag the mayor to our doorstep at this hour.

Before I have time to talk myself out of it, I'm in my room sliding on tennis shoes and a pair of jeans. Then I turn back to my closet and grab a dark long-sleeved shirt and baseball hat.

*Camouflage. That'll be better.*

I stop just short of the threshold.

That's a strange thing to think. *Better than what?*

I shake my head and grab my keys. I better hurry.

The night's warm, but in comparison to the day it might as well be an air conditioner on full blast.

Above, the fingernail moon turns the trees into a line of hulking bodies. The stars wink down at me like they know something I don't. Somewhere in the distance a dog barks.

As I pedal away, gravel kicks up against my ankles. I follow the curve of our driveway until it bends into the main road, then head west toward the mines.

The darkness is thick and deadly quiet except for the scurry of night critters hiding between the shadows of prickly pear and cypress trees. I click on my flashlight and angle it toward the road. Just because I can get to the mines with my eyes closed doesn't mean I want to.

Out-of-towners probably don't even know that the mines exist—there's no sign to signal the turnoff, and if you're not looking carefully, you'd likely mistake the entrance for a dirt path leading into the desert. From there it's another mile until you finally reach the dirt-packed parking lot, and the bumpy ungroomed road is enough to deter anyone curious from getting too close.

I slow down so I don't miss the entrance, squinting until I find the dusty imprint of tire tracks that curl off the main road. I'm careful to avoid the clumps of greasewood plants that sprout between the tread marks making up the path, and I have to slow my pace even more to use the tire marks as a guide. The thin beam coming from my flashlight does little to cut through the inky black desert night.

A small pit of dread uncurls inside my stomach. What am I doing out here alone in the middle of the night? Someone could hop out from a tangle of cacti and I wouldn't even know it until they were practically right on top of me.

This is ridiculous. Dad can take care of himself.

I'm about to turn around when I see a faint light in the distance. Every nerve in my body is screaming at me to go home. But I don't listen, because something else tugs me forward.

As I get closer, I see that the lights in the trailer they use for the main office are on, and about a hundred or so yards behind that, the mouth of the mines is illuminated. There are nearly a dozen cars parked in the lot, like it's any old weekday when people are at work. Can this really be where my dad went? Who would want to spend their night inside a cave? And what kind of work can even be done at the mines in the middle of the night?

I hop off my bike and turn off the flashlight, then crouch behind one of the parked cars to get a better view out of sight. Between the lot and the mines there's nothing but desert and dark, with clusters of yucca, bear grass, and greasewood shadowed across the dusty landscape. And beyond the mines, Mexico stretches out into a black expanse indistinguishable from the sky.

The light illuminating the opening is just bright enough that I can see a line of people lurking outside of it, like they're waiting for something. The mayor stands in front of them, flanked by my dad and two large burly-looking men. Based on the way his arms are flapping around him, it looks like the mayor is giving a speech.

I creep closer, past the trailer, crouching low as I leave the safe covering of the parked cars and enter the dark section of desert that leads to the mines. On a normal evening, the path would be brightly lit and buzzing with activity, with trucks weaving to and from the mines carrying the day's quarry. But given the late hour, the space feels vast. Almost ominous. When I'm close enough to hear some of what's being said, I duck behind a large jumble of plants. The trailer is less than a dozen yards behind me, but I'm far enough in the shadows that the light from the window can't quite reach me. And I'm counting on my dark clothes and the barely there moon to help me stay hidden.

The mayor's still wearing his sunglasses. The lights illuminating the craggy mine opening cast shadows across the spectators' faces, so it's hard to make out their exact expressions. But if I didn't know better, I'd say they look scared.

". . . efforts won't go unrewarded." The mayor lifts the bill of his hat and wipes at his forehead. "This is purely a precaution."

He motions to the large men standing next to him just as they both step forward. That's when I notice they're carrying guns. Big ones braced with black leather shoulder straps, like they're about to march into battle.

*Oh my God.*

As if choreographed, the two men simultaneously lift the barrels and point them toward the line of people. One man ducks. Some folks jump back, hands held out protectively in front of them. Others cry out or cover their faces, like their palms might provide a strong enough barrier between them and the weapons. I gasp, then crouch lower behind the plant in case someone heard me. My hands are trembling so hard I drop the flashlight, sending a cloud of dust into the air as it rolls away. What the hell is going on?

"No need to panic," the mayor explains. "Just do as you're asked, and no one'll get hurt. Understand? Again, this is just a precaution." Then he turns to another man standing there, off to the side—

My father.

The mayor looks at him expectantly and Dad shuffles forward, shoulders slumped, fingers working the crease in his brow. Then without a word, he grabs the hands of the first man in line. Dad's back is to me, but I don't need to see his face to know what he's saying to the terrified-looking man.

*Tell me what you want to forget.*

But no. That can't be right. It doesn't look like this man *wants* to forget anything.

A second later the man's mouth goes slack, and he sways a little in Dad's grip.

My heart is a rabbit inside my chest. Dad still cuts the crusts off his peanut butter and jelly sandwiches. He goes to bed before ten, even on Saturdays, and once grounded me for saying the word *hell*. He's not the kind of man who hangs out with armed men in the middle of the night. And he's certainly not the kind of man who takes people's memories without their permission.

I need to get out of here. I need to get out of here *right now*.

I turn, ready to hop on my bike and ride back to the house as fast as I can, but I run smack into someone's chest.

A hand clamps over my mouth before I can even scream.

# 5

"*You have to be quiet.*"

The voice is a hiss in my ear.

Every bone in my body tells me to do just the opposite, but my throat feels like I swallowed half the desert. The hand covering my mouth tastes like salt, which only makes it worse.

"I'm not going to hurt you."

The grip on me is light—too light for someone trying to hold me against my will. All I need to do is give a small shove and I could make a run for it. "There's someone in the trailer and the walls are like paper. If I take my hand away, do you promise to be quiet?"

An elbow to the ribs would do it for sure. But there's something about the timbre of that voice.

I *know* that voice.

So I nod once. The hand slips from my mouth. I tamp down my instinct to run screaming into the night and turn to face him.

Marco Warman.

He looks at me from underneath the brim of a dark low-slung hat, his face flat and unreadable. His cheeks are smeared with smudges of camouflage, making his eyes and teeth gleam white against the night sky. He looks like he wants to blend into the desert, not like he wants his uncle or the men with the guns to know he's out here.

He presses a finger against his lips and points to the trailer about ten yards behind us, like I might not have gotten the message the first time. I narrow my eyes at him. What's he doing here? How do I know he's not a lookout for his uncle?

If I make a run for it, it would get the attention of the armed men down by the mines. If I don't run, the mayor's nephew might . . . what? Kidnap me? Turn me in to the mayor so I end up facing the men with guns anyway?

But my dad is down there. I may not know what's going on, but I know he'd never let anything bad happen to me. He'd never let anything bad happen to anyone. This whole thing has to be a big misunderstanding.

Marco's eyes are wide and pleading as they flick back and forth between me and the opening to the mines, like he can tell there's a scream on the tip of my tongue. Then they open even wider and he grabs my arm and tugs.

I manage to wrestle free from his grip. "What do you think you're doing?" I whisper.

He motions silently toward the line of people. The man my father just finished unburdening is walking toward the parking lot, looking like he doesn't yet have his wits about him. And he's headed straight for us.

I freeze, looking for a viable place to hide that isn't in the direction Marco went in case this is all a big setup somehow, but there's nowhere else that doesn't place me in plain view of the man marching toward us.

"Lucy!" Marco hisses, eyebrows arching expectantly, as if following him is the obvious choice and he isn't dressed like a kidnapper. But he's right—this is my only option.

I take a deep breath, then crouch-crawl toward the cluster of plants Marco's hiding behind. I have to press in close to make myself fit and keep both of us hidden. My arm heats when it connects with his.

A few seconds later the slack-jawed man stomps straight through the place I'd been hiding a moment before. His foot makes contact with the flashlight I dropped earlier and it scuttles across the dirt, disappearing into the darkness. The man doesn't so much as flinch; he continues forward at an unwavering pace.

There's something about the way he moves. It's . . . odd. When people leave the Memory House without their burdens they look light as clouds, like there's barely enough gravity to tether them to Earth. But this man is moving like he's got boulders strapped to his back.

I hold ramrod still, straining my eyes to see as he crosses the parking lot, climbs inside a dust-covered sedan, and turns the ignition, all with the robotic movements of someone not quite right in the head.

Once he's gone, I let loose a long breath. I feel Marco relax next to me, too. We turn back to look toward the mines.

The mayor paces the stretch of people, his mirrored sunglasses glinting beneath the lights strung around the mine opening. The armed guards are on opposite ends of the line, guns poised and ready.

Dad releases the hands of another person and they begin the same glassy-eyed march toward the parking lot as the previous man, jaw slack, back hunched, and arms swinging loosely as if something inside them got snipped from their center and they don't quite know how to move without it.

*What is happening?*

Marco's mouth is pressed into a thin line, his face unreadable behind the camouflage smearing his cheeks. He sits so still I'm not even sure he's breathing. His eyes are fixed squarely on his uncle.

The mayor stops in front of the next person my dad's about to unburden. It's Missy from Patty's Pie Pantry—she works the weekend breakfast shift and always gives me an extra pancake when I come in. Her eyes have gone round and her lips are moving, whispering something I can't make out from this distance. The arch of her brow makes it look like she's on the verge of tears.

Mayor Warman places his hand on her shoulder. I strain to hear what he says. "Missy, I really am sorry about this. It's just a precaution, that's all. It'll all be over soon. You understand, don't you?"

Missy nods uncertainly just as the man behind her steps out from the line, the fury on his face burning a hole into the night. It's Mr. Lewis, the mailman. He pulls the hat from his head and crushes it in his hand, waving it in the mayor's direction.

"Why are you doing this to us?" Mr. Lewis raises his chin, like he's ready for a fight.

"I told you, it's just a precaution. It's for your own good." The mayor's voice is placating, like he's talking to a small child.

"Like hell it is." Mr. Lewis steps closer, his mouth twisting into a grimace. Even from all the way back here, I can see he's shaking. "What you're doing out here—it isn't right."

The mayor takes a slow step toward Mr. Lewis, raising his palms as if in surrender.

"Come on now, Pete. No need to get so upset. We're all friends here. Just calm down, all right?"

"Don't tell me to calm down. You're stealing our memories because you don't want us telling anyone what you're doing, aren't you? It's not right!" His voice raises to a roar, and he steps so close he's practically nose to nose with the mayor.

Mr. Lewis is barely there for a breath before one of the armed guards grabs him by the shoulders and hurls him into the dirt. He crumples into a heap. Mayor Warman takes a step toward him and shakes his head.

"Every time, Pete. Why do you have to do this every single time?"

Mr. Lewis looks up at him from all fours. "What are you talking about?"

The mayor says something to one of the guards, and he disappears into the opening of the mineshaft. A few seconds later he emerges with a jar. There's something black inside of it.

"What do you mean, *every single time*? Has this happened to me

**47**

before?" Mr. Lewis pulls himself up so that he's on his knees, his hat clutched tightly to his chest like he's praying.

"I really hate that you're making me do this, Pete. I really do. Just remember, it didn't have to be this way." The mayor lets out a bark of laughter and slaps his knee like someone just told him a hilarious joke. "Aw, who'm I kidding? You're not going to remember a thing."

The guard with the jar marches toward Mr. Lewis just as the other guard grabs him from behind, pinning his shoulders so that he can't move. Then they press the jar to Mr. Lewis's lips and pull his head back by his hair, forcing him to drink some of the thick black concoction inside.

At the same time my father lurches forward, but the mayor seizes him by the arm.

"Stop it! You can't keep doing this to people—"

"Easy there, Charlie." Mayor Warman yanks Dad backward. "Wouldn't want to have to hurt you or Lucy again, now would I?"

Dad goes still. The night is a fist squeezing around me. What does the mayor mean by *again*?

All at once Mr. Lewis's face crumples and his body goes slack. The guard releases him, and he falls to the ground. At first I think he's unconscious—that whatever they made him drink knocked him out. But then he starts to sob, a low keening sound that makes me want to cover my ears. He places a hand over his heart, shaking his head, and the sob becomes a wail. He starts to rock back and forth. Tears shine on his cheeks. All the while his hand is pressed to his chest, like he's trying to hold his heart together.

"What's wrong with him?" I whisper to Marco, but I can tell by the look of horror on his face that he has no more of an idea than I do.

The mayor leans down to Mr. Lewis and whispers something in his ear. Mr. Lewis sways, nods, and says something that seems to satisfy, because the mayor gives him a pat on the back and motions toward his men.

The guards grab Mr. Lewis under the arms and drag his sobbing form into the shadows.

The mayor glances up and down the length of the line, his gaze lingering on each person. "Anyone else got something they'd like to say?"

Wide eyes stare back at him. No one moves. The night seems to hold its breath until finally, *finally*, Mayor Warman nods and the remaining guard resumes his pacing. Then the mayor claps my dad on the back, like they're old buddies on a fishing trip and my dad just lost a big catch. "As you were, Charlie. They won't give you no more trouble."

In the dim light, the mine opening looks like a gaping, screaming mouth. But the only sounds are the pumping of my heart, the desert crunching against the guard's feet, and Mr. Lewis's fading sobs.

My dad's the one who fixes broken people, not the one who causes them to break. He can't really be a part of this, can he? I want him to turn around so I can see his face. I need to see his eyes so I can know for sure. But all I can see is the slump of his shoulders as he shuffles slowly back to Missy.

The mayor's words from earlier slice through my memory: *We both know what will happen if you don't.*

I turn to face Marco, heat firing in my cheeks.

"What is this? What the hell's going on?" My voice is louder than I mean for it to be.

Marco pushes me lower behind the plants, shushing me with his other hand. He pauses, listening to the rhythmic sounds of the guards' pacing. Once he's sure no one heard, he looks at me full-on for the first time. His jaw is clenched as tightly as his fists.

"I don't know," he hisses. "I swear. My uncle's been coming home in the middle of the night for the last two weeks. And he's been acting really sketchy, so tonight I followed him. First to your house, then here. I don't—I have no idea what's going on."

We're sitting so close I can feel the heat of his breath against my cheeks when he speaks. The furrow in his brow looks pained, like he's genuinely confused by what he just witnessed. But it all feels too convenient.

"How do I know you're not here as a lookout for your uncle?"

"Don't you think I would have called someone over here by now if I was? I'm not gonna hurt you." His voice is urgent. "I promise, Luce."

*Luce.*

My nickname rolls off his tongue like he's said it a hundred times before. And he's looking at me the same way he did this afternoon—as if he can see inside of me.

My hand shoots up to the necklace I found on my dresser. I press one of the points of the star to my finger; there's something so familiar about the feel of it . . .

And then I see another flash of us together, just like I did when he was with Manuela at Mama's swing this afternoon.

*His hand brushes the hair back from my face, then he reaches behind me and clasps something around my neck. I feel coolness land against my collarbone, and when I look down, there's a delicate chain with a single gold star hanging from it.*

*"It's like the stars on your map," he tells me. "So you can always find your way back home."*

*My heart is the sun inside my chest. Marco's crooked smile spreads across his face, and then he says my name, once, like it belongs to him.*

*I love you, Luce.*

Then the vision is gone, sliding away from me before I can understand it.

I blink numbly back at Marco as his face swims in and out of focus. The camouflage smears on his cheeks blend against the desert sky, and for a second all I can see are his eyes—twin moons against an empty expanse.

"Lucy? Are you okay?"

I shake my head once, twice, trying to steady myself, but it feels like the world is turning to mush around me and I'm sliding down, down, down.

"I need to go home," I say at full volume.

Marco's eyes go wide and everything snaps back into place. That's when I realize that I'm no longer crouched next to him— I'm standing up, and I've stepped far enough back that whoever's inside the trailer can probably hear. I'm only a few yards away.

There's a hush at the mines, but I don't dare look.

Above me, the moon smiles wanly. Behind me, the trailer door squeaks open. Then quick footsteps crunching in the dirt.

There's a sigh, and that's all I need. Because I'd know that sigh anywhere. I hear it at least a hundred times a day.

"Not you two," says Vivi. "I swear, you're like magnets and iron the way you keep finding each other."

**6**

*"Mom? What are you doing here?"*

Marco's still crouched by the bush, his face pale behind the camouflage paint smears.

Vivi moves toward me. Her fingers circle tightly around my wrist. She keeps her eyes on me, like she doesn't want anyone to know Marco's there, but her next words are for him.

"Never you mind that," she whispers. "You need to get out of here. Now. Your uncle can't find you here again."

*Again.* What is she talking about?

I can feel the heat of eyes pointed in our direction. I'm standing close enough to the trailer to catch some of the light, so anyone looking this way can probably see me. Marco's hidden in the safety of the shadows. What was I thinking?

I try to wrench my wrist free from Vivi's grasp, but she squeezes harder. Her long nails dig into my skin and I bite the inside of my cheek to keep from crying out.

"Not you. They've already seen you." Her eyes blaze at me. "Marco, if your uncle finds out you followed him here again . . ."

Vivi shakes her head and pulls the arm with the cast close to her chest, still looking at me even though she's addressing Marco.

"What do you mean, followed him *again?*" Marco's brow creases, his confusion matching mine.

"Never mind, he's coming this way. Just . . . stay hidden. Please, Marco." Then she raises her voice and calls down to the mines, where the mayor and one of the armed men have already started toward us. "It's Charlie's daughter."

"She alone?" the mayor calls, his sunglasses glinting in the moonlight. Behind him, the people at the mines are quiet as the dawn.

"Yes," Vivi answers. She squeezes my wrist again, the message clear. *Don't say anything.*

"You sure?"

Out of the corner of my eye I see Marco slink further into the shadows until he's nothing but a sliver of empty desert night.

"'Course I'm sure." Vivi lets out an annoyed huff, but there's a slight tremor in the hand gripping me.

"Charlie," the mayor calls, tipping his head toward my dad without slowing his gait. "Best you come with me." His tone's not unkind, but it's clearly not a question. He sounds like a master telling his dog to sit.

Dad hesitates, just for a second, then begins lumbering toward the trailer, careful to avoid the clumps of bear grass and yucca littering the path. He stares at the desert floor like he can't bring himself to look at me.

I think of Mr. Lewis and the way he looked like someone had ripped his heart right out of his chest. My pulse hammers inside my throat.

"Why can't you just stay away from him? You need to leave each other alone. It's for your own good." Vivi's breath is a hot hiss against my ear. It smells like coffee and spearmint gum.

*Stay away?* Is she serious? Marco barely looks in my direction on a good day.

But the questions shrivel on my tongue. The inside of my mouth is a cactus. I squeeze my eyes shut, like maybe if I squeeze hard enough I'll be back in my room, asleep, and none of this will have happened.

When I open my eyes, the mayor is in front of me, face large as a moon. His smile is a slow, crawling thing, stretching across his mouth like afternoon shade from a tree. A guard stands a few feet behind him, gun at the ready.

"Lucy, Lucy," he drawls. Then he clicks his tongue against the roof of his mouth. "What are we gonna do with you?"

He glances around the desert again. "You positive she's alone? You checked?" He's looking at Vivi, but I catch sight of my stricken face in the smudgy reflection of his sunglasses.

"Yes." Vivi nods, somehow managing to appear bored despite the electricity crackling in the air. "Anyway, I can't believe you thought you could prevent this from happening. You and Charlie are about as quiet as tornadoes sneaking out of that old house. How'd you expect *not* to wake her up?" She shakes her head at her brother and lets out another annoyed huff. But I can still feel the quake in her fingers. "I have paperwork to finish. Can we get this over with?"

The mayor studies her for a beat, and even though I can't see his eyes through his aviators I imagine them sliding past Vivi, searching the night for something she might've missed. I search the darkness again for Marco but can't see anything but a stretch of black.

"Go on inside." He gives a dismissive nod. "I'll take it from here."

"Tell Charlie to get an alarm installed in his house. Please." Then Vivi releases her grip and I stagger forward. My wrist throbs. She catches my eye, giving me a look I can't quite decipher. Anger? Fear? Guilt? Then she turns away, and I'm left staring at her back.

A few seconds later the trailer door snaps shut with an efficient click.

"My sister, always business." The mayor's tone is apologetic, as if Vivi's abrupt exit is the thing I'm worried about. He tilts his head to the side and studies me, a small smile on his face. "You look more and more like your mama every day. I bet you grow up to look just like her. That's a compliment. Amelia was a very beautiful woman."

Her name sounds all wrong coming out of his mouth. Mama was a blue sky twirling above a tire swing, the curve of a highway just as it bends to reveal the ocean. The mayor is desert, dirt, and all the things that live there. He doesn't deserve to so much as think her name, let alone speak it.

I have the urge to launch myself at him and rip the smirk right off his face. But then my dad is at my side, and every ounce of fight whooshes out of me.

He looks like one of the memory-burdened people who spill out of their cars after making the long drive to Tumble Tree—one step away from falling into the ground from the weight of what he's carrying.

"Lucy." His face is a crumple of frown lines.

"Dad, what's going on? What are you doing here?"

"Oh, Luce. You shouldn't have come." He takes a long, heaving breath and steps toward me. His face is too pale in the wan moonlight.

"Dad, please," I beg, though I'm not sure what I'm begging for. An answer? An apology? Only I don't think there's anything he could say to me right now that would make what I just saw at the mines okay.

The people that come to visit my father willingly give their memories to him because they need him. Because they trust him with their pain. No one standing outside of that mine came willingly. No one asked for his help. Maybe that's why they looked so broken walking toward the parking lot—because he took something from them they didn't want him to have.

Which means that what my father is doing out here is theft. No. Worse—deceit. And there's no explanation good enough to justify it.

His hands reach for mine. I step back before he can touch me.

"How could you do that to those people?" I jerk my head toward the line. Everyone is turned in our direction, though I doubt they can hear what we're saying.

"You don't understand. Please, Luce, you have to believ—"

"Enough." Mayor Warman cuts Dad off. "Let's get this over with."

The guard's rough hands grab me from behind and push me forward. I dig my heels into the dirt, pressing back against him, but he only shoves me harder.

"Let go!" I struggle, trying to wrench my body out of his grasp. I twist to the right and for a second I'm free, but then there's a sharp pain at the back of my leg as something hits me with a *thwack*, and suddenly I'm kneeling in the dirt, taking deep gulps of dusty air. Pain shoots down my leg.

Dad shouts my name and lunges to help me, but the guard grabs him by his shirt and jerks him backward.

"Don't hurt her," Dad says meekly, and I'm struck by how powerless he is in this moment. It's like someone replaced my father with a helpless old man.

"You're making this harder than it needs to be." The mayor's mouth is too close to my ear when he speaks. He smells like sweat and desert.

I force myself to look at my dad. At his watery brown eyes. At the half-moons carved deep into the skin below. At the crease between his eyebrows that he rubs when he's anxious. There are a million questions in my head, but only one bubbles to the surface, hopping out like it's been waiting for me to find it all night. I think of Mr. Lewis again as I speak.

"I've been here before, haven't I?" My voice is as sharp as the mayor's fingers digging into my shoulders. "This isn't the first time I followed you."

Dad closes his eyes and turns away. It's all the confirmation I need.

"Charlie," the mayor says, his voice edged with warning.

Then the guard steps toward me. The gun that hung loosely at his side is now clutched tightly in his hands. The barrel points directly at me.

"We don't have time for this nonsense," the armed man says, then spits at the ground.

The mayor grabs hold of me; his fingers feel like fire against my skin. He forces my chin upward so that I'm staring directly into Dad's eyes.

I don't need to ask what's about to happen.

"Dad, please," I say, unable to hold back the sob in my voice. "Please don't do this."

He looks at the mayor pleadingly. "What if we let her go? Maybe if she remembers, she won't follow us again. I promise she won't tell anyone. You won't, right, Luce? She's a good kid. Please."

"You know I can't risk that."

"Please don't make me do this again." Dad puts his head in his hands. "Please. I can't keep doing this."

"Enough!" the mayor roars. "I don't want to be here all night.

Either you do it right now, or I'll tell Lucy what really happened to her mama."

I freeze. Dad's face blurs in front of me, pooling against the night sky. "What's he talking about? Dad?"

Only he won't look at me. His eyes are fixed on the ground.

Does the mayor know why Dad's memory of Mama turned guilt-red?

I push back against the mayor, trying to free my arms, but he holds on tight. The armed guard steps even closer.

"Tell me what he's talking about!" A string of spittle flies out of my mouth when I yell. There are spots on the edge of my vision and my heart sounds like a machine gun hammering in my ears. My knees buckle again and I'm crouching in the dirt, the mayor's hands the only things holding me up.

*Mama was in an accident.* I've always known this. I feel the weight of her ring against my finger, and then everything smears into black. Images flash in front of me.

*A dark road.*

*Someone yelling, repeating the same words over and over again.*

*Hands at my back, pulling me away.*

There's a rushing in my ears, like ocean waves crashing against a shore. I blink and see her face. I blink and I see the barrel of the guard's gun pointed at me.

*Ladybug, one day we'll fly away from here. We'll leave this place to the dust and the lizards.*

Something happened to Mama. What was it? There's a sharp

pain inside my head, like something inside me is trying to claw its way out. Mama's ring seems to pulse. I can almost see it—almost grab onto it. Almost—

Then just as quickly the pain is gone. The sensation that I was about to catch something disappears. The night slides back into view. My eyes snap back into focus. Dad's face looms in front of me.

I think of my training session with Dad this afternoon and our conversation about Echoes, and suddenly I know what I have to do.

*Sometimes people subconsciously hide things, and that's when we get the Echoes.*

"Lucy, it's going to be okay," says Dad. "You're going to be okay, do you hear me? I love you, Luce."

I let myself fall forward, pretending I've fainted. My hand hits the ground with a jarring *thud.*

Dad reaches out to steady me.

"Luce, you okay?" He grabs my shoulders, fingers trembling.

I shake my head once, twice, as if I need to shake off the cobwebs. As if the fall was an accident. But as I push myself upright, I close my fist around a handful of dirt.

"I think so," I say, bending at the waist like I'm catching my breath. At the same time, I shove the fistful of desert into my pocket.

The black gun barrel hovers a few inches away, gaping like a mouth. No one seems to have noticed what I just did.

"I'm sorry." Dad's voice is nearly a sob. "Please forgive me."

I let myself slump against the mayor's grasp as though I'm too numb and tired to fight anymore. Fingers grab my chin and point it upward, forcing my eyes to meet my father's.

I touch my jeans pocket and feel the lump of desert hiding there.

*Remember. You have to remember. You have to try to create an Echo.*

Behind Dad, I can just make out the handle of the Big Dipper glowing against the night sky. Out here the stars are more than old light—they're memories of planets and stars and all the secrets they keep. I want them to keep mine—I want them to hold on to this moment and send it back to me so that I don't forget what happened tonight.

So I don't forget that my dad is a thief and a liar.

Dad's eyes are twin headlights beckoning me to look. I feel myself being pulled inside of them, as if hands reach out from the dark of his expanding pupils and grab hold, until I am swept into the blackness beyond.

Then I hear his voice, soft as a whisper—

"Tell me what I want you to forget."

The words are quicksand.

And I sink.

. . .

. . .

. . .

# 7

*My eyes snap open to a too-bright room, the sun streaming in through* the curtains, demanding to be noticed. My blankets are tight and twisted around my body, like I spent the night doing somersaults. There's a dull thudding at the back of my eyelids and my mouth feels like I swallowed half the desert. I reach for the glass of water on my nightstand and take it down in a single gulp.

My head feels like somebody used it as a baseball. I press my temples to push the pain back in—why in the world does it hurt so bad?

That's when I notice the quiet, as if the house is holding its breath. Our house is *never* quiet, except for maybe in the middle of the night. The guests usually arrive with the sun, thumping their way over the pothole outside so that it's impossible not to hear them. What time is it?

I glance at the alarm clock. Holy hell, its 11:02. Vivi must be freaking out.

Why hasn't she beat down the door and dragged me out for morning chores? Maybe hell's frozen over. Or maybe she got bitten by a rattlesnake and is lying helpless in a ditch somewhere between here and El Paso. Those are about the only reasonable explanations I can think of for why she'd let me sleep so late.

I jump out of bed and trip over the tangle of bedding.

*Ow.*

There's a sharp pain at the back of my right leg. I twist around to look at it and see a large purple bruise ballooning from the back side of my knee. I touch the darkest spot in the center and wince. I don't remember hitting it yesterday. Maybe I banged my leg and my head at the same time; this headache is unreal. Could I have done it in my sleep?

The floor groans when I carefully make my way to standing. I go to the bathroom and swallow down two Tylenol, then survey the heap of clothes in the middle of my floor.

My jeans are in an inside-out pile instead of in the hamper, where I usually put them. I barely remember climbing into bed. I must have been so exhausted last night I couldn't be bothered to toss them in.

I stick my arm through the legs to turn them right side out, one then the other, but sand pours out from one of the pockets.

That's odd.

I reach my hand inside the left, then the right pocket, and pull out a handful of sand and bits of what look like a greasewood plant.

It's not unusual to have sand in my clothes; I live in a desert. But there's way more of it than usual, like I've been digging holes and decided to take home some of the dirt. How in the world did I manage to get this much grit in my pocket?

I toss the sand in the trash can, then tiptoe down to the landing and listen for Vivi. I'm relieved when I hear someone moving around in the kitchen, but still—there's too much calm inside a house that's never calm. The unease that prickled when I first woke up starts to spread, landing like a rock in the pit of my stomach.

The hallways seem larger than they did yesterday: big and empty, like they grew a few inches in every direction overnight. The door to Dad's office stands wide open with no sign of him inside. There are no files on his desk, no half-eaten sandwiches he's snuck in before Vivi could stop him.

But when I enter the kitchen, that's when I freeze.

A woman busy at the stove. Dark hair piled on her head. Jeans hanging low on her hips. An apron tied loosely at the waist. The smell of cinnamon and caramelizing bananas wafts over.

Mama had a thing for alliteration, and in the summer she would make these huge breakfasts that started with the same letter as the day of the week: Taco Tuesday, Waffle Wednesdays, French Toast Friday. She started to run out of ideas by the end of the summer, so we'd have to eat strange concoctions she invented just to make the first letters match—Macaroni Monday, Thanksgiving Surprise Thursday—and every morning I came downstairs ready to laugh at whatever bizarre meal was waiting for me.

*Maybe I dreamed the whole thing. Maybe she's been here in the kitchen all along.*

I open my mouth, ready to ask her what she's making today, even though I already know the answer. I can smell her famous Monday Monkey Bread.

Then she turns and the mound of curls spilling out from the bun at the crown of her head gives way to another face. And I remember that it's Friday, not Monday.

Of course she isn't Mama. She can't be.

"There you are!" Vivi's smile is wide. She's wearing Mama's old KISS THE COOK! apron and her hair is piled haphazardly on top of her head in a mass of tangled curls, just the way Mama used to wear it. Vivi's jeans are wrinkled and her T-shirt has a small smudge of sauce just under the neckline. And she's not wearing lipstick. Vivi *always* wears lipstick. "I was wondering when you were going to finally wake up, sleepyhead. I'm making monkey bread and eggs!" She waves a spoon as if in proof.

I swallow the tears burning at the back on my throat.

"What's going on?" I ask. The woman before me and her too-casual appearance is not the Vivi I know. And since when does Vivi say things like *sleepyhead*?

"I'm making breakfast," she says, like that explains it. "I remember your mama used to make banana monkey bread for you sometimes. I thought you might like it."

I blink back at her. The mention of Mama makes my breath catch, and my heart seizes at the hole in my chest. The hole that makes me wonder if life is just a series of people leaving, each one taking a piece of you with them until one day there's nothing of you left and it's your turn to leave a you-sized hole in someone else.

"Did something happen?"

Vivi huffs out a laugh and turns back to the stove. "Don't be silly. Can't I just do something nice for you?"

I press my lips together and let the silence stretch. She spins back to look at me, like she can feel my skepticism.

"Look, your father isn't feeling well and I thought a nice breakfast might cheer him up. And you seemed like you could use the sleep, too. You don't have to act like I'm some kind of monster to you all the time."

*Except you are.*

"Fine," I say. "But where is everyone?" I press my fingers to my head. The Tylenol can't kick in fast enough.

"Well, since your dad isn't feeling well, I sent everyone home. He's taking a sick day."

"A sick day? Like, the *entire* day?"

Dad doesn't take sick days. Ever. On the rare occasion he's not feeling well it's all we can do to get him to take a few extra hours to rest. He never makes the burdened guests *leave*.

A scowl fights the unnatural smile on Vivi's face. "He's a human being, you know. Sometimes people need a day off to rest. I thought you may be coming down with something, too, so I let you sleep."

I blink again. "Why?" The last time I told Vivi I wasn't feeling well, she told me to take some Tylenol and suck it up.

"What do you mean, *why?* And what's with all the questions? Can't I do something nice for you and your dad without getting the third degree?"

I start to say no, but stop myself. My stomach grumbles. The monkey bread smells amazing. I can't remember the last time I had it.

So I bite my tongue and slide into an empty chair at the table. But when my bruised knee bumps against the seat I can't help but wince.

"Is Dad okay? Does he need to go to the doctor?"

"He'll be fine, he just needs some rest and quiet. Let's let him be for today, okay?"

"Maybe I should just check on him—"

She glares at me from under heavy mascaraed lashes, looking for a second like she'll return to her usual bossy self, but instead turns back toward the stove. "Just let your father rest, okay? He could really use it."

There's a knock on the back door then, and we both jump.

"Probably someone for Dad. I'll tell them to come back tomorrow." I move to slide out of my seat, but the back door springs open before I can get to it.

"Afternoon, Vivi. How's my favorite sister today?" the mayor's voice booms.

The hairs on my arms start to rise. "And Lucy. Good to see you. How's the summer treatin' you?"

He adjusts the sunglasses on the bridge of his nose, like I'm the sun trying to get in the way of his view. Something about the gesture makes my skin crawl.

"Fine," I answer. His cheeks are tanned and ruddy and his beard has smudges of dirt in it, like he's spent the morning working outside. Even though I can't see his eyes through the mirrored lenses of his aviators, I don't like the way it feels when he looks in my direction. It's like he's searching for something.

"Charlie mentioned he's teaching you the family trade this summer. That must be exciting." He steps farther into the room like he owns the place, not bothering to wipe his snakeskin boots on the welcome mat. A diamond-encrusted ring flashes from his right ring finger.

"How's that going? You take anybody's memories away yet?"

I shift uncomfortably in my seat. I wish people wouldn't pry into my business. Not that I can blame the mayor, exactly—the Warmans have lived in Tumble Tree almost as long as our family. They helped build the mines, and Mayor Warman's great-great-grandpa was the first in a long line of Warman Mayors, which I guess makes Mayor Warman a bit like Tumble Tree royalty, if dust bowl towns can have such a thing. Not that it gives him any right to march around town like he owns it. And it certainly doesn't give him any right to go poking around in my business. Doesn't he have better things to do?

I want to say something smug, or tell him that it's only a matter of time before I'm running this place and he won't be allowed to just bust on through the back door without an invitation, but the words won't form on my tongue. Because I can feel Vivi watching me, and it would be just like her to tell him and anyone else that will listen what an epic failure my first memory-taking session was yesterday.

"Not yet." I keep my eyes on the table, hoping he doesn't ask any more questions. Hoping he takes the hint and leaves. "But we only just started yesterday. Dad's not feeling well, if you came by to see him. He's taking a sick day."

For some reason my voice is shaking when I talk. I slide my hands into my lap, trying to hide their unexpected tremble. I hope I'm not coming down with whatever Dad has.

Vivi is all smiles as she sets a plate of eggs on the table, followed by a pile of oozing cinnamon-covered bread. She follows it up with a tall glass of sweet tea before turning to face her brother.

"I can let Charlie know you stopped by when he's feeling better," she says, wiping her hands on the apron. There's something plastic-sounding in her voice, like she's putting on a performance. "Unless you want to join us for breakfast?"

My eyes go wide. Mayor Warman joining us for breakfast is a terrible idea. Except I'm a tiny bit curious to see if he keeps his sunglasses on while he eats. I don't think I've ever seen the man without them.

The mayor steps over to the stove to inspect Vivi's work, then he reaches a bare hand into the pan of eggs. I watch with disgust as he plucks out a finger full of food and tosses it into his mouth. He makes a low *mmm* sound at the back of his throat, then grabs a piece of monkey bread from the steaming plate on the counter and takes a bite. He turns to look at me, smiling as he swallows.

"Thank you, but no. I wouldn't want to interrupt you ladies."

*Except you already have.*

Regardless, I relax a little. Vivi's shoulders seem to do the same.

"I just came by to have a little chat with Charlie and say hi. I'm going to send a handyman over to do some work we discussed. Name's Archie. He won't be any bother to you, just fixing a few things around the house Charlie said needed fixing. You'll let him in when he comes by in an hour or so?"

"Of course."

"The fan we keep on the front porch stopped working yesterday," I say. "Can this Archie guy take a look at it for me?"

The mayor lets out a huff and shakes his head. "He's not that kind of handyman."

I want to ask what kind of handyman Archie *is*, exactly, and why my dad asked Mayor Warman to send someone over instead of calling up one of our local guys, but I don't want to encourage him to stay any longer than necessary.

"Sure I can't make you a plate for the road?" Vivi says, reaching for an empty dish. "There's way too much for just me, Charlie, and Lucy."

Mayor Warman's smile is slow as he tips his hat in my direction. "Maybe next time. Y'all enjoy. Best of luck with your memory lessons, Lucy. I bet you'll make a fine addition to the family business."

He gives me a slippery smile as he crosses the room in a few long strides, snakeskin boots kicking up dust as he goes. I don't look at him when he opens the back door, but I can feel the weight of his gaze on me just before he steps back out into the heat.

"Have a nice afternoon, ladies."

Then the door creaks shut, and I'm left staring blankly at my breakfast with a sick swirling feeling in the pit of my stomach.

"Something wrong?" Vivi asks, plunking down a bottle of Tabasco.

I shake my head and force the eggs into my mouth. I barely taste them as they slide down my throat. For some reason, I'm not that hungry anymore.


I offer to clean the kitchen, but Vivi shoos me away, telling me to go out and enjoy my summer break for a change.

"Don't worry," she says with a too-wide smile. "I'll still pay you. I know how hard you've been working to save up for that car."

I have to pick up my jaw off the ground.

Whatever's gotten into her is making me uneasy. She was chatty as a Pie Pantry waitress while we ate, gossiping about people in town, the upcoming church bingo night she's organizing, and other non-business-related things, as if we were two girlfriends gabbing over lunch rather than two people who usually spend the day bickering.

But I know better than to look a gift horse in the mouth.

I wait until Vivi's elbow deep in soapy dishwater before tiptoeing to Dad's room. The door's shut, but I can make out the low hum of the radio coming from the other side. Hopefully that means he's awake. I twist the knob as slowly as I can and push the door inward just enough so that I can squeeze inside without making the rusted hinges scream.

The air is thick and sticky, like it's been days since anyone opened a window. The curtains are drawn tight so that only small ribbons of light seep in through the edges, casting shadows across the piles of clothes littering the usually tidy space. There's a mound on the bed. Dad doesn't move.

I step farther into the shadowy room.

"Dad?" I whisper.

His boots are tossed into a heap on the floor and I almost stumble over them. "You awake?"

He grunts, shifting his body so he can peer out from under a plaid comforter. His fingers reach out and turn down the radio.

"Vivi said you were sick. Are you okay? Can I get you anything? Some water maybe?"

"Luce." His voice sounds like gravel crunching against a shoe. He pats the empty space on the bed next to him. "Come sit. How are you feeling this morning, sweetheart? Did Vivi make you a nice breakfast? She said she was going to make monkey bread. You always did love monkey bread."

I blink and sink down onto the corner of the mattress. What is with everyone today?

"Are you all right? Vivi said she sent everyone away. You

never turn people away. Maybe we should get you in to see a doctor?"

He reaches out and pats my hand. His fingers are ice. "Don't worry about me, Ladybug. I'll be good as new tomorrow. We can even get back to your training. You'd like that, wouldn't you? Maybe you can try to make me forget that I took a sick day today, how about that?" His voice is high and eager. His eyes shine in the dim light.

"Are you sure you're feeling okay? I'm pretty sure you just *volunteered* to let me unburden someone. Haven't you been trying to talk me out of that for, like, my entire life?"

He chuckles lightly. "A promise is a promise, Luce, and I promised that you could try again. I'm a man of my word." He clears his throat, like the last sentence got stuck on its way out.

First Vivi lets me sleep in, now Dad's offering to let me wipe memories. Has the whole world gone mad?

"What's going on?" I don't bother hiding the suspicion in my voice.

Dad pinches the space between his brow, his smile tight. "Nothing's going on. I just need some rest. And Vivi and I both agreed that you could use a day off, too. No harm in taking some time off now and then, is there?"

I furrow my brow. He's not wrong, but still. I didn't even get a break from my chores on my birthday.

"Why don't you go to the library? You haven't been there in weeks. I'm sure Mrs. Gomez misses you. She probably thinks you've fallen into a hole. You'd be doing me a favor by showing her we aren't working you to the bone around here."

He smiles.

"Yeah, all right."

I've been working a lot more hours this summer so I haven't had as much time to spend at the library. Mrs. Gomez probably has a stack of travel books waiting for me, collecting dust. "You sure you're okay? There's nothing I can get you?"

"I'm sure, don't you worry about me. I just need a little rest, that's all. You go and enjoy the day, okay?"

Then he reaches over and turns up the radio again, like the matter's settled, and I'm left with a feeling that there's something I missed—only I can't put my finger on it.

# 8

*When I go back upstairs, my room looks just like how I felt when I woke* up this morning—disheveled. My sheets are in the twisted pile on the floor where I left them, and the sand-filled jeans are still in a heap.

I walk over to the jeans and put my hand into the pocket; another handful of desert comes loose. There's too much of it—you don't just happen to get this much sand in your pockets by accident. But why would I fill my pockets with sand and broken plant bits?

I try to think back to last night.

I went for a walk, got tired, then went to bed. Nothing out of the ordinary.

*I went for a walk, got tired . . .*

I press the greasewood between my fingers. Something niggles at the back of my brain. It's weird, because when I think back to last night I can see my feet in front of me on the path like I'm walking the usual trail from the house to Mama's tire swing, one flip-flopped foot in front of the other. But at the same time, I can see the ground rush past me faster, gnarled trees flying by in quick flashes like I'm in a car. Cypress, prickly pear, yucca, a dusty path off a darkened road—and at the same time the slap of plastic against my heels, the crunch of gravel against my flip-flops as I walk down the path.

*I went for a ride* . . . I blink. No, that's not right. I went for a *walk.* Then I came home and went to bed because I was tired.

But that doesn't feel right, either. Nothing about this day feels right.

I dig around in the top drawer of my dresser until I find a pair of shorts and a tank top. I'll take a walk to the tire swing and retrace my steps. Get some fresh air. Try to get my head on straight before I go to the library.

I'm blasted with heat the second I'm out the door. It's another one of those cloudless afternoons where the sun's got no place to hide and the ground feels like a stovetop. The yard looks odd without the usual parked cars filling it—an empty patchwork of dirt, tire marks, and dead grass. Vivi's put up the chain that blocks the turnoff into our driveway. There's a handwritten sign hanging from the center of it: CLOSED. PLEASE COME BACK TOMORROW.

I make my way around the bend, trying to remember how it felt to do this last night.

*I went for a walk. Got tired. Went to bed.*

The steps are familiar, but then again, I've done this walk a million times.

I veer off toward the park. The dull hum of cicadas fills the afternoon air, but otherwise the only sound is the crunch of my shoes against the dirt. When I round the corner, I'll find the lonely tire swing and empty picnic table waiting for me as usual.

Only it's not empty.

Marco Warman's sitting on the bench, his fingers tracing the woodgrain in the picnic table. He jumps up when he sees me, practically tripping over his feet as he stands. There's a faint flicker of a smile on his face, and once again I'm reminded of a crooked stretch of highway leading somewhere far away from here.

"You came." He says this as if he's been expecting me. He shoves his hands in his pockets, then pulls them back out like he's not exactly sure what to do with them. "I wasn't sure if you would, but I didn't want to come to your house. I figured it was worth trying the park where I saw you yesterday."

Suddenly the air feels warmer than it did on the walk over. I open my mouth, then close it. Why in God's name would Marco Warman be looking for me?

"What are you doing here?"

Marco's smile twists into a frown. "You should sit down." He motions toward the picnic table. "We need to talk."

"About what?" I don't mean to sound as incredulous as I do, but I can't help it.

"Please?" His face is serious, almost pleading.

I can't begin to imagine what Marco Warman and I have to talk about, but I find myself nodding as I walk toward the table.

I sit on the corner, as far from him as I can get. Any minute he might bust out laughing or Manuela and a group of kids from school could jump out from the bushes and throw something at me. This whole thing is just plain suspicious.

Marco bites at the edge of his lip and looks down at the finger that's gone back to tracing the wood. Behind him, the tire swing sways slightly.

"Do you remember anything from last night?" he asks. But he doesn't look at me when he says it.

"Last night?"

He looks up. "Do you remember seeing me?" I feel him search my face, mouth pressed into a thin line.

I laugh. "Obviously. You were here with Manuela. Where is your girlfriend, anyway?" I stand, because this whole thing is ridiculous and I don't want to play whatever weird game he's playing. But he grabs my arm to stop me. His skin feels warm against mine even though my arms are already blazing from the heat.

"She's not my girlfriend. And anyway, that's not what I mean." There it is again: That pleading frown. That searching look. "I'm talking about last *night*. Do you remember going to the mines? Seeing me? Anything?"

I shake my head, suddenly wanting to be as far away from Marco as I can get. A slow creeping dread sinks into the pit of my stomach and starts to spread.

*I went for a walk. Got tired. Went to bed.*

"I don't know what you're trying to do, but—"

"You don't remember." It's not a question.

"Remember what?"

Marco runs his hands through his hair and lets out a frustrated grunt. He places both hands on the table, fingers splayed out, and takes a deep breath before leveling his eyes to mine.

"Look, I'm not sure how to say this, so I'm just going to say it. And I'm not sure how much your dad took away from you last night, so this will probably sound ridiculous. But it's not ridiculous, okay? You have to believe me."

What is he talking about?

He stands from the picnic table and starts to pace, shoes kicking up a spray of gravel as he walks.

"Last night you were at the mines with me. We both followed my uncle and your dad there, and they caught you. Well, actually, my mom caught you. And then your dad, he—I think my uncle made him do it, but your dad took away your memory of what happened. That's why you don't remember anything from last night. And I know this is going to sound even more bizarre, but I think they've done it to you before. To both of us. I think you and I may have been something once. Friends or maybe even—"

"Stop it." The dread creeps up from my stomach, spreading to my chest and head. There's a dull roar in my ears that grows until it seems to come from everywhere, humming like a freight train driving straight through my skull. I shake my head to make the noise go away, but it doesn't work.

The pile of sand and greasewood I found in my pocket flashes like a beacon.

"Whatever it is you're trying to do, just stop it. This isn't funny."

There was too much of it to be an accident.

"I'm not trying to be funny. Lucy, if you'd just try to remember—" His fingers brush my arm. They feel like fire.

And at the same time, they feel familiar.

"There's nothing to remember!" I shout, jumping up from the bench. My hands cover my ears in an effort to drown out the sound. I can't tell the difference between the cicadas and the buzzing in my head; it's all one giant roar of noise, like the whole world is shouting. Every muscle in my body is screaming at me to stay as far away from Marco as humanly possible. It's a trick. A cruel trick Manuela or his other friends put him up to.

"Lucy?" He sounds concerned.

I squeeze my eyes shut. "You're wrong." I try to make my voice sound confident. "I was home last night. Then I went for a walk. Got—

"—tired. Went to bed?"

Marco finishes the last part of the sentence with me, as if it's some mantra we've chanted together a hundred times before.

I blink back at him, startled. The cicadas continue their dull, whining buzz.

"That's not what happened to you last night, Luce."

*Luce.* The way he says my name . . .

This time when his hand touches my arm I don't pull away.

"That's what your dad *told* you happened—right after he took your memory away. Right before my uncle put you in his truck and had my mom drive you back to your house. I know because I was there, too. I saw it all happen. I should have done something. I should have—"

He looks up at the sky like he's searching for the right words, then levels his dark eyes at me and sighs. I reach up and touch the star necklace. I know that look. Something deep inside of me knows the depth of it, even knows the weight of his hand against my arm, warm and familiar.

I blink. Something tugs at the edge of my memory. The world hums with noise, an image blurring in and out of focus. Too fuzzy and quick for me to grasp.

"Let me ask you this," Marco says, his tone like something you'd use to coax a dog out of a hiding place during a thunderstorm. "Do you remember climbing into bed last night? Do you remember coming home?"

"Of course I do." I want to sound strong, but my voice is so soft that I'm not sure Marco can hear me.

Because I don't remember climbing into bed. I don't remember walking into the house. I don't remember changing into pajamas. I don't remember brushing my teeth. All I remember is that one horrible sentence: I went for a walk, got tired, went to bed.

*And sand. A handful of sand to make me remember.*

"Stop it," I whisper. "Please."

His hand is still on my arm. My skin feels too hot beneath his fingers, but I don't want him to move. I'm afraid if he does I might collapse.

"Lucy, I'm telling you the truth. We were both there. There was this line of people waiting outside the mines, and your dad was making them forget. And there were guards with guns—they hurt Mr. Lewis. They made him drink this stuff, and he started sobbing uncontrollably—"

My head jerks at the mention of our mailman. "What do you mean? Why would someone hurt Mr. Lewis?"

"One of the guards knocked him to the ground and made him drink this black sludge out of a jar. I think because Mr. Lewis was pretty angry, saying he wasn't going to let them make him forget. He was yelling at your dad and my uncle. But then once he drank the sludge he got all weird. He started sobbing and, I don't know, it was like all the fight *whooshed* out of him. You have to believe me, Lucy. There's something going on at the mines. Something they don't want people to know about. Something they don't want the people working there to remember." He stops, his eyes scanning my stricken face. "I'm sorry, I know this is a lot to take in." He pulls away, and I'm untethered.

I squeeze my eyes shut again. The cicadas *buzz, buzz, buzz*. My mind is swimming.

There has to be some kind of explanation.

"Come with me. To the mines. Maybe there's something there that will trigger your memory."

"What, now?"

Marco glances down at his watch, then back in the direction of the house. "No, not now. I have to get back. My uncle will be looking for me. How about tonight? We can retrace your steps. See if that brings any of your memory back. Does it work like that?"

I shake my head. It *shouldn't* work like that. Outside of the occasional Echo, when a memory is gone, it's gone. Unless . . .

I touch my pocket.

The sand.

There was sand in my pocket this morning.

Could I have put it there on purpose? To help myself remember? If that's the case and if Marco's telling the truth, would going to the mines trigger something else?

Marco must sense me waning because he grabs my arm again. "What do you have to lose? Come on, Lucy. Just come with me. Please. They took away your memories for a reason. Don't you want to know why? Or see for yourself that I'm telling the truth?"

I want to tell him that he's lying and he needs to leave me alone. I want to turn around and pretend I never found Marco waiting for me; that he never told me his version of what happened last night. I want to say a million other things, but instead I feel my head nod.

"Which window is your bedroom?"

"The one on the top right, on the side yard. Why?"

He nods once, flashing his crooked highway smile. "I thought so. This probably sounds like a weird thing to ask, but is there a map on your ceiling? For some reason I keep picturing a map with red stars on it."

The cicadas *buzz, buzz, buzz.* My head swims.

The rational part of my brain tells me that Vivi must have told him about the map on my ceiling and the red stars that mark the places I've been. But the other part of my brain—the part that feels like something just cracked it in half—tells me that Marco knows exactly what my room looks like. It tells me that the sand I found in my pocket wasn't an accident. It tells me that Marco's version of what happened last night is the truth, and I need to listen.

"Listen, Lucy, I know this must seem ridic—" Marco stops suddenly, head tilting to the side.

He puts a finger up to his lips.

I strain my ears over the cicadas, trying to hear whatever Marco hears.

There—the steady crunch of footsteps on dried earth. Just past the bend in the direction of the house.

"I have to go. My mom can't see me here. She can't know that I told you what really happened." Marco's voice is barely a whisper. "I'll come by tonight. After everyone's asleep. Don't tell anyone you saw me here, okay? Especially not my mom. She can't know, do you understand?"

I nod and swallow back the lump forming in my throat.

"And Lucy?" Marco's dark eyes are serious as they search my face. "You might want to write down everything I just told you.

We both should. Just in case something happens and they try to take our memories again."

*Again.*

Then he turns on his heel and is gone. And I'm left standing alone, feeling like the entire world just split in two.

## 9

*My eyes trace the squiggles of highway that run along my ceiling* map. I-10 past Fort Stockton into San Antonio, then north up I-35, past Austin to Dallas. Mama used to love to drive the I-35 corridor running north into Oklahoma, especially at night when it was mostly just her and the truckers sharing the road. She said the flat stretch of winding black tar between Hillsboro and Dallas felt like what she imaged the Autobahn felt like— with nothing but her, the wide expanse of star-flecked sky, and the black road beneath her tires. I bet the air smelled cleaner once she left the dry desert heat behind. I bet the wind coming in through the open windows felt like a story waiting to be told.

Staring at this map makes me feel like myself. Grounded. Connected to Mama—almost as though I'm staring at her fingerprint.

I try to keep my brain focused on the twists and curves in the roads and the names of cities marked along the way, on the stories Mama used to tell me about the road trips she took before she met Dad. But my eyes keep drifting down to the red stars I've drawn marking the places I've been to.

The red stars that Marco knew about even though he's never been in my room.

So what if Vivi mentioned the map to him at some point? The real question is, why would it matter what's stuck to my ceiling? Why would Marco care enough to remember something as silly as a worn-out map hanging in some random girl's bedroom?

But the main thing that's bothering me isn't about the map. And it's not the fact that I can't think of a reason why Marco would lie to me, either. It's not even the unexplained bits of desert and greasewood I found in my pocket this morning, or Vivi's and Dad's weird behavior all afternoon.

No.

What I can't figure out is how a boy who's lived in the same small town I've lived in my entire life could feel like a complete and total stranger. Even though his mom has worked in my house for nearly five years. Even though his mom was a close friend of Mama's long before that. How is it that Marco and I know so little about each other? And why I can't shake the feeling that *despite* that, we have some kind of history, even though we've never spent time together?

The thought turns my stomach into a fist, because that can only mean one thing. But Dad's not a memory thief. I know him. He wouldn't do that.

I trace I-35 toward Wichita, through Topeka, Kansas, and all the way into St. Paul, Minnesota, until I hit Lake Superior. Maybe someday I'll go that far north. Maybe I'll keep driving until I get to Canada, where the ground stays wet from snow and the sun doesn't burn so hot.

*Tap.*

A sharp thump on my window makes me bolt upright.

The clock shows that it's nearly eleven. Outside, the cicadas drone. Beneath me the house is still. I listen.

The tapping comes again, this time more than once—*tink, tink, tink* against the windowpane. And louder. Definitely intentional.

I jump down from my bed and push the curtains aside, heart thumping hard against my rib cage. Marco's standing directly below my window. His hand is raised like he's about to throw something again, but he lowers it when he sees me. White teeth flash a grin.

He actually showed.

He puts a finger to his lips. Then he points to the place where the dormer window meets the roof, followed by the trellis below. He wants me to climb down.

He's kidding, right? I could fall and break my neck.

I shake my head no. He rolls his eyes, then motions for me to open the window.

I put a finger up. *Hold on*, I mouth. Then I tiptoe out of my room and listen for sounds of movement. There's nothing other than the squeak of floorboards beneath my feet and the house breathing its normal nighttime sighs. I heard Vivi leave hours ago, and as far as I can tell Dad hasn't come out of his room once today. I could probably walk right out the front door and no one would be the wiser.

I gently close my bedroom door and go back to the window. Marco's looking the other direction, one hand shoved deep in his pocket and the other sliding back and forth across his lower lip like he's deep in thought. His dark hair curls around his ears, longer than he wears it during the school year. I have the sudden desire to reach out and touch one of those curls.

He looks back up and smiles when he sees my face at the window. My stomach does a tiny flip.

Then I open the window latch. It makes a loud *snap* that cuts through the quiet.

Marco jumps and looks around the yard, like the sound of the window latch might have awoken some sleeping creature lurking in the dark. He motions for me to hurry.

I press my palms against the glass and push up. The window slides open. Warm air seeps in.

Then a high-pitched siren cuts across the night.

I jump back from the window. What the hell? It sounds like someone's trying to make a break from prison. Down below, Marco stands wide-eyed and stone still.

The alarm keeps blaring. I cover my ears and look around my room for the source of the horrible screeching. Where is it coming from? Downstairs? Outside?

"Lucy?" Dad's voice booms from the bottom of the stairs. A few seconds later he busts through my bedroom door, his hair sticking up in wild tufts.

I can barely hear him over the pulse of the alarm.

"What's wrong?" he shouts over the noise. "What happened?"

"I don't know! I just opened the window and—"

Dad pinches the skin at the bridge of his nose and shakes his head, like he's trying to shake out the sound. "Crap. It's the alarm. Vivi must have turned it on when she left. Hang on."

Alarm? What alarm?

Dad marches out of my bedroom before I can ask, bare feet slapping back down the stairs. At the landing, he bumps into something and curses loudly. Then a few seconds later the house is filled with silence.

I let out a breath. My ears ring from the screeching.

I listen for Dad to come back up the steps, but when I don't hear him I quickly cross back over to the window and look out. The front yard is nothing but shadows. If Marco's still down there, he's hiding.

Downstairs I hear Dad's muffled voice. He must be on the phone, maybe with the police, assuming the alarm triggered something.

Since when do we have an alarm? And more importantly, why?

I glance once more out the window toward the empty yard, then tiptoe into the hallway so I can hear better.

". . . in her room. I'm telling you she's been here all night." Dad sounds agitated. I step closer to the stairs, straining to hear.

"You're overreacting. Her bedroom is upstairs, for Chrissake. It's not like she can fly out the window." There's a long pause, followed by Dad's frustrated sigh. "Fine, I'll check. But I'm telling you it's nothing."

"Everything okay?" I call down once I'm sure he's hung up the phone. I try to make my voice sound as innocent as possible even though my mind is racing, trying to make sense of it all. Who was Dad talking to? It didn't sound like the police.

"Everything's fine. I'll be right back. Stay upstairs."

He rummages in the kitchen for something, snapping drawers open and shut. Then a few moments later the front door creaks open.

I run to the window and look outside. Dad stands in the front yard with a flashlight clutched in his hand. Shadows scuttle back from the beam of light. It bounces across the yard, illuminating the empty parking lot and the desert beyond. He sweeps it back and forth like he's looking for something. Or someone.

He walks to the side yard, cutting the beam toward the bushes below my window. My pulse speeds up.

*Please don't let Marco have been foolish enough to hide in the bushes.*

Dad continues along the side of the house, the light moving side to side until he's out of view. I hold my breath, waiting.

After a few minutes the front door closes and the lock slides into place. Then footsteps toward the kitchen and the low rumble of Dad's voice again. Did he find something?

I start to make my way to my bedroom door, but hear Dad coming back up the stairs. I jump back into bed, trying to look like I've been waiting here the whole time. My fingers dig into the rumpled blankets.

Dad looks exhausted. His robe hangs open, revealing an old white undershirt, boxers, and pale, skinny legs. He crosses over to the window, looks out, then slides it shut.

"Dad, what is—"

"What were you doing opening the window in the middle of the night?" His voice is gruff. Accusing.

I don't want to lie. So I don't answer the question.

"Since when do we have an alarm?" I counter.

Dad pinches the bridge of his nose, staring at me like he can't figure out what to say next. It could just be that he's tired, but he looks . . . angry. Like he knows that I opened my window because there was a boy outside of it. But he must not have seen Marco; Dad would say something if he had.

"There's—" He clears his throat and pinches the bridge of his nose again. "There've been some break-ins in the area so I had an alarm installed this afternoon. You need to keep the windows closed at night. It's too hot to have them open."

"Break-ins? In Tumble Tree?" Most nights we don't even bother to lock our back door, and I'd bet good money no one else in Tumble Tree bothers to either. What's there to steal, anyway? If someone wants to take the junk Dad lets people pay him with, they can have it.

Is that what the mayor's handyman was doing in our house this afternoon—installing an alarm?

"Dad, what's going on?" I ask, searching his face. "Who was that on the phone?"

"No one, just the security company. Everything's fine. Just . . . keep the windows shut, okay?" His eyes bounce around my room, looking everywhere but at me. "You should get some sleep. We both should. I'll see you in the morning." He nods at me once, like there's nothing more to discuss, then closes the door behind him with a definitive *click*.

I listen to the sound of his footsteps retreating, then walk back to my window.

Outside, there's nothing but shadows.

## 10

*The next morning, it's business as usual, and I'm tending to the many* people waiting to see Dad.

"Water?" I say to the scowling man at the back of the line. The porch creaks beneath our feet.

He looks from me to the empty glass in his hand like he can't quite figure out what he's doing there, then holds it out for me to fill. He arrived early this morning, the sun barely poking out over the horizon when his white Honda thumped over the pothole and made its way into the already-filling lot. New Mexico plates, which means he should be familiar with the desert heat. Hopefully he won't complain as much as the others.

But the slump in his shoulders and shadows under his eyes look different from most of the other folks waiting. There's a hard set to his jaw, and his dark eyes are locked on the ground.

*Guilt.*

I study the deep lines that splinter around his face like cracks in the dried earth. He has the look of someone who wants to forget something that's been keeping him up for many, many nights. Which probably means he's done something he wishes he could undo.

"How long do you think it will take?"

I fill his water glass, studying the stretch of people that curves around toward the door—an Asian woman wearing a dress too stylish for the Tumble Tree dust, a lanky white man with a scraggly beard and holes in the knees of his skinny jeans, a twentysomething Black man in a Phillies baseball cap who keeps looking at his watch, and so many others. The front yard is filled with cars—if we get anyone else they'll have to park down the road.

At the front of the line, the Oklahoma woman sits on a metal folding chair fanning herself. If Dad hadn't been sick yesterday, she'd probably be well on her way back home by now, feeling as light as a cloud wisp.

The New Mexico man chews on his lip nervously, waiting for me to reassure him.

"Hard to say how long, exactly," I finally answer, shifting the pitcher to my other hand. This is the part where I would usually tell him that what my father does is beautiful, where I would comfort him by promising that everything will be okay and if he just waits patiently with everyone else his turn will come and his burdens will be lifted.

But today, all I can say is, "Will you excuse me?"

Then I march back toward the front door. I almost run smack into Vivi on her way out of the house, clipboard pressed tight against her chest.

"Oh!" Her lipsticked mouth flattens into a thin line. All signs of yesterday's cheeriness have been swept back up into her usual bun and crispy exterior. As if to make up for her casual appearance yesterday, she's wearing a snug red dress with leopard trim and matching leopard heels. It's almost too much, even for her. She looks from me to the people waiting, and I know from her frown that she's checking to make sure I've done a good job serving all the guests.

Behind me, metal squeaks and floorboards groan as people stand from their folding chairs and shift upright from their slouching positions against the wall. The whole porch seems to rise and stand at attention. The sight of Vivi means that Dad is ready to see his first guest.

Vivi studies her clipboard, then eyes the Oklahoma woman. She looks so full of hope that she might just explode and leave bits of the Sooner State all over the front porch.

"Regina Tuck? Mr. Miller will see you now. Please follow me."

Oklahoma's mouth makes a silent O as she steps forward. The rest of the line slouches with resignation, resuming their waiting stances. Vivi motions toward the door, allowing Regina to step inside, then turns back to me.

"Did you clean the bathroom this morning?"

"Yes, Vivi." I'm surprised she didn't check my work before asking. Not that it matters—I scrubbed that thing until it shined like a desert sunset. If I want any hope of getting time for myself today, I can't give Vivi reasons to make me redo work.

"Your dad wants to see you later this afternoon for another session."

As if on cue, the Oklahoma woman clears her throat on the other side of the threshold and crosses her arms impatiently.

"Oh. Okay." My skin prickles and I realize I'm frowning. I plaster on a smile and try to look like that's the best news I've heard all week. Vivi searches my face.

"You feeling all right?"

"Fine. Great." I smile wider.

Vivi narrows her eyes. "When you're done here, how about taking out the trash? But no dawdling this time. You should stick close to the house so you're ready when your dad calls for you. He's got a lot of people to see today and no time to waste. Seems like the line's gotten longer, no?"

She looks like she's about to turn around, but her eyes snap to my chest and her mouth falls open.

"Where did you get that?" Vivi reaches for my necklace. Her voice is sharp, accusing.

I step back so she can't touch it, suddenly feeling protective. There's something comforting about the feel of it against my skin.

"I found it." My fingers curl around the star charm. Vivi's frown deepens.

"Found it where?"

"The porch," I lie. But it makes sense. How else would it have found its way onto my nightstand?

Vivi's eyes jump back and forth between the necklace and

my face, like she's trying to work out whether or not I'm telling the truth.

"Um, ma'am?" The Oklahoma woman clears her throat again. "Should I go see Mr. Miller?"

Vivi shoots an exasperated glance at the woman before rearranging her face into something more pleasant.

"Of course, right this way," she says to Oklahoma, then she points a finger at me. "You really shouldn't just take things you find without asking. It's practically stealing."

I hold back my eye roll until she's inside the house, then feel my shoulders slump with fatigue.

It was dark when I woke up this morning, but since Vivi usually arrives with the sun, getting an early start was the only option if I wanted any time by myself to try to figure out the alarm code. I fought the exhaustion pressing at the back of my eyelids and forced myself out of bed.

I found the alarm on the wall by the front door—a single light glowing red inside the white plastic casing that holds a three-by-three keypad. Red isn't usually a good sign, so I figured Dad probably reactivated it before going back to bed last night.

First I tried his birthday. Then mine. Then Mama's. After each attempt, the red light flashed once, then returned to its steady glow.

By the time I heard Vivi's car thud over the driveway pothole, the sky was starting to streak with purple and I was running out of hope that I would ever figure out the damn code. There could be hundreds of thousands of possible combinations.

I spent the rest of the morning knocking down my chores one by one, waiting for a chance to escape to the park. But every time I tried to slip out unnoticed, Vivi emerged with another chore that kept me anchored to the house.

Until now.

I grab the trash and practically sprint down the path that leads to the tire swing.

Then I see the mail truck parked at the end of the drive.

"Afternoon, Mr. Lewis," I call. A hand waves back, but it doesn't belong to Mr. Lewis. Or at least not the Mr. Lewis I expect to see. Instead, his brother, Hank, emerges from the truck. He's softer around the middle and more unkempt than Mr. Lewis the mailman. His sandy hair sticks to the nape of his neck and his shirt's come untucked in the back. There's a brown splotch staining the front.

"Well, hey there! My brother ain't feeling so well so I'm taking his shifts for a few days." He stuffs a stack of mail into the rusting letterbox.

I nod like that makes complete sense, but a coil of dread tiptoes down my spine as I think about what Marco told me yesterday. Was he right? Did someone hurt Mr. Lewis?

"He all right?" I ask.

Hank hesitates. "Yeah, I reckon he'll be all right. Just not feeling like himself at the moment." He dabs at a line of sweat trickling down the side of his face. "I'll send your regards. Gotta get a move on, though. I got a late start. You have a good one."

Before I can ask anything else, he gives me a wave and backs up the truck.

What'd he mean, *he's not feeling like himself at the moment*? Seems like an odd way to describe someone who's sick.

I walk the trash to the dumpster and wait until the mail truck is out of sight. Then I race toward the park.


*Please be there, Marco.*

I picture his face under my window last night—the way the heat made his dark hair curl around his ears and the white flash of his crooked grin, bright and easy in the fading light.

A swarm of ladybugs circles in my stomach, and I hate myself just a little bit for it. Who cares what Marco looks like? It's silly to get all swoony over some guy I barely know, never mind that he's the mayor's nephew, or that he hangs around with girls like Manuela.

Still, my heart is pumping as I round the bend, as much from nerves as from running. I can feel the dust clinging to my legs and the grime from a morning of chores crusting underneath my fingernails. I probably look like the crawl space under our house chewed me up and spit me out. I wipe my hands on my pants self-consciously before stepping into the park.

My heart drops to my feet. There's no one there. The only sound is the ebb and flow of the cicadas singing their summer song.

But what did I expect? That Marco would spend the whole day

waiting for me just because I found him here yesterday? Of course he has better things to do than sit around waiting for me in some sad little park. Unless he already came and went . . .

But I guess I'll never know.

I look around, circling the space in case he's hiding, which is silly. First, there aren't many places to hide here. Second, why would he need to hide?

Finally, I plunk down on the tire swing and tip my head toward the sky as it swoops backward, letting the disappointment wash over me with the afternoon air. I reach upward, grabbing for the chains so I can dip lower and let my head hang back—

My fingers brush against something tucked into the metal links.

It's a piece of paper.

I set my feet on the ground to stop the tire from swinging. Someone's carefully folded it into a long, thin rectangle and woven it between the chain links so that you'd have to really be looking to find it.

I yank the paper free and unfold it. There are smudges of ink across the page, like whoever folded it didn't have enough time to let the ink dry. I squint against the sun to read the tiny all-caps writing.

L:

Sorry I can't stop by today. My uncle has me driving our handyman Archie around town because his car broke down. I'm taking him to install alarms, like the one you have.

*Supposedly there've been a bunch of break-ins and my uncle wants to make sure everyone's secure. Too bad Archie's not the sharpest knife in the drawer—he programs the same code every time. Any robber who can make a backward letter L could figure it out.*

*Would you meet me at Miracle Lake tonight? I should be there around nine. I'll wait for you as long as I can. Hope you can make it. Don't tell anyone you're meeting me.*

*M*

As if it isn't already clear the note is meant for me, in the lower right corner of the page there's a lumpy sketch of the state of Texas with stars drawn on it, just like on my ceiling map. The map he shouldn't know about, let alone be able to draw since he's never been in my room.

I fold the piece of paper and stuff it into my pocket, smiling.

Marco wants to meet tonight. And he's just told me how to disarm the alarm. It's risky, even if I can manage it.

But first, I need Dad to give me some answers about what happened last night. He owes me that much.

## 11

*Dad's at his desk when I get back, with the remnants of what looks like* another of Vivi's tuna fish sandwiches spread out in front of him. I wonder if he'll have me attempt to make him forget it again. There's a box of junk sitting next to him filled with what looks like a stack of old encyclopedias, a vase, and a painting of a barn. I can only assume the Oklahoma woman used this to supplement her payment in exchange for Dad unburdening her. Great. Because we didn't have enough junk filling the house already.

Dad doesn't hear me when I enter even though the floorboards squeak in announcement. His eyes are fixed on the framed picture of Mama that sits in the corner of his desk, a pensive look on his face that makes me feel like I'm interrupting a moment I'm not meant to witness.

I lean on the squeaky floorboard again to make certain he knows he's not alone.

He looks up and smiles sadly when he sees me.

"I love that picture," I finally say.

"Me too." He sighs and reaches out a finger to tap the glass.

"Remember how she used to make us drop everything and go outside on nice days? Even when you were a baby. I took this at one of her spontaneous picnics. You're just out of the frame, asleep in your stroller, and your mama was trying to get me to put the camera away. She was afraid we'd wake you up. You were such a fussy baby." He laughs to himself, looking from me to the picture as if he hasn't told me this a hundred times before. In it, Mama's looking at the camera, or maybe at Dad since he's the one holding it. Her dark hair is wild as a storm cloud around her face, smile wide and mouth slightly open in a laugh. She is so beautiful and so impossibly alive that it hurts to look at her.

"She looks so happy."

"She was. I know I told her a joke to make her laugh just before I snapped the photo, but I can't for the life of me remember what it was. I was just sitting here looking at it, and I realized I have no idea what joke I told to make her laugh like that. Not that it was that hard to make your mama laugh." He smiles another sad smile.

I nod, afraid that if I speak my voice will give away the lump forming in my throat. I wish I could give that moment back to him. I wish I could jump inside the photo and be that fussy baby again, if only for a few seconds, so I could hear Mama laugh one more time.

I'd planned to come in here guns a-blazing about last night and grill Dad about the alarm, the mysterious phone call, and the strangeness of everything else that happened yesterday. But I can't. I know better than to prod Dad when he's clearly having one of those days where the rooms in the house seem both too full and too empty of Mama—and of the space she left behind. I know it the same way Dad knows not to interrupt me when I'm looking at Mama's scrapbook or tracing the outlines of highways on my ceiling. It's our unspoken father-daughter pact—sometimes, you just need space to remember.

"How about I try to make you forget the sandwich again?" I force enthusiasm into my voice. A subject change and a peace offering. For now.

Dad stands and motions for me to follow him to the couch.

"Sure, yes. The sandwich." He clears his throat and sits. I do the same. Then he stretches his fingers out to me, looking the tiniest bit lighter now that he has something else to focus on. "You remember what to do?"

I nod, but hesitate, searching his face.

"Can you—is it possible to pick and choose what memories you take from people?"

Dad frowns. "What do you mean?"

"Like what if you wanted to *make* someone forget something instead of asking them what they wanted to forget? Could you do that?"

Dad's nose twitches. There's a long pause before he answers.

"We only take what we're given, Lucy. It's the cardinal rule. You know that. Now come on." He pushes his hands into mine, and I can't help but notice that he didn't answer the question. "Ask me what I want to forget."

I think about pressing more, but his hands are hot inside mine and I can hear the crowd impatiently shifting their weight against the porch. So I level my chin with his, look directly into his eyes, and say the magic words.

One second I can hear the folks outside, then next the afternoon sounds blur into quiet. Just like before, there's a little snag inside my head and Dad slides out of view. Pictures start to take shape, but they're smeared and jumbled together, until at last the fragments slip into place and a single image comes into focus.

Only it's not a sandwich like I expect.

There, on the center of the stage inside my mind, is the most beautiful woman I've ever seen. Her hair is dark and wild. Her mouth is open and laughing.

"Stop, Charlie. You'll wake the baby."

The woman's words sound garbled and slow, not quite matching the speed of her mouth as she says them. She shakes her head and laughs again, just as I feel my finger press down on the button of the camera I'm holding. There's a loud *click*.

*Mama?*

I'm not sure if I say it or think it, but I'm certain it's her sitting in front of me just like in the picture. My hands are curled around a camera—I can feel its heft in my hands just the way my dad must have all those years ago.

Mama looks as real as a sunrise. Her laugh is everywhere, all around me in a swirl of sound. And then the image flashes gold and everything seems to shimmer with light, and I'm enveloped by an overwhelming sensation of love so enormous that I feel like I could drown. It's everywhere—as big as the sky and as deep as the ocean. He loves her so much it almost hurts. I can *feel* it in every pore of my body just the way that he must have, only it's like his love for her belongs to me.

*Love is gold*, I realize.

I try to reach for her, but her image dances away, rippling backward like a broken reflection in a pool of water. Then there's another burst of color and the golden feeling of warmth and love that surrounded me just a moment before is replaced by a cold so deep I shiver.

And everything goes red.

I see a flash of Mama's face again, this time walking away, a suitcase in hand. Another flash. Now she's behind the wheel of her Buick, her face determined. *Flash*. Someone screams the same words over and over. *Flash*. She laughs for the camera. *Flash*. Her back, suitcase in hand. *Flash, flash, flash*.

Images soar past me, some in a blur of motion, others in quick static bursts. Everything is red, red, red. It's hard to make sense of what I'm seeing.

But then I'm filled with that same horrible empty sensation I felt the first time I tried to make my dad forget, and the same thought bursts into my consciousness—*red means guilt*. I can feel it—I can *feel* guilt—the same way I felt my dad's golden love for Mama just a moment before. Only this feeling is thick and empty and horrible.

A scream rips from my mouth as I fall back from the bursts and flashes of Dad's recollections. One moment I'm staring at red smears of memories, my chest on fire from the pain of it. The next I'm on the floor, staring up at my dad's face.

What. Just. Happened.

Dad's eyes are wet with moisture. The color's drained from his cheeks.

"What the hell was that?" he asks.

I open my mouth, then close it because I can't seem to form any words. There's a dull thudding in my temples and my stomach's clenching like I might throw up.

Dad's still holding his hands out in front of him, as if he's waiting for me to take them again. They're shaking.

"Mama." I finally find my voice but it's barely a whisper. I squeeze my eyes shut. "I saw Mama on the day from the picture, only it . . . it changed."

His brow furrows. He looks from me to the desk and back again, like he's trying to make sense of it. Did he see it too? Or does he have no idea what I'm talking about?

He stands from the couch, stepping past me as he makes his way to the desk and the framed picture of Mama. For one horrible second I wonder if I've accidentally taken away the afternoon with Mama from him instead. But then his finger traces the beveled frame and his eyes soften, and I know he's remembering her the same way he was when I first entered the room.

"I was picturing the sandwich." Dad lifts the photograph off the desk, turning it over in his hands like it can somehow offer an easy explanation. "But maybe because we were talking about your mom just before, I subconsciously thought of her instead?" He looks back at me like he wants me to reassure him, so I do.

"Yeah, that was probably it." But even as I say the words, I know I don't believe them. Because we weren't talking about Mama that first day when I tried to make him forget the sandwich, and I saw the same flashes of red then. Felt the same, horrible guilt clawing inside of him that day, too.

"That's enough practice for today, don't you think? Clearly my head's not in the game." Dad smiles at me like everything's just fine. I smile back, trying to hide the fact that I've gone cold all over. I stand up so that I can hide my shaking hands behind my back.

"Sorry about that, Ladybug. We'll try again tomorrow." He walks toward the door and I follow, forcing my face to look as neutral as possible, even though two questions blare like last night's alarm inside my head.

First, even if it wasn't intentional, why would Dad think of Mama when I asked him what he wanted to *forget*?

Second and most confusing of all, why would one of his memories about Mama turn red from guilt? There's no way to simply explain that feeling away. It was real. I felt it, painful as a knife. Maybe I could have ignored it the first time because I'd never taken a memory before and I didn't know what to expect. But twice?

"Tell Vivi to give me fifteen minutes or so before she sends up the next guest, won't you? Oh, and can you ask her to come up here and pick up these boxes?" He motions to the encyclopedias and another box of memory-filled jars. The memories swirl inside the glass. The dark core of the shimmering fog seems to pulse. There are nearly a dozen—the Oklahoma woman must have had a lot of memories to get off her chest.

I look straight into Dad's eyes, willing him to say something, *anything*, that tells me he knows what I just saw and can explain it. But there's nothing. Just the soft, tired-looking bags under his eyes and an apologetic frown for having once again failed to teach me how to take memories away.

"Sure, I'll tell Vivi," I reply.

Then Dad looks at me like he has no idea what I'm talking about, his mouth falling into a tiny O. But just as quickly his eyes go wide and a big smile stretches across his face. He claps his hands and runs back to his desk, scooping up the picture of Mama.

"I just remembered what I said to your mom to make her laugh that day!" He looks from me to the picture, grinning wide. "What's a pirate's favorite letter?"

"A pirate's favorite letter?" The question is so absurd that I laugh a little. "Um, *R*?"

"No," he says in a pirate voice, squinting one eye and bending his right hand into a hook shape. "It's the sea." He doubles over, slapping his knee and laughing until tears pool in his eyes. "Get it? *Sea* like the ocean, *C* like the letter? That joke always made your mama crack up. I can't believe I forgot it!"

He looks so happy and so sad at the same time. He loved Mama. He loves *me*. I know it in my heart, and I felt it in his memories, golden and warm as sunlight.

There has to be a reasonable explanation for what I just saw.

"How about I tell Vivi to wait half an hour before sending anyone up here, to give you some time?" I ask him, but before I finish the sentence he's already back at his desk, smiling down at the picture of Mama like he's remembering the day all over again.

I tiptoe out of the room, leaving him alone with his memories and the love I can see so plainly in his eyes. The love I *felt*.

Yes. There's an explanation for all of this, I'm sure of it.

I just need to figure out what.

# 12

*It's well after ten when I finally hear buzz-saw snores rumbling from* inside Dad's bedroom. My neck is cramped from pressing my ear against the door. I've been standing here for the better part of an eternity waiting for Dad to finally conk out. At this rate, I hope Marco hasn't gotten tired of waiting for me and left.

Next to the front door, the red alarm light glows menacingly.

*Any robber who can make a backward letter L could figure it out.*

Here goes nothing.

The numbers are lined up in a three-by-three block. Vivi punched in four numbers, which means the bottom side of the L must only be two numbers wide. That leaves two options: seven, eight, five, two, with the longest side of the L running up the center, or eight, nine, six, three with long side running up the far-right column.

I try the far-right option first. The light blinks once, but stays red. Just like all my failed attempts this morning. I heave out a breath.

*Please don't be wrong about this, Marco.*

My fingers shake as I type in the last combo. The lights on the keypad flash twice, then go dark. The red light disappears.

It's disarmed.

I check Dad's room one last time to make sure he's still asleep. Then I slip out the front door into the summer night.

My bike rests against the side of the clapboard latrine where I left it. If Dad's so concerned about thieves and break-ins, why not have me chain it up? It's not fancy, but it's worth more than a lot of the junk we have inside the house.

I walk the bike along the far edge of the driveway where darker shadows pool and there's no gravel for the tires to crunch against. Once I'm on the other side of the bend, out of view, I hop on and start the ride into town.

It usually takes me about twenty or so minutes, but I pump my legs faster than usual; every second that passes is a second closer to Marco giving up and going home. He said he'd wait as long as he could, but it's pushing 10:30. What are the chances he's still there?

I turn right onto Maple, then wind my way toward Oak, the main thoroughfare leading to the center of town. Whoever did the city planning had one hell of a sense of humor, because none of the leafy season-changing trees the streets are named for exist in Tumble Tree. Nothing around here but angry shafts of bark and branches poking at the sky.

Small, squat houses surrounded by neat picket fences zip past me. My neighbors may not have much, but what they do have they take pride in. Above me, the stars glow bright against the blacktop sky. The moon is a grin. The cicadas hum a song to the desert. It's almost peaceful, except for my racing legs and thudding heart.

On nights like this—when the heat feels like a warm whisper; when the moon hangs high and bright and paints the desert silver; when the sky seems to be made of more stars than darkness, so close it seems I could reach out and touch them if I tried—I can almost understand why Dad doesn't want to leave Tumble Tree.

Almost.

I turn right onto Elm, passing the Dollar General, Mr. Whitcome's Snow Cone Stand, the Texaco, Patty's Pie Pantry. The storefronts are all dark.

Up ahead, the sign for the Dairy Queen looms. I pass it and make a left, turning onto the dirt-packed winding road that leads to Miracle Lake.

Miracle Lake's not nearly big enough to be a real lake, but it's definitely a miracle. Some people say it doesn't have a bottom; that the water goes all the way down to the center of the Earth. Maybe they're right—at least that would explain how a crystal-clear pool can subsist in the Tumble Tree heat.

It's been here as long as I can remember, and long before that, too. Mama and Dad taught me how to swim there when I was little, and in the summertime we'd join the rest of the town with our picnic blankets, towels, and bags of snacks, spreading out along the water's edge and taking turns daring each other to climb up one of the nearby trees and jump into the water. Now, Dad and I steer clear of the lake, no matter how hot the sun burns. Without Mama, it's nothing but a cold hole in the ground.

The parking lot is empty, but as I get closer, I can see a cluster of cars and bikes lined up near the water's edge. Around them, kids mill about, some dancing, some talking, some doing a little bit of both. A few people are in the water, their faces pale against the black surface of the pool even though there's a sign that clearly says NO SWIMMING ALLOWED AFTER DARK.

I should have known.

Marco didn't say anything about other people being here, but on weekends during the school year the lot next to the lake fills with all the kids who can't find anything better to do than hang out in a parking lot and take turns blasting music from their car stereos. Why would summer be any different?

My heart rate quickens.

The twangy hitch of country music blares from the open door of a large green van. Jessica Rodriguez leans against the door frame, her foot tapping to the music. Her mouth pops open when she sees me and she nudges the girl next to her. Manuela's head snaps up, her stop-sign red lipstick impossible to miss. Wisps of hair escape the bun at the crown of her head and her darkly lined eyes shine with shimmery eyeshadow. She looks like she belongs on a crowded New York City avenue, weaving her way between skyscrapers and flashing billboards.

We have absolutely nothing in common.

More heads turn my way as I lean my bike against a pole. I wave at a few people, trying to act like I do this every night, like I'm just another kid in Tumble Tree who treats Miracle Lake as their second home. I ignore the nervous glances they give me and the fact that a few people step back to put more distance between us. As if by just looking at them, *poof*, their memories will disappear.

When I was younger, kids at school would ask me about unburdening all the time. Some of them would even try to get me to practice on them. But Mama and Dad's rules were clear—no memory-taking until I was older. Unburdening wasn't a party trick. Even as a little kid I knew that what my family did was beautiful and important. We took away people's sadness. We helped people stop hurting. That wasn't the kind of thing you messed around with just because people thought it was cool.

But in middle school things changed. People would corner me in the lunch line or after school at the bike rack, begging me to take something from them or someone else. Most of them believed me when I said I didn't know how to do it yet. But some of them didn't. Some of them got mad. Some of them thought I was being selfish and stuck-up. Some of them were tired of me talking about memory-taking like it was something to be revered, like I was better than them.

Then stories started sprouting up about me taking things without permission and people began to keep their distance. Which was just fine by me. I had more important things to focus on. I had the Memory House to help run, chores to do, and burdened guests to help. Plus, I had no intention of sticking around Tumble Tree long enough for any of it to matter. Dad and I were going to leave this place to the dust and the lizards, just like Mama always said we would.

Manuela's red mouth twists into a grimace when she sees me approach. A few others look at me like I've sprouted a second head, probably trying to figure out what Lucy Miller is doing at one of their parties. The song ends, and the silence before the next one feels like an empty chasm punctuating my footsteps. Suddenly I have no idea what to do with my arms as I walk toward the lake.

Then Marco steps out of the crowd and his crooked-road smile stretches into a full-wattage grin, and all the other faces melt away.

"You made it." He sounds genuinely happy to see me. "I was worried you wouldn't find my note."

"I had to wait for my dad to fall asleep. Thanks for telling me how to disarm the alarm. I never would have figured it out."

"No worries. You want something to drink?" He jerks his head toward a truck and leads me toward it before I can answer.

Manuela's eyes narrow as we pass but she doesn't say anything. The music's switched from country to something thick and bass-y and she grabs Jessica's hand, pulling her in to dance. I know Manuela is just pretending to have fun; I can see her staring right at Marco. He either doesn't notice or doesn't care to. I hope it's the latter.

The truck bed's been folded down to make way for two large coolers. Marco hops up onto the lip and digs through one of the ice chests, then holds out a Coke. I reach for it.

"Some of the guys bought stuff to spike it with, if you're interested?"

I shake my head. "This is fine."

"I'm interested." Manuela's suddenly at my side, smiling a pouty grin. I get the sense that she's trying to prove something. Like I made the wrong choice by only having a Coke.

Marco shrugs and digs through a bag at the far end of the truck bed. He passes her a silver flask without a word.

"What brings you here, Lucy?" Manuela's voice is sweet as a Pie Pantry pecan pie, but she's looking at me the way a snake does right before it strikes. "Someone call you over here to do some brain scrambling?" She unscrews the cap and takes a long swig from the flask, her eyes never leaving mine.

"Manuela, come on." Marco shoots me an apologetic look.

"I wasn't planning on doing any brain scrambling tonight." I match her sticky-sweet tone and take a step closer. "But I'd be happy to make an exception for you if you'd like." I don't have to fake my grin when I see the look on her face. I turn to Marco. "Can we go somewhere to talk? Alone?"

"Yeah, sure. Just give me a sec."

He pulls Manuela away from the truck and steers her back toward Jessica. I can't make out what they're saying, but it's clear neither one of them is happy with the other.

A few minutes later, Marco's back at my side. Manuela glares at us from across the parking lot, but she stays put when Marco leads me in the opposite direction.

"Sorry about that." He points toward a white Yukon parked at the very back of the lot. After he hops onto the hood, he pats the space next to him.

"Your girlfriend seems nice," I say, making sure my sarcasm is clear. Then I set the Coke down and raise myself onto the hood. Marco grabs the Coke to keep it from spilling and reaches out to steady me. His hand is warm against my arm.

"She's not my girlfriend."

I raise an eyebrow. "Does she know that?" Our fingers brush as I take my drink from his hand. And I shiver.

Faces keep turning to look at us. Manuela's gone back to dancing with Jessica, but she keeps her body turned in our direction and every now and then her eyes cut over to me. I feel like I'm on display.

"Did you get in trouble last night? For setting off the alarm?"

I shake my head and take another swig of Coke. "I thought for sure he would find you when he went outside. Where'd you go, anyway?"

"The crawl space under your house. I didn't have time to run anywhere else without being seen."

"Oof. Sorry."

"Yeah, you guys should have it looked at. It smells like something died under there."

"Don't say anything about it to your mom. She'll have me digging underneath the house for the rest of the summer, and I am definitely not getting paid enough for that. Sometimes I think she's trying to kill me with all the chores she pawns off on me. You'd think she broke *both* of her arms."

I mean it as a joke, but Marco's smile disappears. His face turns somber.

"Has she said anything to you about . . . me?"

"No," I say. "She's mostly just been keeping me busy with work. Why?"

He looks back at the crowd. Most of them have lost interest in us, turning their attention to the music and their drinks.

"She told me to stay away from you and that if I tell you about what I saw at the mines the other night, she'll have my memory wiped, too. She said I have to keep it a secret because . . . it's dangerous. Listen—" He reaches out and grabs my arm, eyes large and pleading. "I know you think your dad would never do something like that to you, but you have to believe me. It happened. I saw it. And I saw the way you looked after it was over and they were leading you to my uncle's car. You were . . . all wrong, Luce. Empty."

*Luce.*

I look at Marco. I think about his words.

"I swear, I'm not making it up. There's something going on around here that isn't right."

I tip my head to look at the wide stretch of black sky and winking stars. I find the Big Dipper almost immediately, glowing brightly against the cloudless expanse. I feel a tug inside my head, like something is trying to get out, and my hand instinctively reaches for my pocket.

*A fist full of desert to help me remember.*

I shake my head, trying to loosen the thought. But it's stuck there.

"There's something I didn't tell you yesterday at the park." I turn to look at him. My pulse thuds in my ears. Once I say it out loud, I know I won't be able to take it back. It's as if just breathing the words will make the world crack open and the truth come oozing out, and I'll never be able to change things back to the way they were.

I take a deep breath.

"When I woke up yesterday, I found dirt and bits of plants in my jeans pocket. There was too much of it to have been an accident, and I keep having these . . . flashes." I swallow and take a sip of Coke to keep the words from sticking.

"Flashes?" he asks.

I try to read Marco's expression, but I can't. So I keep talking.

"I think I may have put the dirt in my pocket on purpose. To make myself remember something."

"What exactly *do* you remember?"

He runs his thumb back and forth against his lip as he watches me.

"Not much. I mean, it's kind of jerky and not entirely clear. But I keep having flashes of being in the desert, and falling forward, only it's like I'm doing it on purpose—I can feel the intention behind the fall, if that makes sense. And then I grab hold of a fistful of dirt just before I tell myself to remember. I think it's an Echo."

I look at Marco, and suddenly my lower lip is quivering. I wipe at my eyes with the back of my hand, embarrassed but unable to stop myself. His face and the moon and the night sky smear into a watery blur of darkness and light.

"What happened, Marco? I need to know. I need you to tell me all of it."

For a moment, I don't think he'll tell me. But then he takes a deep breath and the words tumble out, one on top of the other, each one cutting deeper than the last.

The music thumps. Laughter floats back from the crowd. People splash lake water back and forth. Above us, the Big Dipper burns and the stars wheel on, watching like a hundred pairs of knowing eyes.

At some point Marco takes my hand in his and I squeeze it hard, not giving it a second thought when he weaves his fingers between mine. When he tells me how the guard hit me on the back of my leg, the tender spot behind my knee pulses with proof. Not that I need any more evidence—Mr. Lewis's absence this afternoon, Dad spending the day in bed, even Vivi's afternoon of acting like a normal human being for once—it all makes sense now. And deep down, I know that everything Marco is saying is true. I can feel the pieces sliding into place, like they've been waiting for me to put them together.

"You looked like a hollowed-out doll after it happened. It was like you were you, but you were empty. Even when they walked you to my uncle's truck, your eyes were open, but I don't think you were seeing anything. It looked like you were just sorta staring blankly as they dragged you. Is that what happens to people after they leave your house?"

"No, not at all. People look . . . light. Happy, even. Like the burdens they'd been carrying were boulders, and without them they're finally free. It must be different when the memories are taken instead of willingly given."

"I should have done something to stop them. I should have . . ." Marco trails off, averting his eyes.

"Come on. What could you have done? Those men had guns." Marco sighs.

"What do you suppose they're hiding down there that's so important?" I ask.

"I don't know, but I think we should try to find out. Whatever it is, it can't be good."

I nod and turn away from him. "My dad's a good person. I don't know why or how he got mixed up in all of this, but there has to be a rational explanation." I'm not sure if I'm saying this to Marco, myself, or both, but I have to fight to keep my voice from cracking.

And then I close my eyes and see Mama's face from Dad's memories, the image splashed red with guilt. It doesn't make any sense.

When I open my eyes again, Marco is staring at me. Hard. Like he's about to say something, but suddenly the volume of the music spikes and he jerks away.

The bass is thumping so loudly it causes the speakers to rattle. More people have started dancing near the water's edge, their voices raised to shouts so they can be heard over the percussive pulse. A few more people have jumped into the lake, clothes and all. Manuela's still on the shore, her arms swung round the neck of Nick Brewer, grinding and laughing as they pass a flask back and forth. They raise their arms to ward off splashes.

"Will you excuse me one sec?"

Marco slides his hand out from mine before I can answer and hops off the hood. I assume he's going to pull Manuela away from Nick, but instead he marches toward the green van and reaches inside. The music volume cuts to a dull hum.

"You can't play it that loud," he says, eyeing the group of people standing near the open truck door. "You're gonna get the cops called on us again."

As if on cue, a police car pulls into the parking lot, followed by a large black pickup truck. Marco's eyes go wide and he turns to look at me, frantically motioning with his hands for me to get down off the hood.

*Hide*, he mouths, then quickly turns back toward the two approaching cars. Manuela pitches the flask underneath the van and a few other people throw similar containers away. The kids in the lake frantically pull themselves ashore, water dripping from their hair and clothes. I hop down, not really sure what is going on.

Then I see who's behind the wheel of the black truck, and I understand.

It's the mayor.

# 13

*The police car stops just after the entrance to the parking lot, blocking the* exit so that no one can leave. The mayor pulls up behind him and hops out, boots thumping against the pavement. For once, he's not wearing sunglasses. Someone's turned off the music, making it seem like all the sound's been sucked out of the night.

I crouch low next to the Yukon and jiggle the front door handle. *Damnit.* It's locked.

I recognize Officer Lewis immediately. He looks like a slightly pudgier version of his dad. Mr. Lewis has told me at least half a dozen times that his son was recently promoted. Maybe that's why he puffs out his chest as he surveys the lot, like he's trying to make himself bigger. I suppose we're supposed to call him Chief Lewis now, but the title doesn't suit him.

I duck before he can see me. Taking a page from *The Marco Handbook of Hiding,* I flatten myself against the pavement and wriggle underneath the car. Dirt and grit stick to my skin as I belly-slide as far back as I can go. At least it's better than the crawl space.

"It's kinda late for a party, don't you think?" Officer Lewis calls. "Thought we agreed you kids wouldn't stay out here past eleven. And I sure as heck hope none of you were swimming in the dark. We posted those signs for a reason. It's dangerous."

"Sorry, sir." A deep voice I don't recognize answers. "We must've lost track of time. We were just about to shut it down."

From my place under the car I can only see about waist-high, but I recognize the mayor's custom snakeskin boots as he walks toward his nephew. Manuela's feet are so close to Marco's that she's practically on top of him. I wonder if she's holding his hand. The thought makes me grit my teeth.

"You kids ain't been drinking tonight, have you?"

"No, sir," Marco responds, his tone all business. "We were just listening to music and talking. It's like they said, we just lost track of time."

"Otis, go check that cooler, won't you?"

Officer Lewis's dark shoes stroll toward the truck bed housing the cooler. The lid makes a loud bang as it flips open. Ice falls to the ground and water sloshes. Then there's the crack and fizz of a can being opened, and I can only assume he's grabbed one of the sodas for himself.

"Just a bunch a Cokes, sir." Officer Lewis lets out a loud belch.

"Check around, just to be sure."

More ice hits the pavement, followed by the thumps and bumps of Officer Lewis digging around for contraband. It sounds like he's inspecting every single can of Coke. While he searches, the mayor weaves in and out of the crowd, pausing in front of each person. His boots *thunk, thunk, thunk* against the pavement.

I hope there aren't more flasks beyond the one Manuela took—if Officer Lewis or the mayor find them, they might not be quick to leave. The mayor already seems to be taking his sweet time as it is; it's like he enjoys making the kids in town squirm. My nose itches and my left hand's gone numb. I don't know how much longer I can stay smashed against the pavement like this.

"I'm not finding anything else, sir, 'cept a pack a Marlboros," calls Officer Lewis. "I think the kids are telling the truth."

"All right, then." The mayor finally makes his way back to Marco. Manuela's standing way too close to him. Her legs shift from foot to foot like she's barely able to stand still.

"Manuela, you all right?" The mayor takes another step toward her. "How've you been? My nephew treatin' you okay?"

"Yes, sir," she says, her feet continuing their two-step. "I'm sorry, sir, but I really gotta pee. I don't think I can hold it anymore. Too many Cokes, I guess."

A few people chuckle, the mayor included.

"Yeah, all right. Go on ahead. Bathroom's closed and locked up for the night, though I reckon you know that."

"Yes, sir," she says, "I'll be real quick."

Then Manuela turns and freight-trains toward the Yukon.

My heart pumps in my ears. I try to press myself into an even flatter pancake, praying it's dark enough under the car that she won't see me.

Her shoes slap past me toward the back of the Yukon.

*Shit.*

I hear rocks crunching under her feet as she squats right there behind Marco's car. I can't bring myself to look, so I squeeze my eyes shut and grit my teeth, as if that will make a difference.

Because I'm lying right downstream of her.

Another shuffle. Another crunch of ground beneath shoes as she settles in.

No way. I can't do this. Mayor or no mayor, I can't let Manuela *pee* on me.

I try to slide over, away from the path, heartbeat thundering inside my head.

"I know you're under there."

I open my eyes. I'm facing the other way, but I can see the shadow her body casts from the back of the car where she's crouched. My stomach clenches.

"Why are you hiding from Marco's uncle?" Her voice is louder this time. I get the feeling she's doing it on purpose.

"Manuela, please," I hiss back. "Be quiet."

"Are you dating Marco again?"

*Again.*

From the parking lot Marco calls, "I should probably get Manuela home." He must be saying it to the mayor, but his volume makes me think it's meant for me and Manuela. "I didn't realize how late it was."

"You kids need to stick to our agreement—no hanging out

here past eleven." The mayor's boots thump. It sounds like they're backing away. "The next time Officer Lewis and I won't be so forgiving. I mean it."

There's a chorus of *yes, sir*s and *sorry, sir*s, then the sound of footsteps retreating in different directions. They're letting everyone go.

Car doors open and close. The truck bed slams shut. Engines rumble to life. I heave out a relieved breath.

Manuela stands. I hear someone marching toward the car.

*Please let it be Marco.*

"I'll be home soon," Marco calls to the mayor, closer now, and I remember that Vivi and Marco live in the mayor's large house at the edge of town.

Then Marco's feet are next to Manuela's and it looks like he's steering her toward the passenger side of the Yukon.

"What the hell were you trying to do?" he hisses.

"*Me?* What the hell are you doing bringing Lucy Miller here? Are you going to tell me what's going on, or am I going to have to ask your uncle?"

"Just get in the damn car. Where'd Lucy go?"

"She's crawling on the ground like a bug, where she belongs."

I grit my teeth and bite back a retort.

Manuela climbs into the front seat, then a few moments later Marco's head appears underneath the car. His crooked smile is not far behind when he sees me wedged beneath the undercarriage.

"He's gone now. You can come out."

I belly-slide out, then stand and shake my stiff limbs loose. I'm covered in dirt and grime. My neck feels like someone sat on it.

"You all right?"

I roll my shoulders to get the kinks out. "I think so."

Marco opens the back door and motions for me to get in. "I'll take you home. Probably better that you're not out on the streets in case Officer Lewis is patrolling."

"Right, okay. I just need to get my bike." I jerk my head toward the place where I left it.

Marco nods once, then crosses the lot to retrieve it. I wipe the grit from my hands and clothes and slide into the back seat.

Manuela's inspecting her lipstick in the passenger mirror like it's her job. Her eyes flick to my face and narrow. "Don't tell me he's giving you a ride home, too." She snaps the visor shut and crosses her arms over her chest.

"What is your problem with me, exactly?"

"My problem"—Manuela spins to face me and jabs a finger in my direction—"is that you aren't supposed to be here. You aren't supposed to be in his life anymore."

My mouth suddenly feels dry. I reach for the star pendant around my neck and a wave of vertigo rocks my vision.

*Marco's thumb against my palm—*

*The sound of my name when Marco whispers it—*

*The feel of Marco's breath on my cheek—*

"I have no idea what you're talking about," I hear myself say, but the words sound like they're coming from someone else's mouth.

Because I do know. The same way Marco knows about the map on my wall. The same way my fingers knew the way his hand felt before tonight.

We're two forked roads finally merging.

Again.

I lean forward and grip the headrest, just as Marco opens the back of the Yukon and heaves my bike inside.

"What happened between me and Marco? Please, you have to tell me. I—I can't remember."

Manuela studies me with the same intensity Dad uses when unburdening someone. Her bright red lips disappear into a thin line.

"Please," I add once more. "What do you know?"

The front door jerks open and Marco slides into the front seat. The jangle of the keys slices through the quiet inside the car. His eyes jump back and forth between us.

"What'd I miss?"

Manuela looks down at her hands, studying the blue chipped nail polish. Her fingernails are bitten to nubs.

The silence stretches.

Marco's eyes find mine, but I don't know how to respond.

"Fine. You really wanna know what happened?" Manuela looks right at me. "You had each other erased. After you guys broke up. You had Lucy's dad make you forget that you ever knew each other."

I can't breathe.

The darkness has hands. They close around my throat, my chest—my heart.

"How exactly do you know this?" Marco clutches the black vinyl steering wheel so hard his knuckles are white.

Manuela looks out the passenger window, studying the trees that line the back of the parking lot. They look like gnarled fingers pointing up toward the night sky.

"The mayor told me. He told all of us. He showed up at Miracle Lake one night and told us all that you'd broken up and had each other erased. He said we shouldn't mention Lucy's name in front of you. That it would be too upsetting. That it was better if we let you both just go your separate ways. He said it's what you wanted."

She looks up at Marco, her eyes large and round. "I thought you couldn't remember her—that you didn't want to. I thought that you were over her and that I was . . ." She trails off, shaking her head. Her lower lip wobbles. "Never mind. Just take me home."

# 14

*The drive to Manuela's house is silent. Like the air has been sucked out* of the car. Or the world.

I avoid Marco's eyes in the rearview mirror and the reflection of Manuela's tear-streaked face in the passenger-side window. Instead, I watch the jagged trees slide past; the moon smiling high in the sky; the dark line of the desert horizon in the distance where Texas and Mexico collide.

*You had each other erased.*

It isn't unheard of for kids from my school to show up at the Memory House asking to have someone that hurt them erased, but Dad's rules are firm—he won't take memories from anyone under eighteen. Why would he make an exception for me and Marco?

The roads are empty and we pull up to the entrance of Manuela's cul-de-sac a few minutes later. The car has barely even come to a stop when she wrenches the door open and jumps out.

"Manuela, wait. Will you just give me a—" Marco leans across the seat like he wants to grab her, but she's gone. The door slams, putting a perfunctory exclamation on the evening.

We watch her recede into the night, practically running toward a tidy double-wide with a rainbow-colored pinwheel sticking out of the dusty front yard. She doesn't turn around.

It's Marco who finally breaks the silence. "Do you want to sit up front?" He angles his body to look at me.

"I probably shouldn't. What if your uncle is still patrolling?" It's a practical response, but the truth is that I like the distance created by the seat between us and the fact that he can't get a good look at me. I'm afraid he'll be able to see my hands shaking. That he'll hear my heart pounding.

"Right, good point." He nods, like he agrees with me, but his voice is tinged with something else. Disappointment?

He turns back around and eases the car onto the road, taking care to look both directions even though Tumble Tree is a ghost town. His eyes linger a second too long in the rearview mirror, catching mine.

I feel my face flush and roll the window down a crack to let the night inside. The warm breeze feels good against my sticky skin.

Would I really have asked Dad to erase Marco? I close my eyes and think about the way my skin heats when he's near. It's hard to imagine wanting to forget that. But I can't deny the gaping holes in my thoughts or the flashes of unexplained things I saw that day I bumped into Marco and Manuela at the park. The wreckage of Echoes and missing thoughts are there—and there are too many to ignore.

If what Manuela says is true, that still doesn't explain *why*. Dad says we're never allowed to take a memory we aren't willingly given. So why would he have taken so many of mine?

"Just so you know, I wouldn't have done that," Marco says, like my thoughts are on display. I meet his gaze in the rearview mirror. His eyes are dark and serious. "I wouldn't have had you erased. I don't care what Manuela says, she's wrong."

The inside of my mouth feels like sand. Once I say this, I can't take it back.

"Marco, I've seen flashes—of us. The other day you asked whether there was a map on my ceiling. You even drew it on the bottom of the note you left me."

"Yeah . . ."

"Well, there is. And it looks exactly how you drew it—because you've seen it, haven't you? You've been in my room." It's not a question. "We had something once."

He looks at me with the saddest expression.

"I think Manuela is right," I add.

"I know. But that's not what I meant."

"What do you mean?"

"When I said I wouldn't have done that, I meant I wouldn't have *asked* to have you erased. There's no way I would willingly want to forget you. Ever." He swallows and drops his gaze. My chest flares with warmth, and I think about how his hand felt when we were sitting on his hood. Soft and familiar.

He's right. I wouldn't want to forget that—forget *him*—either.

"So you think Manuela's lying?" I ask.

Marco shakes his head. "No, I don't think she'd lie about that. Manuela's many things, but she's not a liar."

I try not to linger on what *many things* Manuela is—was— to him.

"Okay, so if Manuela isn't lying, then that would mean your uncle is. Why would he tell everyone we had each other erased if it's not true?"

Marco's Adam's apple bobs up and down. "What if it wasn't our choice? What if they forced us, just like they forced people to forget at the mines?"

No.

"My dad wouldn't do that. He wouldn't take something that important from us unless we wanted him to. That's the cardinal rule of unburdening. Not to mention it's against our policy to take memories from minors." I try to make the words sound strong, but there's a wobble in my voice.

"Then how do you explain the other night, Luce?" His voice is gentle, but the words sting all the same.

"I don't know. But there has to be a good reason."

*Except I can't think of a single one.*

The Yukon veers off the main road, heading toward the bend that leads to my driveway. Marco turns off the headlights, leaving us in darkness as he pulls up slowly. In the wan light of the moon I can just see the outline of the chain and the CLOSED sign blocking the entrance.

He cuts the engine. His shadow is rigid, hands gripping the

wheel. Outside, the cicadas buzz. Time seems to stretch around us. I can't tell the difference between a second and a minute.

Finally, Marco clicks on the overhead light and turns to look at me. His face is oddly pale in the bright light. There's a small mole on his right cheek, and I have the sudden urge to reach out and touch it.

His eyes rove over my face, like he's studying me, too. They land on the star necklace resting against my collar bone.

"Where'd you get that?" He leans across the center console and reaches for it, his fingers brushing my neck as they lift the charm.

My skin goosebumps.

"That seems to be a popular question," I say, recalling Vivi's expression when she saw me wearing it. "I found it. On my night-stand. I must have picked it up somewhere and put it there without thinking—"

Marco shakes his head and leans even closer—close enough that I can feel his breath against my skin. I realize that I'm leaning forward, too, shrinking the space between us.

"I know this necklace. I've seen it before, I just can't—" He squeezes his eyes shut. Dark eyelashes rest against his cheeks. When he opens them I notice what a deep shade of brown they are—warm, like fresh coffee in the morning. "I think I gave this to you."

He drops the charm but doesn't move away. He doesn't look away, either. He watches me, and I wonder if he's studying the color of my eyes, too, or if he's counting my freckles, or memorizing the curve of my cheek the way I'm trying to memorize his.

"When?" I ask, the word barely a whisper.

"I don't know. But I know I gave it to you. I can *feel* it, if that makes sense."

I nod. Is that why I can't remember how the necklace ended up on my nightstand—because it's a remnant from when Marco and I were together? I think of the flashes I've been having of Marco; the way there's something about him that seems to be on the edge of my thoughts, just out of reach.

"When we unburden people, we tell them to get rid of any physical objects tied to the memories they want to have erased. Because objects with emotional ties can trigger an Echo." I press my lips together. He's so close that he must be able to hear my heart beating—the sound seems to fill the cabin. I have the sudden urge to close the distance between us, like there's an invisible thread pulling me toward him.

Marco looks out the window, thinking. "The other night at the mines, just before you got caught—you were holding the necklace when you sort of spaced out. It was like you forgot where you were for a moment. And you were looking at me like, I don't know, like you *knew* me, if that makes sense. Could that have been an Echo?"

I think of the way Marco looked at me that day at the park—like he could see inside me.

"Maybe," I say. "None of this makes any sense."

He leans back and runs his hands through his hair.

"I know it's hard to believe, Luce, but there's something bad going on here, and your dad and my uncle are at the center of it. I think my mom's involved somehow, too, otherwise why else would she have been at the mines that night? For some reason, they don't want us together."

I open my mouth to protest again, but Marco keeps talking.

"My mom even said something about it when she found us. She said something like, 'Why can't you guys just stay away from each other?' Why would she say that unless they were trying to keep us apart? And then she told me to stay away from you. She said that I couldn't tell you what happened at the mines, no matter what. That it was dangerous."

I swallow. The sick feeling in my stomach is back.

"Okay," I whisper. "But why?"

"I don't know. But I think it has to do with what's inside the mines. I don't think they're mining what they say they are. And I think maybe at some point we figured out what they're really doing."

"And they had our memories erased because of it," I add.

I hate how much sense it makes.

"You said your mom couldn't let the mayor know you'd followed him to the mines *again*. Which means we'd been there before."

"Exactly." Marco's face is shadowed, brows knit. "Have you ever wondered why no one talks about what's actually being mined down there?"

I try to remember, but Marco's right. Most of the town works at the mines. There aren't many other places to work, outside of the few restaurants and shops on the main drag, and even then, most people do shifts at the mines to bring in extra cash. I've lived in Tumble Tree my entire life—shouldn't I know what the town's number one export is?

"I don't know either," he continues, watching my face. "Every time I try to think of the answer, my brain goes all staticky and I can't find the word. It's like it's been plucked right out of my head. And then I started thinking about how other people talk about it. No one ever says what they do, do they? They just say, 'They're going to work at the mines,' or 'My dad works at the mines.' Doesn't that seem strange to you? It's like the entire town has no idea what the heck is happening around here. Like they've all been brainwashed."

The hairs on my neck start to rise. It's hard enough to process the fact that my dad took my memories, Marco's memories, and the memories of everyone working at the mines the other night. But the entire town?

"Look. I hear what you're saying, but I know my dad. He must have had a good reason to do what he did. You said yourself he was held at gunpoint. They *forced* him to take away my memories. He's not a memory thief, Marco."

Marco presses his mouth into a line. The silence stretches as he studies my face, and I can tell there's a war going on inside his head. There's something he's not telling me.

"What?" I finally ask. "What aren't you saying?"

He opens his mouth. Closes it. Shakes his head.

"It's late. Maybe we should talk more tomorrow, once we've both gotten some rest and had a chance to let all of this sink in."

"No way. Whatever it is, I can take it. I mean it can't be any worse than anything else you've told me tonight, right?"

I mean it as a joke, but Marco's expression darkens.

"Just say it," I whisper. The air suddenly feels too thick inside the car.

"It's something my uncle said right before your dad took everything from you." He pauses. "I—I don't even know how to ask you this."

"Just say it, Marco." This time I don't whisper.

"It was about your mom."

"My mom? What do you mean?"

*Mama's face splashed red; the cold, hard feeling of guilt slicing through me . . .*

Marco runs his hands through his hair and lets out a long exhale. "Luce, how did your mother die?"

I flinch and swallow back the familiar lump that forms whenever someone brings her up. "She was in an accident." I turn my head toward the direction of our park. There are trees blocking the view and it's too dark to see much of anything anyway, but I can feel it out there, like a living, breathing shadow of Mama.

*Ladybug, I love you bigger than Texas. Bigger than all the stars in the sky.*

"What kind of accident?" Marco's voice is gentle, but I still feel like I've been slapped.

"Why are you asking me this?"

"Just try to answer the question. It's important. What kind of accident was it?"

Suddenly my hands are shaking so hard I have to grip the lip of the seat. The edges of my vision start to blur, tunneling inward so that all I can see is Marco's shadowed face. My temples throb.

"She was in an accident," I say again, then I close my eyes so I can't see the concern on Marco's face. "She . . . She was in . . . She had . . . She . . . it was . . . an . . . acci . . ."

Sweat drips down the back of my neck from effort. My whole body quakes. I bang my fists against the seat, trying to force the answer.

"She was in an accident!" I spit the words in one continuous string, my voice rising to a shout.

Because it's the only thing I can say.

Because I can't answer the question.

Because I have no idea how my mother died.

# 15

*The Memory House doesn't open until noon on Sundays, so I'm left with* a blissfully free morning. Dad's banging around in the kitchen like he usually does when Vivi's not around to feed him, so I take advantage of his distraction.

"I'm heading out for a bit, Dad. I'll be back before we open!"

I force a smile into my voice and avoid eye contact, then run past him out the front door and hop on my bike before he can stop me.

I can't face him right now. I have no clue what to say. Last night I tossed and turned, Mama's face swimming in and out of focus. I have a right to know what happened to her. I *need* to know what happened to her. But right now, I just want to get to Marco.

Patty's Pie Pantry looks more like a house than restaurant, with gingham curtains lining the windows and rocking chairs peppering the wraparound porch. By noon, the place will be packed with the after-church crowd, but for now the rocking chairs are empty and most of the cars in the lot belong to the staff. I spot Marco's

Yukon in a parking spot near the front, and my stomach squeezes. I reach for the star charm, pressing the points against my fingers like that will somehow calm my nerves.

The bell above the door tinkles when I open it, and I'm hit with the scent of pancakes, eggs, and bacon frying on the griddle.

"Lucy!" Patty grins at me from her usual place at the hostess stand, her smile broad and welcoming. "What a pleasant surprise. I haven't seen you in here in weeks. Where've you been hiding?"

"Oh, just working longer hours at the Memory House this summer. Hoping to save up to buy a car."

Patty looks at me like I just told her I landed on the moon, the parentheses around her mouth deepening with surprise.

"Well, look at you, Miss Independent." She reaches for two plastic menus, as if everyone in town doesn't already have the menu memorized. "Seems like just yesterday you were toddling around in diapers and here you are talking about cars. Time really does fly, doesn't it? Is your dad parking?" She looks behind me expectantly.

"Actually, it's just me today. I had a craving for blueberry pancakes and he'd already eaten, so here I am." I shrug, searching the restaurant for Marco. "Okay if I just grab an open seat at the bar? No need to take up a table if it's just me."

"Sure thing. Head on back and Missy will be with you shortly. So good to see your face!"

"Good to see you, too, Patty."

I wave off the menu that she offers and make my way toward

the back bar where Marco is sitting. He looks up just as I pull out the stool next to him.

"Not there." He motions to the next seat over, leaving a wide space between us. "Just in case one of my uncle's men comes in, I don't want it to look like we're here together."

I nod and move one seat down, feeling a twinge of disappointment. Vivi and his uncle are with most of the town at Sunday service, so the risk of being seen is low. But still, he's right to be cautious. Especially since he feigned a headache to get out of church. At least, that's what he said he was going to do last night when we agreed to meet up here.

"How're you holding up?" Marco takes a sip of the coffee that's in front of him and watches me. Shadows from last night ring his eyes.

I shrug, because I don't know how to describe the buffet of emotions I'm feeling—anger and sadness, with a heaping side of confusion?

"I don't know," I say instead. "It's . . . a lot to digest."

"That's one way to put it." He gives me a crooked grin, and I feel myself relax. "Thanks for meeting me."

"Who can say no to Patty's famous pancakes on a Sunday morning?" I smile and try to pretend that's all this is: breakfast between friends rather than two people trying to figure out how to put the pieces of their missing past together.

"If you wanna know the truth, I'm more of a waffle guy. Don't hold it against me?"

My cheeks heat at the notion of being held against Marco and I instinctively reach for my star necklace. I can't stop tracing the way his hair curls around his ears or noticing how it looks black, except when the sunlight reveals coffee-colored streaks that match his eyes. Why didn't I take a menu so I would have something else to look at?

Missy appears next to me, notebook in hand, and I'm grateful for the distraction.

"What can I get you, hon?"

Her curly hair is teased in a mound on top of her head like usual. It reminds me of cotton candy, if cotton candy were bright red and frozen in place with a gallon of hair spray. Missy's worked at Patty's Pie Pantry for as long as I can remember. When I was little, she used to sneak me crayons and coloring books while Mama and Dad ate. Now she always gives me an extra pancake when I sit in her section. And she's forever in a good mood—the building could be on fire and Missy would still find a way to smile and laugh it off.

She pulls a pencil from the pocket of her blue-and-white-checked Pie Pantry apron and raises her eyebrows expectantly.

"The usual, thanks, Missy."

Missy tips her head to the side and blinks her large green eyes at me. "Which is what, exactly?"

I stare at Missy, waiting for her to erupt into one of her giggle fits and tell me she's kidding or make fun of me for being so gullible. But she just taps the pencil against her notebook and looks up at the fork-and-knife clock hanging on the wall.

"Blueberry pancakes and a large sweet tea, please," I finally say.

"You want bacon or sausage?"

"Er—neither."

I always get the same exact thing. Most days she puts in the order as soon as she sees me walk through the door. How can she not remember?

Missy snaps her notebook shut and gives me the same smile she gives out-of-towners.

"I'll be right back with that tea, hon." Then she sashays back to the kitchen.

I wait until she's out of earshot. "That was weird. She acted like she didn't know me."

"Same," Marco says, shaking his head. "Maybe she's tired. She was one of the people working at the mines the other night. Maybe she worked last night, too?"

I recall her telling me she was saving up to go to nursing school a few months back, so maybe she's picking up extra shifts to help make ends meet. But still, after what Marco told me, the idea of Missy working at the mines makes me go cold all over.

She comes back with the sweet tea and scurries away without so much as a word. Missy's usually as boisterous as her hair, but today there's something stiff about the way she moves, like she can't quite remember how her legs work.

Marco must see the worry on my face because he reaches across the bar for my hand. Then just as quickly, he yanks it back.

"Sorry," he says, shaking his head. "I keep having this urge to grab your hand. It's like this . . . pull, if that makes sense. Do you think it's one of those Echo things? Like my body remembers what it was like to be your boyfriend even though my mind doesn't?"

The word *boyfriend* hangs heavy between us, feeling somehow wrong and right at the same time. Last night it felt so natural when he grabbed my hand—as though there were a thread wound taut between us, inching us closer.

"It's weird," I say, looking at my hands so I don't have to look at him. "Supposedly we have this entire past together, but I don't know anything about you, like what your favorite food is or what you want to do after you graduate."

The left side of Marco's mouth twitches into a smile. "It's a tie between chocolate chip ice cream and Patty's shrimp and grits. And as for after school . . ." He shrugs, looking at the mug clasped in his hands. "My uncle wants me to follow in his footsteps and become mayor someday. It's what all the men in our family do." He deepens his voice so that it has the same gravelly sound as his uncle's. "You come from a long line of Tumble Tree mayors, Marco. It's our legacy to keep this town safe."

"But you don't want that," I say, because it's clear he doesn't. "So what then?"

"It's probably a long shot, but the University of Texas has a pretty good writing program. SMU up in Dallas, too, though it's really expensive. I thought maybe if I could get a scholarship . . ." He shrugs, looking toward the window. "But it's a long shot."

Judging by their giant house on the edge of town, I'd always assumed the mayor had plenty of money. But maybe money's not the problem. Maybe he just doesn't want Marco to leave. Family legacies aren't the kind of thing you can just walk away from. I would know.

The star charm is warm against my throat, and suddenly—

*Marco is leaning against a tree, a notebook in his hand. The sun is high and bright in the sky, giving his hair a warm brown sheen that matches his eyes. I'm in the tire swing, head tilted back as I listen to him read one of his stories. It's a story about a girl who can never get lost. A story about a girl who sees the world for what it could be rather than what it is. A story full of roads and magic and possibilities.*

"'The Girl with a Compass for a Heart.'" The title slides out of my mouth like it was just waiting there for me.

Marco blinks in surprise. I wonder if this is what I looked like when he asked me about my ceiling map.

"I think maybe you read it to me once, in the park by the Memory House."

Marco nods, and I wonder if he has seen a flash of that day, too.

I scan the knickknacks covering the restaurant walls, as if I'll find a clue about our past nestled in the decor.

"You think we ever came here together?"

"Definitely," Marco says, grinning. "But I bet I took you somewhere nicer for our first date, like outside of town. I would have wanted to impress you."

Heat creeps back into my cheeks as I try to imagine what it would be like to go on a date with Marco. Maybe I would have stressed over what to wear. Maybe he would have been nervous, fumbling with the handle when he tried to open the car door for me. Maybe our hands would have slid together on the drive, and sometime during the night, maybe there would have been a kiss.

*A first kiss.*

With a pang, it hits me that I probably had my first kiss with Marco. And I'll never be able to get it back.

"I wish I could remember it," Marco says, his voice edged with anger.

"I know. Me too."

He looks at me. "Okay, there's something I need to tell you."

Oh no. I don't know if I can handle anything else right now.

"I went to the mines this morning."

"You did *what?*" I can't stop my voice from rising.

Marco shushes me, then glances around to make sure no one's paying attention to us.

"Why didn't you wait for me?"

The plan was to meet here and then go to the mines together. Like most things in town they're closed on Sunday, so we figured we could check it out in the daylight to see if it jogged any memories, or if we could find clues about what they were up to down there.

"I wanted to make sure it was safe before I brought you there. I only planned to do a quick drive-by."

He shrugs and bites his lip, avoiding my eyes, and I wonder if he purposely waited to tell me; if, like me, he wanted to spend a few normal minutes together first, where we weren't talking about the mines or what's been taken from us.

"So, what did you find?" I keep my voice low this time.

He shakes his head. "Nothing. There's a guard positioned at the entrance. I couldn't even make the turn in. I don't think there's a way for us to get in without being seen, unless we want to try again tonight. Or I can try going by myself, so we don't put you at risk again."

"No way. If anyone should go, it's me. You at least have your memories of what happened the other night. If they catch you, we lose everything."

"Well, I'm not letting you go by yourself," he says, jaw set.

"Then I guess we're in this together." I match his determined tone. Something hitches in my chest when I say the word *together*. "What could they be hiding that they need to protect so badly on a Sunday?"

Marco opens his mouth to respond, but there's a shout from one of the other tables.

A man jumps to his feet, his pants covered in dripping brown liquid.

"What the hell is wrong with you?" he shouts, motioning to Missy. She's leaning over his table, a coffeepot in her hand, pouring liquid into an overflowing cup. It pools on the table and drips onto the floor in a brown, steaming waterfall. Missy's eyes are wide and unblinking. Her mouth opens and closes, opens and closes, but no sound comes out.

"Missy!" cries Patty, running to her side. "Missy, what are you doing?"

She presses a hand on top of Missy's, forcing her to finally stop pouring. Missy's eyes seem to refocus. She looks from the coffeepot to the man, then back to Patty, brow furrowed like she can't quite work out what's happened.

"Missy," Patty says again, more gently this time. "Are you okay? What's gotten into you?"

Missy clutches the coffeepot to her chest, hands trembling.

"Who's Missy?" she asks. "And who are you?" She looks around the room. "Where am I?"

A tear slides down her cheek. The coffeepot slips from her fingers and crashes to the floor. Shards of glass skitter across the restaurant.

I jump to my feet at the same time as Marco. From the kitchen, I hear shouting. Someone yells to call for help.

Missy drops onto her heels and starts rocking, a low moan escaping her lips. Patty squats next to her, whispering in her ear, while the rest of the staff scurries to sweep up the broken glass and wipe the still-dripping coffee from the table.

My heart seizes as thoughts knock around inside my head. It's like she's forgotten who she is—like she has no memory . . . of herself.

But that doesn't make any sense.

Marco and I look at each other. Freaked.

"Lucy," he says. "Do you think the Memory House could have

had something to do with this?" Marco's voice is gentle, but it doesn't stop the question from feeling like a slap.

I shake my head. "No. Unburdening doesn't work like that. We take away specific memories—snippets of people's past that they don't want anymore. We don't take away an entire person's sense of self. I don't even know how that would be possible."

I think of all the jars Dad would have to fill, of how long that would take. Even if he wanted to erase someone, there's just no way.

Marco's hand is on my arm, fingers hot against my skin.

"Luce—"

"No! I'm telling you, even if my dad could do something like that, he wouldn't. Plus, why would he do that to Missy, of all people? It doesn't make sense."

Patty has Missy seated at one of the tables now, a cloth pressed to the back of her neck. The sobs have subsided, but her breathing is loud and quick.

"Wait a sec. Missy obviously showed up to work today, right?" I ask, an idea taking shape. "She must have woken up and gotten dressed in her uniform, knowing that she was coming to the Pie Pantry. Which means my dad couldn't have just wiped away *all* her memories—otherwise how would she have known to come here? Something else must have happened."

Marco bites his lip, thinking. "If she works at the mines, she's probably had her memory erased multiple times. That's what my uncle said to Mr. Lewis when he tried to fight back—that it had happened before."

"So if Missy has had her memories erased more than once, too, you think this could be a reaction somehow?"

"Possibly," Marco says. "Maybe having it done too many times makes you forget more than just the memory you had erased."

It's an interesting theory. And it's not like I would know what people look like after having their memories wiped a bunch of times. The people who come to the Memory House are almost always one-time customers, content once their burdens have been lifted. Except . . .

"If that's true, wouldn't you and I be having fits like that, too, though? You said yourself my dad admitted that he'd erased my memories before—that the other night wasn't the first time." Marco frowns and looks like he's about to disagree, but I keep going.

"What about the stuff you said they gave Mr. Lewis—the black liquid he drank that made him act all strange? Do you think they could have given the same thing to Missy? What if this is what happens to you once it's been in your system for a while? Or if you've been forced to drink it multiple times? Maybe it has nothing to do with my dad at all. Maybe it's just that weird drink?"

The front door jangles before Marco can answer and heavy boots *thunk* through the restaurant entrance.

Officer Lewis and another man I don't recognize step through the door. Judging by the look on Marco's face, I can only assume the stranger works for the mayor.

"Shit," Marco mutters, stepping several feet away from me. His face turns ashen.

The man with the boots has a thick beard and aviator glasses, just like the mayor. I can't see his eyes, but I can feel them on me as his head jerks back and forth between me and Marco. Something cold slithers down my spine.

"Tonight," Marco whispers, his head faced forward and his lips barely moving. "I'll come to your window." Then he raises a hand and walks toward the men. "Officer Lewis! Archie. So glad you're here. There's something wrong with Missy Cooper. She needs help."

I focus my attention away from Marco, even though I want to run to him; even though I want to ask him who this man really is, what time he'll come to my house tonight, and if he's going to be okay.

"Patty, is there anything you need?" I say, slipping a few bills on the table for the tea. Patty doesn't look at me; her eyes are focused on Missy. "I'm gonna get out of your hair, but please call if there's anything I can do to help."

She nods and turns away.

Then I march out of the restaurant, past Officer Lewis and whoever this Archie guy is, without once looking back at Marco even as my heart screams at me to go to him.

## 16

*I make my way back home, but I don't even know why. Home is supposed* to be a safe haven. But how can I feel safe when everything I thought I knew about my life and my family is unraveling? My home is a place I don't recognize anymore. It's as if the walls were just there to hold up the lies, and now that I know the truth, everything is gone.

"You're back," says Dad. His voice is cheerful, without the slightest hint of betrayal.

It makes me want to scream, but I hold it inside. I can't let Dad suspect that anything is up.

I stiffen as he marches into the kitchen, an oblivious smile reaching across his face. He moves past Vivi, who's busy emptying the dishwasher, and grabs the PB&J she's left on the counter for him. When he takes a bite crumbs scatter across his shirt front and the floor. Vivi rolls her eyes and hands him a napkin.

"What do you say we have another practice session once we wrap for the evening?" Dad opens the cabinet and pulls out the coffee mug with WORLD'S GREATEST DAD! painted on the front in crooked rainbow letters. I made it for him for Father's Day years ago, when I believed that fathers were worth celebrating.

I force my face into a smile. "Sure."

The lie slides out easily. And why wouldn't it? I've been raised by a lying man in a lying house in a town filled with lies. I press on the points of my star necklace—the necklace Marco thinks he gave me. The necklace I have no memory of getting because of Dad, because of what he took from me.

I want to yell at him. I want to ask him *why*. But I'm too afraid the truth will only lead to more lies. Or worse—that he'll erase my memories again and I'll go back to being an oblivious puppet like everyone else in this stupid town.

I push the remnants of my sandwich around my plate, avoiding eye contact to hide my fury. Making sure I don't accidentally let him see that I know he's a memory thief.

"Great, see you in a few hours," Dad says, raising WORLD'S GREATEST DAD! toward me in a mock toast. I make a mental note to throw the mug in the trash.

I don't know how I'll be able to keep up this charade—but I have to. Until I figure out what the heck is going on around here, I have to.

Vivi finishes with the dishwasher and wipes her hands on a towel, watching me.

"You aren't eating," she says in that way she has of stating the obvious. The bright pink dress and matching pink lipstick she's wearing makes her look like something a Barbie threw up.

"I'm not hungry." I push back from the table. Then I dump the sandwich in the trash and drop my plate in the sink with a *thud*.

"Do you want to talk about it?"

I keep my back to her as I rinse my plate, watching the water slide off the clusters of pink and blue flowers painted along the edges. I can feel her trying to figure out what's crawled inside of me and died.

"Talk about what?" I ask, feigning innocence.

There's a loud sigh, and I don't need to turn around to know that she's scowling.

"It's okay to be frustrated, Lucy. I know how much you've always wanted this. But it doesn't do anyone any good—especially not you—to stomp around the house moping." She pauses like she expects a response. Like I'm supposed to know what the heck she's talking about. "It will come with time. Your dad said you just need more practice."

I almost laugh when I realize that she's talking about my lessons—she thinks I'm upset because I haven't been able to take away any memories yet.

"Right," I say. "Practice."

"You're always so impatient. Just like your mama." She lets out an exasperated huff, as if the statement sums up my entire existence. I wonder what Mama would think if she knew that her friend was helping her husband erase memories from an entire town. Or worse—that he was lying to me about what really happened to her.

Just thinking about Mama and my missing memories of her accident makes me feel sick to my stomach.

"I should get back to my chores," I manage to choke out, clearing the tears from the back of my throat.

I grab the pitcher of water from the counter, head to the front of the house, and begin soundlessly filling glasses for all the people gathered on the porch. I don't reassure them when I see their anxious glances. I don't offer explanations when they squint toward the front of the line, likely wondering what will happen once they cross the threshold to meet with Dad. I don't even take time to walk out to the yard to check the new arrivals' license plates. I just fill the glasses. Take out the trash. Clean the bathroom. Rinse and repeat.

When evening comes around, I grab the half-filled bag of trash from the waste bin and head to Mama's park. Not just because I can't stomach the thought of spending a practice session with Dad, trying to pretend like I don't know he's hiding things from me, but because of what may happen if I'm successful at taking away his memory this time. What if Dad makes me help the mayor? Or worse—what if the mayor doesn't give me a choice?

"Where do you think you're going?" Vivi calls to me from the porch, but I hold up the bag of trash and tell her I'll be back in a bit, then scurry away before she can question me further.

I don't waste any time because I see Mr. Lewis's brother Hank at the mailbox when I pass.

"Hey there!" I call out.

Hank leans out of his truck and dips the brim of his hat to me in greeting.

"Afternoon, Lucy! Something I can help you with?" He shoves a stack of mail into the open slot.

"I was just wondering about Mr. Lewis. Is he feeling any better? Any idea when he'll be back at work?"

Hank frowns. "He's still not quite feeling himself, I'm afraid."

My skin prickles under the weight of the sun. "What do you mean? What's he sick with, exactly?"

"Well, that's the thing—I'm not really sure. He's just—" He clears his throat and looks up at the sky, like he's trying to figure out what to say. "He's just not himself right now."

*He's just not himself*—like the first time, I'm struck with what an odd description that is for someone who's under the weather.

Before he got sick, Mr. Lewis would always tell me the same story about his son getting a promotion. I thought it was just pride that had him boasting over and over again, but what if that's not it? What if he's sick the same way Missy's sick? What if whatever is going on at the mines is the cause?

I think again of the black sludge.

"Maybe I could drop off some soup or something at the house for him? Try to cheer him up?" *Or try to figure out what's wrong with him.*

"That's real nice of you, Lucy, but I think it's best he just focuses on resting and getting better. I'm sure he'll be okay soon. Nothing you need to worry about." He makes a bad attempt to look reassuring. "I'll send him your regards, how's that?"

Hank doesn't wait for me to respond before he starts backing away.

"Hang on a sec," I say.

He lets out an exasperated huff, but stops.

"Mr. Lewis mentioned he moonlights at the mines sometimes. I was wondering if you ever work there, too?" I use my hand to block the sun so I can look him in the eye, ignoring the way his fingers tap against the steering wheel impatiently.

"Sure, most folks around here moonlight at the mines from time to time. Why?"

"Do you ever work there during the day, or just at night?"

"Just night. They don't call it moonlighting for nothing, Lucy." He gives me a sympathetic smile, like maybe I'm a little slow on the uptake.

"Right." I give him a fake smile back. "So what is it they have y'all doing out there in the middle of the night? I mean, seems a little dangerous to have people mining things in the dark, don't you think?"

He drums his fingers against the side of the car and looks in the rearview mirror, and I wonder if he's going to try to back up without answering.

"You're sweet to worry, but there's nothing to concern yourself with. They just have us hauling the day's quarry. Beats the heck out of working in this heat, I reckon. Now, you have yourself a nice afternoon. Tell Charlie I said hello."

He starts to back away, but I'm not ready to let this go.

"And what exactly is the day's quarry?" I raise my voice until I'm certain he can hear me over the rumbling engine.

The truck comes to a jerking halt and Hank looks right at me, his brow creasing.

"What do you mean?"

"I mean, what is it that you're hauling from the mines?"

"The—quarry." His words are stilted, like he can't quite figure out what he's saying. Or like he can't say anything else. He rubs his chin and glances in the rearview mirror, then back at me. His mouth is pressed into a frown. A sheen of sweat forms above his lip.

"You all right?" I ask.

"Yes, I—" He lifts the hat from his head and wipes at his brow. "I should get on with my deliveries. You have a nice day, Lucy."

Then he backs up quickly before I can ask any other questions, and speeds off, like he wants to put as much distance between us as humanly possible.

I watch until the dust cloud following his truck fades, then walk the trash to the dumpster.

When Marco asked me what kind of accident Mama was in, I couldn't get any words out other than to say she was in an accident. I was sweating from the effort. Is that what I just saw happen to Mr. Lewis's brother? Is he not able to say anything other than *quarry* because his memory's been erased, too?

Which begs the question—does anyone in Tumble Tree have any idea what the heck is down there?

The park is quiet when I turn the corner, like it's been holding its breath.

I take a seat on the tire swing and dance my feet in a circle until I'm spinning and the afternoon smears away. On my neck, the star necklace presses warm against my skin. On my finger, I feel the weight of Mama's promise ring.

*Mama.*

I tip my head back so I can look at the blotches of clouds painting the sky.

*What happened to you? What don't they want me to know?*

Last night, the tears didn't come. Not when Marco told me how the mayor had threated to tell me the truth about Mama. Not when Marco whispered how sorry he was over and over again, until his apologies blended with the nighttime hum of cicadas. Not when I climbed out of his car and walked on mechanical legs toward the house that no longer felt like a home. Not even when I heard Dad's snores rumbling from behind his door and realized that everything he's ever told me is probably a lie.

But now, in the quiet of the park where Mama's memory snaps in the breeze like sheets on a drying line, the tears fall. They come in choking sobs and quiet pleas. They come in bursts of red guilt and green regret. I cry until my throat is raw, my muscles ache, and my chest heaves from the mother-sized hole inside of it.

At some point, the tire swing stops spinning and I run out of sounds to make. When I stand, I feel light and heavy at the same time, but more than anything, I feel sure about what I need to do.

Tonight, Marco and I will figure out what's at the mines. And then I'm gonna figure out what really happened to Mama, what's happening to Missy and Mr. Lewis, and just what it is Dad and the mayor are hiding.

# 17

*When I get back to the house, Dad's in with the last guest and Vivi's in* the kitchen, her head bowed over the guest ledger as she works out the day's intakes. I take advantage of their distractions, grab a broom and a feather duster so it looks like I'm working, and start to make my way through the house.

I have no idea what it is I'm looking for, but there has to be something that will give me a clue.

The drawers in the hallway and living room only yield rubber bands, old batteries, a deck of cards, and wrinkled receipts for meals at Patty's Pie Pantry. I slowly make my way toward Dad's bedroom, working the feather duster back and forth along the walls. They're littered with pictures of my family and the generations of Millers who've run the Memory House. I stop for a moment in front of a picture of Dad, the mayor, and Mama. It reminds me that the mayor used to stop by after we closed, and he and Dad would sit on the porch talking late into the evening, like two best friends might. When did they stop being chummy? I can't recall.

In the photo, they're both grinning and raising glasses of iced tea at the camera in a toast. Mama's next to them, but she's not smiling. Her mouth is curved down, like someone's sucked the smile right out of her. She's also holding a glass of iced tea, but hers is darker, like cola. Mama never did like the sweet tea everyone else in town drinks—she drank hers black and kept a pitcher of it in the fridge just for her.

I lean closer, feeling the weight of Mama's ring against my finger. Something tugs at the edge of my thoughts. Something about Mama's expression . . .

The thought slithers away, and I'm left staring at the picture, trying to call back whatever was trying to break through. What was it?

I shake my head and go back to working the feather duster down the wall.

Dad's room is stuffy and dark, the curtains pulled tight over the windows. I cross the room and pull them open, sending early evening light dancing across the floorboards. Dad's not exactly what I would call neat, but he keeps the floors clear and the surfaces mostly free of clutter. I start with the nightstand, quickly sifting through the drawers before moving on to the dresser, but don't find anything other than clothes, pocket change, and a few old photographs of Mama. I run my finger over her smiling face before carefully placing the pictures back where I found them.

The closet is a mass of stacked boxes filled with various odds and ends—shoes I've never seen Dad wear, winter coats, hat boxes, an old clock radio, a stack of DVDs. I can't tell if it's stuff Dad purchased over the years or remnants of the junk guests have left—probably a little bit of both. Regardless, if there's something in here I'm not supposed to see, it won't be out in the open, and there's no way I'll be able to sort through it all now. I'll need to find an excuse to come back and go through it on a day when I have more time.

I lift the dust ruffle at the base of Dad's bed and peer underneath. The space is crowded with even more boxes. I crouch down and slide one of them out. The cardboard gives easily when I unfold the nested flaps. Glass catches the light. It's the empty jars we use to store the unwanted memories. I slide a few more of the boxes out, but they all contain the same—empty mason jars used to store memories. I'm about to slide the last box back under the bed when something catches my eye—a bright yellow label on one of the jars. I pull it out of the box and hold it up to the light, reading the swirly old-timey font.

*Miracle Happiness Elixir*
*A cure for what ails your heart!*

A floorboard out in the hallway squeaks, and I quickly shove the jar back in the box and slide it under Dad's bed. A moment later, Vivi's voice knifes through the quiet.

"Lucy! What are you doing in here?" Her casted arm is clutched tight to her chest and the other hand is fisted against her hip.

"I—just—" I pick up the feather duster and wave it at her. "Cleaning. I figured it's probably been an eternity since Dad dusted around here." Her eyes narrow as she looks around the room.

"You shouldn't be in here. This is your dad's personal space. How would you feel if he went digging around in your room without permission?"

"I was just trying to help." I wave the feather duster again, like it proves I wasn't snooping even though that's exactly what I was doing.

Vivi's eyes scan the room again before landing back on me, and I remember her warning to Marco to stay away from me because it was dangerous. What is she trying to keep from us?

"Your dad just finished with the last guest. Put that duster away and help me shut down for the night."

Then her heels click out of the room without another word.


Vivi stays at the Memory House later than usual, saying something about the ledgers and her accounting being off. But I can't shake the feeling that she's staying late to watch me. It's almost like she knows that Marco's planning to come over and she wants to make it as difficult as possible for me to sneak out. It's nearly ten by the time she finally leaves.

I'm in my room with Mama's scrapbook spread across my lap. Below me, the house is quiet. Outside, the night waits to tell me its secrets. Soon, Marco will come.

I flip another page. Mama's pictures smile back at me like a promise.

She always said she'd take me on the road with her so I could see the world for myself. So many years of promising—why didn't we just get in the car and go?

"What happened to you?" I whisper.

I've looked at these pages at least a thousand times like the key might be buried within. I trace my finger across the embossed writing on a matchbook, scan a phone number scrawled onto a cocktail napkin, search the faces of the people she met along the road. I scour every page, every line of her handwriting, every face in every photo, until I'm almost at the back of the book, where she kept the pictures of her last trip to San Antonio and where she put the photo of us at the rest stop, on our last family road trip. My hand hovers above the picture of us standing in front of her old Buick with her arms raised high above her head, the sky shining behind her. Her grin is white teeth and happiness. Her hair is freedom and chaos.

I close my eyes and picture the scene, trying to force my mind to remember something, anything. I can feel the past there, trying to get out. There has to be a way to make myself remember. I squeeze her ring.

There's a sudden and sharp pain at the back of my head then. I let go of the scrapbook and press my fingers to my temples. The room tilts on its axis.

*Taillights disappearing down a dark road.*

*Someone yelling, repeating the same words over and over again.*

*Hands at my back, pulling me away.*

I squeeze my eyes more tightly and try to give the memory purchase, but the image keeps sliding away just before I can grab hold. I shake my head. What is it? What *is* it?

Another slice of pain pierces my skull.

*Ladybug, one day we'll fly away from here. We'll leave this place to the dust and the lizards.*

What am I not remembering?

I press my fingers more firmly to my head like I can squeeze the memory out, but it's no use. The memory is gone, and I find myself staring at the wall of my bedroom, trying to remember what I'd just been thinking about. Trying to remember what I'm forgetting that was on the tip of my thoughts only a second before.

Something about a car?

Whatever it was, I can't find it, no matter how tightly I squeeze my eyes shut or how hard I will my brain to remember. But I was so close—I can feel it.

I place the scrapbook back on the nightstand and walk toward the window. The desert is shadows. The night sleeps.

Where is Marco?

I grab a notebook from my nightstand and jot down what just happened—how I'd been looking at Mama's scrapbook and almost had what had to have been an Echo. Since meeting Marco at Miracle Lake I've been writing things down like he suggested. Just in case something happens and I'm made to forget again. When I finish, I lie down on my bed and trace the highways pinned to my ceiling, trying to make my mind go back to the place it had been when I was looking at Mama's pictures. Maybe if I focus on something else, I can call the memory forward. Isn't that what people do when they meditate?

East Coast to West Coast. Gulf Coast to Canada. I-80 and I-15 from Chicago to Santa Monica, then Highway 101 all the way north until I hit Turnwater, Washington. At some point, I must close my eyes, because when I open them again my room is filled with ribbons of daylight streaming in through the open curtains.

I fell asleep.

And Marco never came.

## 18

*Marco doesn't come the next night, either.*

And all day leading up to that, Vivi is on me like spines to a cactus. I can barely so much as sneeze without her rounding the corner to see what I'm doing. It's all I can do to break away long enough to continue my search around the house, and even then, the time alone is so limited that I can't do much. It's like she knows I'm up to something. Like she knows that Marco and I are working together and she's trying to keep me tethered to the house so I can't look for him.

Then a thought hits me—

Could she be the reason he hasn't shown up? Did she catch him trying to sneak out and meet me?

Or maybe it was the man in the aviators at Patty's Pie Pantry—he could have told Vivi or the mayor that he saw us together.

By the second morning I'm desperate. I have to find a way to get to Marco. Going to his house feels like walking straight into a nest of rattlers, but I'm out of ideas.

"Lucy! Lucy, get down here," Vivi's voice booms from the bottom of the stairs.

"Give me a minute," I shout back, and brush my teeth for a second time just to make her wait.

She's outside the bathroom door not a minute later, fist banging up a storm. Like I didn't hear her the first time.

"I said I'd be there in a minute." I swing the door open, tooth-brush in hand.

Vivi stands with her uninjured hand on the hip of a brightly patterned dress that looks like an Easter egg lost a fight with a paintball gun.

"I don't have a minute. I need you to manage the guests for the day. I've got some errands in town to attend to. Think you can run front of house without burning the place down?"

"You're leaving?" I don't even try to hide the surprise in my voice.

"Don't look so excited. It's just for one day. And it's not a break—keeping track of all the burdened guests is a full-time job. I need to be able to trust you. Can I trust you to take care of things while I'm gone?"

I nod and wipe a dribble of toothpaste from my chin. But inside I'm jumping up and down. Because if Vivi's not in the house, she can't play watchdog. And if she can't play watchdog, maybe I can finally sneak away from this hellhole.

"Get a move on. People are already getting restless. Your dad's in with the first guest and he said he didn't think they would take long to unburden. You've probably got twenty minutes tops. Don't make me come back up here to check on you again. I need you downstairs in five so I can walk you through what to do."

"I know what to do. I've done it before."

"Not by yourself, you haven't. Now hurry up."

I bite back the sarcasm because I don't want to give her a reason to change her mind. I'm dressed and downstairs a few minutes later. She takes me through her process, the ledger she uses to track the guests and their payments, what to say to them when they leave the Memory House, and so on and so forth. I don't bother reminding her that we've gone over all of this before, and even if we hadn't, it's not brain surgery.

"I'm counting on you, Lucy," Vivi says.

And then she's gone.

The sound of the door closing when Vivi leaves may be the most beautiful thing I've ever heard. Now I just need to deal with Dad.

He finishes clearing the first person a little bit later. I go into his office to collect the unburdened guest and mark down their payment. Dad's eyes are heavy as they watch me. Vivi's kept me so busy that avoiding him's been a breeze. But now, looking at his lined and frowning face, I wonder if he knows it hasn't just been chores that are keeping me away.

"Why don't you drop back in after you've taken care of Mr. Cloverdale here?" he says. "Before you bring in the next guest?"

I nod and gently place a hand on the arm of the smiling man. He has the weightless look of someone who'll finally sleep after many restless nights.

"This way, sir." I steer him down the steps and out the front door, where we squint against the blazing sun.

"You head on home now, Mr. Cloverdale. You're gonna drive straight back, taking care to stop for meals and restroom breaks. When you get to your house, I want you to go right to bed. You hear me? Go right to bed and get a good night's sleep, and when you wake up, all of this will be forgotten along with the burdens you left behind. All you'll remember is that you went for a drive, saw some sights, and came home. Then you'll be just fine, understand?"

Mr. Cloverdale nods numbly, a small smile hovering on his lips. "I went for a drive. Saw some sights. Came home."

"That's right."

But I shiver when I hear the phrase repeated back to me. The words themselves aren't familiar, but something about the idea behind them is.

*I went for a walk, got tired, went to bed.*

I swallow, trying to keep my voice light. "And if you find anything in the house that you don't remember having, you toss it in the trash, no matter what it is, understand? Throw it away because it's not important anymore."

"Throw it away because it's not important anymore," he repeats. "I went for a drive. Saw some sights. Came home."

"Yes, exactly. You drive safely now, okay? You'll feel good as new once you get home."

Mr. Cloverdale gives me a slow smile, and then walks toward his car.

I never thought the stories Dad planted were bad—they seemed like simple, harmless ways to close the gaps in people's memories so they wouldn't remember coming here once their burdens were lifted; so that they could have a fresh start to their new unburdened lives. But now, as I watch Mr. Cloverdale float out to the parking lot where a silver sedan with Mississippi license plates waits, I can't help but think there's something wrong with planting a lie in the empty space that once housed their memories.

I try to push away the guilt as I watch him drive off, then head back up the steps to the Memory House. The line of folks clustered on the porch watch eagerly. Groans follow me inside when I don't take one of them with me.

Dad's sitting at his desk, looking at the picture of Mama. He smiles sadly at me when I enter, and I can see the guilt etched in the lines on his face. Maybe this will be easier than I thought.

"You haven't been to see me in a few days. Guess Vivi's been keeping you busy? I know she really appreciates having you to help pick up some of the slack while her arm heals. You keep it up and you'll have that car in no time."

"Yeah." I look down at my bitten fingernails and sigh. It doesn't take much pretending to make myself look tired and heavy with burdens. "There's been a lot of work this past week. I know I said I wanted to earn more, it's just . . ."

"You okay, Luce?" His fingers work the crease between his brows.

"Of course. Ignore me. I'm just tired today, that's all." I make my voice sound nice and fake, so he knows I'm just pretending there isn't something wrong.

"We haven't really had a chance to talk to each other much lately. And you haven't come up to see me at lunch, or hounded me about lessons. It's not like you."

"I've just had so much to take care of, what with all the work to be done. And now Vivi's got me busy running front of house, so it's looking like it's gonna be another long one. I'll be all right. Like I said, I'm just tired."

The hurt behind his eyes makes my chest squeeze. He's worried about me. He misses me. He has no idea what's really going on inside my head.

"I know you were probably thinking you'd be good at memory-taking out of the gate, and that you'd be helping me unburden people by now instead of doing so much work around the house." He clears his throat and runs his finger along the desk, like he's checking for dust. "I just want you to know that I appreciate everything you're doing. And while I know you're probably frustrated that the memory-taking hasn't happened as quickly as you'd like it to . . . well, maybe that's not such a bad thing, Ladybug. It's not all it's cracked up to be."

Despite myself, despite everything I know, I miss him so much in that moment that every cell inside my body aches. I can't reconcile this kindhearted, worried-looking version of my dad, who clearly loves me so much he wants to shelter me, with the one who stole the truth of what happened to Mama and distrusts me enough that he'd rather steal my memories than tell me what's going on at the mines. But I can't let myself think about that right now. I need to get to Marco. I need to make sure he's okay.

"It's all right," I say, and give him the warmest, widest smile my face can manufacture. "I understand."

"You're growing up so fast, Ladybug. I don't know what I'd do without you." He reaches out and ruffles my hair. My shoulders tense under the weight of his palm, but I hold on to my grin.

"Do you think—" I let out a heavy sigh, then give my shoulders an *aw-shucks* kind of shrug. "No, never mind. I can't ask you that."

"Ask me what?"

"It's silly. It's really not a big deal. I shouldn't have brought it up."

"Come on, out with it. What's on your mind, Bug?"

"Mrs. Gomez got a new shipment of books she's been holding for me. I don't know how much longer she can hold them before she'll have to give other folks a shot. But that's okay, I guess. Maybe once things calm down a bit, I'll have time to swing by the library and read, assuming the books are still there."

Dad's fingers are back at the bridge of his nose, and I can tell by his frown that he's buying everything I'm selling.

"You've been working really hard. A few hours off wouldn't hurt, I reckon."

"I don't know, Dad. Vivi's not here, and someone needs to sign in the guests and make sure they're taken care of. You should focus on unburdening."

"Now, hold on a second. I can take care of signing folks in and managing Vivi's records. Your old man's not a complete waste of space, you know." He winks at me.

"Well, if you're sure, maybe I can pick up the books from the library and read by Miracle Lake for a bit?"

"Of course. Why don't you take the rest of the afternoon off? Don't worry about things around here. I can handle it. Don't tell Vivi, but it's really not that difficult." Another wink, like we're in on the joke together. Like we're a father-daughter duo. It's almost enough to make me feel guilty. Almost.

"You're sure?" I don't have to fake the smile on my face now.

"Positive. Just be back by dinnertime, okay?"

"Okay, thanks, Dad."

I force myself to walk calmly down the hallway, out the front door, and down the porch steps. Then I sprint, leaving all the burdened guests with their mouths hanging open and questions in their eyes.

My bike is leaning against the toolshed where I left it. I rip off the dust cover, and then I'm flying down our driveway, pumping my legs as fast as they can move.

## 19

*Twenty minutes later I turn onto Manuela's street. I spot the house with* the rainbow pinwheel sticking out of the yard and lean my bike against a nearby tree. A dog two houses over announces my arrival. The low guttural growl doesn't match the ten-pound ball of fluff it's coming from. Not that I can blame the poor thing—I'd kick up a fuss, too, if I had to wear a fur coat in the middle of a July desert.

The curtains on Manuela's front window peel back and I catch sight of her scowling before they snap closed again.

She's home. Thank God.

I walk slowly up to her porch, remembering the reflection of her tear-streaked face on the drive back to her house the other night. Maybe I'm a fool for coming here, but she's the only person I can think of who might be able to help.

I've barely lifted my hand to knock when the door flies open. The porch wind chimes clang in protest. Manuela stares back with crossed arms.

She's wearing an oversized T-shirt, pajama pants with little hearts running down the legs, and no makeup.

"What the hell are you doing here?" she demands, eyes narrowed.

"Hello to you, too," I say, not really sure how to answer.

She rolls her eyes. Behind her, an older woman sits in a faded yellow armchair that looks like the sun's bleached the color right out of it. She's staring blankly at a television set. Manuela sees me looking and closes the door farther so I can't see inside.

"What do you want?"

"Have you seen Marco?"

Her face twists into a grimace at the mention of his name, and she starts to close the door. I have to hold out a hand to stop her.

"Wait, please. I'm worried about him. I haven't seen him in a few days. I'm afraid something happened."

"Sounds like you got dumped, princess. Not my problem." She starts to close the door again. I take a step closer and put my foot against the door to block it.

"This is serious, Manuela. Please."

I can see her evaluating my words.

I keep going. "Can you just tell me if you've seen him? I'm afraid something bad might have happened to him."

"What makes you so sure something happened? Maybe he really just dumped you."

"Do you really think I'd come all the way to your house if that were the case?" There must be something in my voice, because this time, she pauses midway through trying to shut the door in my face.

She turns to look at the woman in the faded chair, then back at me. "He hasn't been at Miracle Lake the last few nights. And some of the guys said they haven't seen him around town. I figured he was with you. Why, what's the big deal?"

Dread tiptoes down my spine. Shit.

"Listen, I have a favor to ask."

She lets out a loud huff of laughter and shakes her head. "You must have been dropped on your head a lot as a baby."

"I'm serious. I need your help. There's something weird going on."

"Yeah, no kidding. You've clearly lost your mind if you think I owe you any favors. Now, will you please get off my porch?"

I squeeze my hands into fists, fighting the urge to snap back. She really is a pain in the ass.

"Marco could be hurt, Manuela. Or worse—" I choke on the last word, not wanting to think about what *worse* entails. "Please, I just need you to go to his house and ask where he is. That's it."

"Why can't you go there and check on him yourself?"

"Because I can't. Just trust me, it has to be you. Please, Manuela. I wouldn't be here if I wasn't desperate."

She studies my face, arms still crossed tightly against her chest. "Fine. But just so we're clear, I'm not doing it for you."

I heave out a relieved breath. "Thank you."

"And if this turns out to be some kind of trick—" She points a finger in my face.

"It's not a trick. I promise."

I almost laugh at the idea that she'd think I'd waste time pranking her. As if I don't have a million other things going on in my life.

"Give me five minutes," she says, looking down at her baggy shirt and PJs. "Wait here."

I remove my foot so she can close the door and take a seat on the porch. The dog down the street keeps growling in my direction, pacing as far as the rope holding it will allow. I look up at the cloud-speckled sky and say a silent prayer to the desert.

*Please let Marco be okay.*

Five minutes pass. Then ten. Then twenty.

The hell is taking her so long? I'm about to bang on the door when she finally emerges, fully made up with red lips and all. She slings a tiny pink backpack over her shoulders and tugs at the pockets sticking out from the frayed edges of her cutoffs. Behind her, a younger version of Manuela scowls.

"I'm telling Mom."

"Not if you want to live, you're not. Just watch Abuela. I won't be gone long." When the girl doesn't budge, Manuela rolls her eyes and adds, "You can play with my makeup when I get back." Then she closes the door and looks at me like *I'm* the one who kept *her* waiting.

"Where's your car?" She looks up and down the street.

I point to my bike.

"You've got to be kidding me. How exactly do you expect us to get there?"

"Don't you have a bike?"

She snorts. "Sure, but I haven't ridden it since I was like twelve. I thought your dad was some hotshot business owner. Can't he afford to buy you your own car?"

I grit my teeth. Typical. Everyone at school assumes that because Dad doesn't have to work at the mines, we must be rich or something.

"I'm saving up to get one, but for now it's either bike or walk. Your choice."

She stares at me like I'm something she found stuck to the bottom of her shoe. "You're something else, you know that?"

"I don't see a Porsche sitting in your driveway, either."

She gives a snort of either laughter or disgust—it's hard to tell with her—and then marches to the back of her house. A few seconds later she wheels a bright pink ten-speed toward me.

"If anyone sees me riding this thing, I'm gonna kill you." She holds the handlebar like it's going to bite her.

"When's the last time you rode a bike?"

"I told you. Not since I was twelve."

I try my best to hide my annoyance. I guess she wouldn't need to. Manuela's the kind of girl who's been getting rides from boys since we were in middle school. It's all I can do to keep myself from picturing her in Marco's Yukon, riding around Tumble Tree like she owns it.

"Why don't you take a couple practice runs?" I motion toward the cul-de-sac that marks the end of her street. I can tell by her scowl that she wants to say something snarky—probably about how she doesn't need practice—but then she's wobbling down the street on her rusted bike, her tan legs pumping and her pink backpack bouncing against her back. The image pulls at something in my memory, and just for a second I get the tiniest tug of warmth toward her. Like maybe, in another town in another life, we could have been friends.

"Are you coming or what?" she calls over her shoulder as she rides around and zips past me.

I hop on my bike and pedal to catch up, sending another silent prayer to the desert that I haven't made a mistake by trusting her.

## 20

*Marco's house is on the opposite end of town. Manuela makes us ride* down the back roads and alleys so no one will see her, which adds at least another ten minutes to our trip. Normally I'd complain, but maybe it's not such a bad idea if people don't see us together. Or at all.

"So are you going to tell me what you think happened to Marco that made you desperate enough to come to my house?"

Her dark hair flows in a stream behind her as she weaves her bike back and forth across the dust-covered alley. The clouds from earlier in the week have broken, and the heat's crept back into the nineties. A line of sweat drips from my shoulder blades to the middle of my back.

"You wouldn't believe me if I told you."

"Try me," she says, wheeling her bike back so that she does a circle around me. If I didn't know better I'd think she was enjoying the ride.

The road's lined with clusters of cactus and bear grass. Our tires crunch against the desert floor. The cicadas sing from their hiding places in the trees.

"Your mama works at the mines, right?" I ask, remembering that her father passed away several years ago.

"Yeah. She took over my abuela's shifts when she got sick. Why?"

"Does she work late?"

"She only works night shifts, so yeah. I guess."

"What does she mine, exactly?"

Manuela does another circle around me. "Who cares?"

"Just try to answer the question. What does she do at the mines?"

"She. Mines. Things." She says the sentence slowly, like I don't have the mental capacity to process her words. "What do I care what she does? You're kind of a weirdo, you know that?"

I pedal faster and pass her. My heart is racing. Do I tell her or not? On the one hand, Manuela's given me absolutely zero reasons to think she'd be on my side, or even Marco's, for that matter. But on the other, if her mom's one of the people working night shifts at the mines, that probably means her memories have been erased. Which could mean she'd want to help . . .

"It must be nice," she says, her voice at my back, "to have a dad who doesn't have to work that hard."

"What are you talking about? Just because he doesn't work at the mines doesn't mean he doesn't work hard. He works harder than most people." My teeth clench thinking of the way Dad's back slumps after spending hours clearing one of the heavier-burdened guests. I may not like him very much right now, but that doesn't mean I don't get that what he does is difficult.

She snorts. "Please. You guys haven't had to work a day in your life. You don't even know what hard work looks like."

"And what does it look like, Manuela?" I jerk my bike to the side and squeeze the brake until my bike comes to a stop, blocking the path. I don't mean to shout, but I can't help it. The words are out of my mouth before I can stop them. "Because I don't see you doing much of anything other than putting on makeup, flipping your hair, and plucking wedgies from your microscopic shorts."

Manuela swerves to avoid me. Her bike kicks up a cloud of dust as she tries to pull on the brakes, but she wobbles to the side and ends up almost falling into a cluster of yucca. She jumps off the bike, her hands clenched into fists.

"What the hell is your problem? You're the one who came to me begging for help, remember?"

"My problem," I say, "is that you act like I'm some kind of monster. Like I've done something wrong. And maybe I did. Maybe I did something so terrible that you should never want to talk to me again. But you know what? I have no clue! I have no idea why you're so mad and why everyone is hell-bent on keeping Marco and me apart because I can't remember any of it. I can't remember! Do you have any idea how that feels?"

My breath is coming out in ragged gasps as I pace the length of the trail. The cicadas have stopped their chirping, like I'm a rattlesnake that's entered their den. "I don't remember!" I shout again, this time grabbing on to my bike and thrusting it into the dirt. "I can't remember anything."

I don't realize I'm crying until Manuela's red lips blur into a sunset smear. She's crouched next to her bike, her fingers gripping the handlebars like she might have to launch it at me in self-defense.

"Wow, girl. And I thought I had issues."

My nose is running. I wipe at my eyes, suddenly embarrassed that I let Manuela see me like this.

"Sorry," I finally say.

Manuela stares back at me, biting on her lip. Then she shrugs and looks back up the path, toward Marco's house. "Do you want to keep going or what?"

I nod and pick my bike up, grateful for the subject change. We ride in silence for a few minutes. I stay behind her, matching her languid pace.

"You didn't do anything," Manuela finally says. "To me, I mean. You just, I don't know, act like you think you're too good for this place or something. And you were always with Marco. It was annoying." She pauses. "You really can't remember?"

I sigh. "No."

"He must have really done something terrible to you to make you want to forget him like that."

"It wasn't my choice. Or his."

Manuela slows down her pace and turns to look at me.

"What do you mean?" Her voice is incredulous.

"I don't know much, but I know *I* wouldn't have chosen to have Marco erased."

"So, what, you think someone else forced you into it?"

"Kind of, yeah." It's as honest as I can be right now.

"That is all kinds of messed up."

"Tell me about it." I wipe at the sweat pooling at the back of my neck. "When you saw Marco and me together, did we seem . . . happy?"

"I guess, yeah." She tugs at one of the straps of her backpack. "That really sucks that you can't remember things. My abuela can't remember things. It's why she had to stop working. It's pretty scary, actually."

Something uncoils in my stomach.

"What do you mean she can't remember things?" I think of the woman in the faded yellow chair, staring vacantly at the TV.

Manuela shrugs like it's no big deal, but there's a slight wobble in her chin. It occurs to me that she might not have been at her house this afternoon by choice. Maybe she has to be there to help out her grandma.

"I don't want to talk about it." Her voice is sharp.

"Did it happen recently?"

"I said I don't want to talk about it." She pedals ahead so that all I can see is her pink backpack bouncing against her back. I swallow the rest of my questions and speed up.

"Marco's house is just up here." She points past the incline in the dirt path, like I don't know where the mayor's house is. Everyone in town knows that house. It might not be considered a mansion in other towns, but in Tumble Tree, it's the closest thing we've got, with a large wraparound porch, bright white latticework trim, and large windows overlooking a perfectly manicured lawn and winding gravel driveway. In the backyard, there's a large pool with a fountain made to look like a rocky waterfall, and someone once told me they have a fire pit and a wood-fired oven the mayor uses to make pizzas. No wonder Vivi and Marco live with him—I'd want to live there, too, if I were them.

A few moments later, we round a bend and the two-story house looms in front of us.

I slow my pace as we get closer, then pull over behind a cluster of plants.

"I should stay back here," I tell her. She comes to a stop next to me and rests her bike next to mine. "I don't want anyone to see me."

I can tell she wants to ask me why again, but she just tugs at her shorts and plucks at the backpack straps on her shoulder.

"His car's here," she says, jutting her chin toward the Yukon that's parked at the back side of the house. "What do you want me to say to him?"

"Ask him if he's alone. And if he is, let me know and I'll come to the door." I bite my lip and look at the house. I can't see the mayor's black truck, but it could be in the garage. "If he's not alone, ask if he's okay, where he's been, that kind of stuff. And ask what he remembers from the other night, at Miracle Lake. But don't mention my name. Especially not if Mayor Warman or his mom is there."

Manuela furrows her brow, but nods. Then she turns on her heel and marches toward Marco's house.

## 21

*I crouch low behind the plants, watching Manuela approach the house.*
She rings the doorbell, then knocks a few times, shielding her
eyes like she's trying to see through the small window above the
door.

*No one's home.*

My heart sinks. But then the door opens, casting a shadow on
Manuela's small frame.

Manuela's posture immediately straightens. She tugs at her
shorts, pulling them low enough to cover the pockets sticking out
from the frayed edges. I can't see who she's talking to, but it's
clearly not Marco.

I search the windows. If I know where Marco's room is, maybe
I can come back on my own, at night.

There's movement in the second-story window above the front
porch. The curtains are peeled back and I can see a shadow looming in the opening, but can't make out much beyond the shape of
a person.

A minute later Manuela starts marching toward me. I search

her face for signs of concern, but she gives nothing away. I crouch lower in case the person who answered is watching.

"He's fine," she says when she's a few feet away from me.

"You talked to him?"

"No, I talked to his mom. She said he's fine. Well, not *fine* fine. She said he's sick. I guess he caught something that's been going around town and he'll probably be better in a few days. She said I can check back then, once he's not contagious."

"Vivi answered?"

My stomach clenches. Marco must be the "errand" she was referring to. Marco was fine when we met at the Pie Pantry. Now suddenly he's sick? Something tells me even if he was, he wouldn't have let that keep him from meeting me.

"What?" Manuela says, reading the expression on my face.

I shake my head, looking back toward the house.

The man with Officer Lewis at Patty's Pie Pantry—he must have said something to the mayor. Or maybe Vivi had second thoughts about letting him go that night at the mines. Either way, if Marco's sick because his memories have been erased, then he probably doesn't have any recollection of what's happened the last few days—the mines, the lake parking lot, the incident with Missy.

I look down at my hands. I can still feel the heat from his fingers entwining with mine, the way his palm pressed against my skin, light and warm. A chasm opens in my chest.

I can't go back to not knowing him.

Every bone in my body tells me this has something to do with me. With us. The same way I know he's not really sick. I can't just leave him holed up in his own house like a prisoner. I have to do something.

"Is Marco's bedroom the middle one?" The curtains on the middle window are closed now. Whoever was up there watching is gone.

Manuela nods, her face a question mark. I almost feel bad, like I owe her an explanation. But why? It's not like we're friends. I practically had to drag her out of the house to help me.

"I should get back." I swing my legs over my bike. "Thanks for your help."

"That's it? You're leaving?"

I shrug and look down at the handlebars.

"You drag me all the way down here with this doom-and-gloom *Marco's in trouble* story, and now you're just going home?" Manuela's lips form an angry pucker.

"I told you, I just wanted to make sure he's okay. Sounds like he's fine. Thank you again."

"You don't look like you think he's okay. You look like someone murdered a kitten."

"I don't look like anything." I can't look her in the eye when I lie.

"Please, you're an open book. Something's up. You can't just show up at my door acting like the world's about to end and then be all, 'oops, never mind.' I deserve an explanation."

I bite my lip. I've already told her too much. What if she starts blabbing to people at Miracle Lake? Even if her intentions aren't bad, what's to say she won't let something slip after a few too many sips from a flask? It's too risky.

"Look, I appreciate your help. But I don't want to get you any more involved than I already have. Marco's okay, you said so yourself. That's all that matters, right?"

She watches me, chews on her bottom lip. Then she climbs onto her bike.

"Fine. Don't tell me. Whatever. But don't come crawling back to me the next time your boyfriend ditches you. I'm done helping."

She pauses for a beat, like she's giving me a chance to change my mind. When I don't, she gives a final huff and steers her bike toward the path. A cloud of dust kicks up underneath her tires as she wheels away from me. She doesn't even turn around to see if I've followed.

I wait until she's out of sight before hopping on my own bike and taking the main roads. There's a tiny tug of guilt for ditching Manuela after she helped, but I don't have time to feel guilty. I need to figure out a way to get Marco out of his house tonight.

First, though, I need to take advantage of my Vivi-free afternoon.

# 22

*The Tumble Tree Library parking lot is packed, which isn't surprising.* During the summer the library rivals Miracle Lake in popularity, mainly because it's one of the few places in town with internet access that doesn't cost an arm and a leg. That, and they don't skimp on the air-conditioning.

I'm blasted by cold air and the familiar scent of well-worn books when I walk inside. A glance to the back wall shows me that all of the computers are taken, and I know from experience that most people don't adhere to the thirty-minute-usage policy. Judging by the kids lurking at nearby tables, there's a long waitlist.

"Hi, Mrs. Gomez," I say, waving to a woman sorting books behind the counter. If Mrs. Gomez were a place, she'd be a small, quaint New England town with white picket fences, Fourth of July parades, and chili cook-offs. The kind of place where the biggest secrets are family recipes and missing church on the occasional Sunday.

She looks up and smiles.

"Lucy! I haven't seen you in weeks. Things been busy down at the Memory House?"

"Yes, ma'am. I'm saving to buy myself a car, so I've been help-ing more than usual." I don't bother mentioning that Vivi barely lets me out of her sight.

"Finally going to go on that road trip, then? That's nice. How's your dad?"

"Good." *For a liar.* "Busy as always."

"We got some new travel books in a few weeks ago—I've been saving them for you. Want me to grab them from the back?"

"That sounds great, but actually," I start, trying to think through how to ask for what I want without raising suspicion. "I was hoping to do a little research. About the town. For a school—a summer school—project."

"Oh! Summer school. You really have been busy. Anything I can help with?"

"Yes, actually. I'm looking for info about the mines, specifically. How long they've been there, what people have mined from them, that kind of thing. I'm writing about their—um—history. Do you know anything that might help?"

"History of the mines, huh? Can't say I know much about them myself, other than that they've always been there." Mrs. Gomez furrows her brow, and for a second I think she's going to say they don't have anything like that on hand, but then she nods and motions to the microfiche viewers on the other side of the library.

"You might try the newspaper archives. I doubt anything about the mines has made it into mainstream papers, but we have all of the *Tumble Tree Weekly*s on file going back to the inaugural edition.

Give me a few minutes and I'll bring you the film and get you set up. Do you want me to add your name to the computer waitlist as well? Maybe you can find some stuff online."

"That would be great, thanks."

Two hours later and I'm nearly cross-eyed from reading about pie-eating contests, church bazaars, lost cats, obituaries, and updates on the weather. Spoiler alert: Tumble Tree has been hot since the dawn of time and the weeklies are as exciting as dirt.

I'm about to give up when a headline catches my eye: COPPER MINES TO CLOSE.

The article is from almost eight years ago.

I scan the text, reading that the copper output had been steadily declining over the years while operating costs were increasing, leading a major investor to pull funding. The article makes it sound nearly impossible for the mines to continue to stay open, noting that countless jobs would be lost if they shut down.

Almost everyone in Tumble Tree has worked at the mines at one time or another. What would happen if they actually closed down?

I scroll ahead to the next few issues, looking for more information about the closing, but there's nothing. Which is odd. In a town where most of the "news" is about lost pets and weather that never changes, wouldn't news about the mines closing be a huge story? And they must have been saved since they're still operating.

Wouldn't that also be newsworthy? Definitely more interesting than another church bazaar. Yet the next few months' worth of issues don't even mention the mines.

So I shift my attention to the other reason I came. With shaking fingers, I grab the reel of film that covers the time period when Mama died—five years ago. I slide it into the machine, place the glass over the top of it like Mrs. Gomez showed me, and begin to scan.

And scan. And scan.

I find nothing. No mention of an accident or anything else about Mama. Again, in a town with very little going on, wouldn't that have been big news?

When my turn at the computer comes up, I go straight to Google. I start by looking for info on the Tumble Tree mines, but the search yields more of the same I saw in the *Weeklys*—a few mentions of the possible closing, but then the trail dries up; there are no other mentions. And when I type in Mama's name next to the words "accident" and "obituary," I come up just as empty-handed. Which doesn't make any sense.

It's almost like Mama's accident never happened.

Or like someone worked really hard to cover up the truth.

# 23

*By the time I get back to the Memory House, the sun is starting to set and* the parking lot's cleared out. Dad must have sent everyone home.

I find him in the kitchen with Vivi, who looks at me like I used her underwear as a hat.

"Hi, Vivi. I thought you were out for the afternoon."

"And I thought you said you were going to run front of house for me while I ran errands," she retorts, giving me a fiery look that lets me know exactly how she feels about my absence.

"Oh, don't be so hard on her," Dad says. "She deserved the afternoon off. Everyone can use a break sometimes, and she's been working so hard around here." He turns to me. "How was your day, Bug?"

"Fine. Good." I force a smile and ignore Vivi's glare. More than anything, I just want to ask him about Mama, but I wouldn't dare do so now. I don't want to raise Vivi's suspicions any higher than they already are. "I went to the library."

"That sounds nice. Vivi brought us a casserole." Dad nods to a steaming pile of something cheesy resting on the counter. "We were just waiting for you to get back."

"I made too much," Vivi explains. "Plus I always worry that y'all are eating like bachelors when I'm not around. If I left you to your own devices, you'd probably live off saltines and Campbell's Chicken Noodle."

A few minutes later we're seated around the table with heaping piles of cheesy noodles in front of us. Dad's all smiles, talking more than he usually does at this time of day. The rest of his afternoon unburdenings must have been tame. Or maybe he's in a good mood because he thinks things between us are back to normal. As if normal will ever be possible again.

I stay as silent as I can, focusing on my food and only speaking when spoken to. I'm too afraid I'll say something I shouldn't, that I'll let it slip that I know something bad happened to Mama and someone's trying to cover it up. I'm about to push back from the table to excuse myself when there's a knock at the door.

Vivi and Dad exchange a look.

"I'll get it." Vivi stands and brushes past me. "It might be my brother."

I stiffen. So does Dad.

Vivi flicks on the porch light and voices float in from the entryway—*female* voices. It's not the mayor, thank God. Across the table, Dad's tense shoulders loosen.

"She didn't say anything to us about it. We're in the middle of dinner," says Vivi, an annoyed edge in her voice. "But then again, that's our Lucy."

I squint toward the front of the house, like that will somehow help. Who's Vivi talking to?

There's a high-pitched laugh. I *know* that laugh, but I can't quite put my finger on the owner.

"Maybe I got my nights mixed up. I can go—"

"No, no. Come in. She's in the kitchen. I swear, she'd forget her head if it wasn't attached to her neck."

Vivi appears at the kitchen door, with her good hand on her hip and a scowl aimed right at me.

"Your friend is here," she says, raising an eyebrow. "For your *sleepover.*"

"My what?"

Vivi steps aside to reveal Manuela standing just outside the kitchen with a duffel bag slung over her shoulder and a look that can only be described as victorious.

"Hi, Luce! Did I get my nights wrong?"

She's traded her cutoffs for a loose-fitting pair of overalls and a plain white tee. Her hair is swept into two braids trailing down her shoulders, and her lips are painted light pink instead of bright red. The effect makes her look younger, but her smile is all red-lipped Manuela. She meets my eyes and her grin widens into something wicked.

"I could swear you told me that you wanted me to stay the night tonight. Remember? I mean I can go, but I was *so* looking forward to catching up with you. It's been so long." Her grin is full wattage as she reaches into her bag and pulls out a stack of magazines. "I brought nail polish, magazines, snacks—you name it!" She pauses, a pout on her face. "Oh no, I did get my nights mixed up, didn't I? Dang it, I'm sorry. What a bummer."

If I didn't know any better, I'd say she sounded genuinely disappointed, but there's a mischievous sparkle in her dark eyes that I don't trust for one second.

Dad's mouth is hanging open so wide you could drive the mayor's truck through it. He snaps it shut and stands, motioning to an empty chair.

"What a—nice—surprise. If we'd known you were coming—Lucy really should have told us—what a—surprise."

"It smells really good in here." Manuela bats her lashes and looks longingly at dinner. Man, she is good.

"Oh!" Dad glances from her to the table. "Would you like to join us? We only just sat down." He looks at me, and I can tell from his confused expression and the way he's talking like his tongue's too big for his mouth that he's dying to ask me what the heck is going on. "Lucy, don't just sit there. Fix your guest a plate."

"Are you sure you don't mind?" Manuela turns up the *aw-shucks* in her voice and pointedly ignores the question on my face.

"Of course not. Why don't you just leave your stuff by the door?" Dad looks at me expectantly. "A sleepover, huh?"

"I, um. I must have, uh, well—"

"You forgot, go ahead and admit it." Manuela's smile is as impish as they come. "It's okay." She leans toward my dad and rests her hand on her chin. "We bumped into each other last week and got to talking, and Lucy here was kind enough to invite me over to catch up because my mom's been working late a lot. But I know she's so busy she probably just got her days mixed up. That's what I love about summer—you can barely tell the difference between a Monday and a Saturday. Anyway, are you sure you don't want me to go home? I don't want to impose. We can always schedule for a different night if it's a hassle."

"No, of course not!" Dad looks at me and motions toward the casserole resting on the stovetop. "Please, make yourself at home. It's a lovely surprise to have one of Lucy's—friends—over."

I stand up stiffly and pile a plate for Manuela. I should have known she was up to something when she didn't put up more of a fight this afternoon. Manuela is the kind of girl that puts up a fight for just about everything. She's probably here to get the answers I wouldn't give her this afternoon. Or maybe she has more information about Marco? But if that's the case, why not just come by my house during the day, like a normal person?

"And where is it that you said you bumped into each other?" Vivi's question has a suspicious edge to it. I can feel her watching me in that way she does when she knows I'm not telling her something.

"The park, just around the bend over there." Manuela points, like they don't know where Mama's park is located. "I was just minding my own business when Lucy showed up. Then we got to talking, and, well, here I am! I wasn't expecting to see you here, Miss Warman. How is Marco feeling?"

"Better. Resting. It was nice of you to check on him." Vivi's voice sounds like she thinks Manuela's visit was the opposite of nice.

I *thunk* the plate of food down in front of Manuela a little harder than I mean to and an errant noodle flies onto her shirtfront.

"Slippery little fellow," she says with a grin that dares me to try it again. She plucks the noodle off and pops it in her mouth, still smiling. "This is going to be *such* a fun night. Thanks again for inviting me. Do you have anything to drink? Sweet tea, perhaps?"

I clench my teeth and smile at her. "My pleasure."

"So, Mr. Miller, how's business?"

When I turn back around, tea in hand, Manuela's leaning forward across the table like talking to Dad and eating Vivi's casserole are the best things that have ever happened to her.

"You must get to talk to so many interesting people. Where exactly do you take their memories away? Do you have, like, a special room for it? I've always wondered if you have them sit on a couch, therapist style, or if you have some sort of special chair. You know, for more of a professional doctor- or dentist-office vibe?"

"Just a couch, sorry to disappoint."

"How does it work? Is there some sort of ceremony that you have to do?"

Dad chokes on a noodle.

"Ceremony?" I raise my eyebrows and sit across from her. I thump her foot with mine, trying to catch her eye. She keeps her gaze on Dad. She's enjoying this.

"Sure, why not? Or, like, maybe there's a magic word or, like, *thing* you have to do?" She wiggles her finger in what I can only assume is supposed to be some kind of hocus-pocus motion.

Vivi watches Manuela like she's a math problem that needs solving. It makes the hairs on the back of my neck stand up. Vivi's too smart not to have some suspicions about what Manuela's doing here. On the same day she showed up on Marco's doorstep, no less.

I shovel food into my mouth as fast as I can.

"This is delicious," Manuela says to Dad, taking a slow, leisurely bite, like she could do this all night. I try to send her a mental signal to hurry the hell up, but she either doesn't notice or doesn't care because she's having way too much fun watching me squirm.

"You have Vivi here to thank for that. I don't know what we'd do without her around to feed us," Dad says.

"Someone has to keep you two from starving to death," says Vivi.

Manuela points her fork and moves it back and forth between Vivi and Dad. "Are y'all like a thing or something?"

It's my turn to choke on a noodle. Vivi almost spits out her sweet tea.

"Oh! What? No, we're just—" Dad sputters through a mouthful of noodles.

"Colleagues." Vivi offers for him. But she's turned three shades of pink and starts tucking her hair behind her ears like she can't quite figure out what to do with her hands.

Even just the thought of Vivi and my dad—I have to hold back a gag. I glare at Manuela with enough force to shake the table.

"You finished yet?" I nod toward Manuela's half-finished plate. "'Cause you look like you're finished."

She narrows her eyes and pats her mouth with the napkin. "I suppose I should save some room for snacks. We can't have girl talk without junk food, am I right?"

"Right. Girl talk. May we be excused?" I look at Dad so I can avoid Vivi, but even out of the corner of my eye it's impossible not to notice her flushed cheeks. Dad looks relieved. Vivi stands suddenly and walks toward the oven.

"Okay," Dad says, resting his fork on his plate. "Do you need anything? For the—sleepover?"

"We can figure it out." Manuela stands. "Don't worry about us, Mr. Miller. We'll try to keep the giggling down so we don't bother you."

Giggling?

I practically leap from the table to grab Manuela's bag.

"My room's upstairs." I lead the way two steps at a time.

"Good night," she calls to Dad and Vivi. "Thanks again for dinner!"

I grab her arm and yank her into my bedroom, snapping the door shut behind us. Then I drop her duffel bag on the floor.

"What the hell are you doing here?"

# 24

*Manuela paces the length of my bedroom, eyeing the maps, travel posters,* and photographs pinned to the walls. She stops to inspect a picture of the Eiffel Tower, then moves on to one of the Grand Canyon.

"You haven't actually been to any of these places, have you?"

"No. Now are you gonna tell me what you're doing here?" I say again.

She plops down on my bed and kicks off her flip-flops. "That's no way to treat your guest."

"'Guest' implies you were invited. You just barged in here. So what's going on?"

She shrugs, stretching her legs across my bed like she belongs there. Her eyes trace the highways on my ceiling map, jumping between the red stars. "Wait, are those the only places you've actually been to? You've never left the state of Texas?"

"Not yet," I answer through gritted teeth. "Manuela—"

"For someone who's never really been anywhere you sure do have a lot of maps and travel pictures." She pops her thumbnail into her mouth and starts chewing. "I haven't been that many places, either. We have cousins in Tulsa and family near Guanajuato, so when I was little we went there to visit. Tulsa's all right, although anything's better than Tumble Tree, right? But Mexico was amazing—even though my family lives in this industrial area, it still felt more alive than it does here. More vibrant, you know? And Guanajuato—it's huge! There are like a million people who live there, and the hills are covered in these brightly colored houses. There are always people hanging out in the plazas and walking around the streets. We were supposed to go there again this summer, but then my abuela got sick, so we're stuck here except for the occasional day trip to El Paso. But I guess that means I have more stars than you. And I've left the state *and* the country, which should be worth, like, double map stars, don't you think?"

"Manuela." My pulse is starting to thud against my temples. She's giving me a headache. "What are you doing here?"

She ignores me and points to her duffel bag. "Pass me that, will you?"

I toss it onto the bed.

"After you ditched me today, I thought about all those questions you kept asking me about my mom and the mines. So when she woke up, I asked her what she did last night." I notice that Manuela's fingers are shaking as she unzips her bag. "She got really weird. She just kept repeating that she 'worked at the mines' every time I asked. It wasn't like her. It was almost like she'd been brainwashed. It was—scary. So I came here, because you seem to know what's going on. But I figured I couldn't just show up at dinner without a good reason." When Manuela turns to look at me, all her bravado is gone. "Something weird is going on. Something happened to my mom, didn't it? At the mines?"

I nod slowly, and it finally hits me just how many people have been hurt by the mayor and my dad. All those people working night shifts—they're people like Manuela's mom, probably working extra shifts because they need the money. They have no idea that the whole thing is a charade. And then there's Missy, Mr. Lewis, and maybe even Manuela's grandma—something bad is happening to the people who work there. Something very, very bad.

"What's going on, Lucy? And don't say 'nothing.' If my mom's being hurt—if someone—" Her lower lip trembles and she looks away from me.

I sit down on the bed and follow Manuela's gaze to my ceiling map. I think of Manuela at the lake, dancing with her friends and sipping from the flask.

"How do I know you won't tell your friends?"

"I won't," she says, her voice serious, and I remember what Marco said the other night. *Manuela's many things, but she's not a liar.* "Please, tell me what's going on."

Downstairs, I can just make out the sound of dishes clinking. Voices murmuring. Vivi and Dad must still be in the kitchen.

I scan my map—I-10 through Houston into Baton Rouge, then left on I-55 into Jackson, Mississippi.

Then I take a deep breath and tell Manuela everything I know.

Manuela is silent for a long time, chewing on her lower lip.

"We were in Walmart the first time I noticed my abuela was acting strange. She wanted me to try on this ugly shirt, and I was being a total brat about it. She always tried to get me and my sister to try on clothes we hated." She lets out a dry laugh at the memory. "Then all of a sudden she looks at me, and her eyes go all unfocused, like she can't see me. I thought she was messing with me, but then . . . then she started to cry and asked me where we were. *Who* we were." Manuela pauses to wipe at her eyes, her chin wobbling. "She used to work at the mines a few nights a week because she said she wanted to help out. If I'd known . . . If I'd had any idea . . ."

"You couldn't have known. No one seems to know, that's the problem."

"Do you think they've erased my memories, too?" she asks.

"Maybe," I say. "I don't know."

"And you think they got to Marco?"

"I don't know for sure, but probably, yeah. He was supposed to meet me here. We were going to go back to the mines a few nights ago, to see if it would trigger anything for us." I walk over to the window. Shadows pool in the yard like dark splotches of sky got tangled up in the dried earth. The sky is bright with stars, sprinkled across the night like sand on a blacktop. I wonder if Marco's looking up at the same sky, trying to make sense of the blank spaces in his memory; if I'm there between the cracks, or just another missing piece.

"He wouldn't have *not* shown up at my house unless something happened. It's the only explanation that makes any sense. I think Vivi may have something to do with it—she told Marco to stay away from me. Maybe she figured out he didn't listen to her?"

"Or maybe the mayor caught him. I always knew that man was a creep. Who wears sunglasses at night?"

"I think it's to protect him from my dad," I say. It didn't occur to me until the night at Miracle Lake, when he wasn't wearing them. Whenever he's around me and Dad, even if he's inside or it's nighttime, he always has them on. Why would you wear sunglasses if your eyes didn't need protection from the sun? "You have to make eye contact to take away a memory—it's the most important part. I think he wears them so my dad won't take his memories away."

"If they're working together, why would the mayor need protection?"

"I don't know," I answer, annoyance creeping into my voice. With every answer a new question seems to sprout, like branches spindling off a tree. I think of the picture in my hallway, of the two of them toasting the camera. They were friends once. Now my dad looks like he's ready to bolt at the mere mention of the mayor.

"We have to go to the mines. My mom's working a shift there." Manuela glances at the clock on my nightstand. "She's probably on her way there right now. Maybe we can get to her before they do—"

"Are you kidding? Did you not hear anything I just said?"

"That's why we have to go there! What if they do something to hurt her? What if she gets sick, too? You said yourself that you and Marco were planning to go there again. How's this any different? Please, we have to help her."

I open my mouth. Close it. She has a point. But that was before they got to Marco. If they catch me and Manuela, who will be left to remember?

"So, what, you're gonna go there and demand that your mom comes home?" I ask.

"Maybe. Why not?"

"And what if they decide you've seen too much and erase your memories, too? What good will that do anyone?"

She throws up her arms in frustration. "I don't know! But I can't just sit here all night worrying about her. I at least need to see if she's okay. I'm not gonna get any sleep anyway." Manuela reaches into her duffel bag and pulls out a pair of tennis shoes, like she's going to the mines right this second. "Stay here if you want, but I'm going down there. I can't just sit around reading newspaper articles, hoping to stumble across an answer. I need to *do* something."

I wince.

"Sorry. I—" She lets out an exasperated sigh. "What if it was your mom?"

Her voice is gentle, like she's tiptoeing around the fact that I don't have a mother anymore. But it's enough to make her point.

*Ladybug, let's leave this place to the dust and the lizards.*

I look at Mama's scrapbook perched on my nightstand. If Mama was working at the mines I wouldn't hesitate. I'd be down there as fast as my bike could carry me. And maybe Marco was right—maybe going back there will trigger an Echo. Sitting around here certainly hasn't gotten me anywhere.

"Okay," I tell her. "But we stay hidden. We're only going to make sure she's all right, understand? We can't let anyone see us." I grab the notebook I've been keeping by my nightstand. "And we write everything down before we go, just in case. So we have a record of it."

Manuela nods and reaches for the notebook, but I rip a page out and hand it to her instead. I don't want her reading something from an earlier entry. More specifically, I don't want her reading an entry about Marco and his crooked-road smile, or how I can't stop thinking about what our first kiss must have been like.

"You need to borrow another shirt. You'll stick out like a flashlight beam wearing that."

Manuela looks down at the white shirt peeking out of her overalls. I move toward my closet to grab her something dark to wear, but she grabs my arm.

"How about tomorrow we go to Marco's again? Maybe I can get him to go for a walk or something so you can talk to him." She smiles, and I know this is her version of saying thank you.

"Yeah, I'd like that. Thanks. Now let's go see about your mom."

# 25

*We wait until we're sure Vivi has gone home and the house is sleeping,* passing the time by taking the ridiculous quizzes in Manuela's magazines. Manuela tells me more about her trip to Guanajuato and promises to bring me a picture to add to my travel wall. I tell her about Mama and all the places we planned to visit, and even flip open the scrapbook to show her a few pictures. When the house is silent, we tiptoe downstairs to disarm the alarm. Manuela manages to hit every squeaky floorboard along the way, like making noise is her superpower.

"Be quiet," I hiss, pressing my finger to my lips. She gives me a look like I'm the one stomping through the silence.

Then we're outside breathing in the desert, the night sky stretched above us like a map to the heavens.

We walk our bikes until we get to the end of the driveway, then I angle my flashlight west, toward the mines. The night hums with electricity, the cicadas providing a steady current of sound. Skeleton trees line the roadway, their branches changing to dark, spindly arms. Even though I know the roads and the tree line as well as I know the way to Mama's park, I'm grateful not to be alone. The darkness feels too big. The road too empty.

Behind me, Manuela's breath comes out in short rasps. Her bike creaks. The dirt crunches beneath her tires. Maybe she's listening to the sound of her heart beating inside her chest, too. I don't think I've ever heard her go so long without saying something.

We slow down when we get close to the turnoff, both of us searching the thin stream of light to make sure we don't miss it. I spot it first, then we're riding down the bumpy dirt road, slowing our pace so we don't slip against the clusters of dirt and plants that make up the unpaved stretch.

The quiet seems to deepen as we get closer to the mines. The road reaches outward like a ball of black yarn unwinding. If I didn't know any better, I'd swear it was growing longer, trying to push us back the way we came. Doubts worm their way into my mind, and I'm starting to wonder if maybe we should turn around. Why am I doing this again?

As if in answer, the fading bruise on the back of my knee begins to throb, pulsing in time to my pedaling. Whatever it is they're hiding down there, it's bad enough that it needs to be protected by armed guards. Bad enough that they're keeping the entire town in the dark by stealing memories. If they catch me this time, a bruise and a wiped memory may not be the only things I leave with.

"Did we miss it?" Manuela asks, her voice too loud for the quiet night.

"I don't think so." I squint, looking for lights to signal where the parking lot is. It feels like we've been riding forever. "Maybe we should go back?"

"No. Not until I know she's okay." Manuela's eyes shine bright against the thin moonlight. "You promised."

Long minutes creep by, and I almost tell her we should go back again. But then the lights from the parking lot split the night and we pick up our pace. I'm not sure if I'm relieved or terrified.

There are just under a dozen cars parked in the dimly lit yard. I recognize the mayor's truck immediately. My heart hammers inside my chest.

"Follow my lead," I tell her, even though my head is screaming at me to run. "And stay low to the ground, especially while we're in the parking lot."

Manuela nods, looking relieved to have someone between her and the men with guns.

We leave our bikes at the edge of the parking lot, just outside the circle of light cast from the nearby trailer. I crouch low, dodging between cars, taking care to stay in the shadows. Manuela does the same.

Once we get past the glow from the parking lot, the desert stretches black and huge. Shadows of prickly pear and yucca glower. Something skitters in the dirt. Ahead, I can just make out the opening to the mines. Lights glow from somewhere inside them, but outside there's nothing—no people waiting like Marco said there were last time. Instead, lights are strung up on poles circling a patch of desert to the east of the mines. Piles of dirt dot the desert landscape. The night is filled with the sounds of scrapes and grunts. Are people digging?

I motion for Manuela to stay behind me, then lead us in a crouch toward the sounds. As we get closer it becomes clearer that people are indeed digging. The desert horizon is peppered with small mounds of dirt. Next to the mounds of dirt are shallow holes, and in between those are wooden crates. I see someone wipe at their brow, a gardening shovel in their hand. Then they lift something out of a hole and place it into a nearby crate, cradling the object as if it might break when they lower it down.

What could they be collecting in the middle of the desert?

On either side of the workers, two men stand watch. They're facing away from me, but I can tell by the way they move they're holding something in their hands, like a gun. Between them, the mayor lumbers with crossed arms, sunglasses glinting.

Manuela runs smack into me when I stop.

"What are you doing?" she hisses, and I put a finger to my lips to shut her up. I motion to a cluster of plants and move to crouch behind them.

But Manuela doesn't stop—she keeps moving.

"Manuela," I hiss, trying to get her attention. She waves a hand at me and flattens herself so low against the ground that her stomach must be scraping the dirt. She continues to edge forward, closer and closer.

What is she *doing*? She'll get us caught. I can barely see her in the wan moonlight, but that doesn't mean the mayor won't catch the motion from the corner of his eye and turn in our direction. That doesn't mean he won't see—

*Her shoes.*

My breath hitches in my chest. I hadn't noticed before because she was riding behind me. But now, as she scuttles closer toward the lights illuminating the mine, I see it. Her shoes have a swoosh of white splashed on the sides. The kind meant to make sure people can see you when you're riding your bike at night.

The kind designed to reflect light.

I bite my lip to hold in a curse. I should have checked what she was wearing more carefully. We should have worn all black. We should have planned better.

We never should have come.

"Manuela," I whisper, but it's barely a puff of air. She keeps skulking forward, oblivious, only stopping when she's dangerously within viewing range, bending low behind a triangle of desert plants. The white shoe swoosh glows every time she shifts, reflecting the lights strung around the area where people are digging.

My pulse races faster. My vision starts to blur. I have a sudden sensation like I'm falling, the world rushing past and smearing around me. A burst of pain slices through my skull.

*The Big Dipper. Hands digging into my back. A fist full of desert to help me remember.*

I feel my hand reach into my pocket like I'm trying to grab something, but there's nothing there.

What was I just reaching for?

I place my hand on the ground to steady the tilting sensation in my head.

It flashes past me then—the pocketful of desert. I must be having Echoes of the last time I was here. My thoughts feel rushed, panicked. It's like my body is telling me to turn back even though my head wants to stay.

I blink once, twice, until finally the scene in front of me stills and I can make sense of my surroundings. Manuela's so close to the work site that they could probably hear her breathing if they listened hard enough. There's no way the mayor won't see her. He just needs to glance to his right, to catch sight of the white mark on her shoes, and she's caught. *We're* caught.

The mayor says something to the people digging. His back is to me so I can't quite make it out, but Manuela must be able to hear every word.

A man stands from his work area and lifts one of the crates. The mayor motions past them to the glowing mouth of the mines. One of the guards steps forward, gun glinting in the dim light.

The man holding the crate walks cautiously forward—maybe from the weight of the box, or maybe because there's a weapon pointed at him. He cradles the box like it might shatter if he drops it. When he gets to the opening of the mines, he hesitates, his wide eyes shining in the light.

The mayor motions him forward. "Into the mines, please. All the way to the back."

The man's eyes go round and white when he sees the guard

step forward, and then he walks forward until he's swallowed by the yawning entry. When he emerges a few minutes later, the package is gone. The mayor claps him on the shoulder, says something in his ear, then bellows to the workers.

"Get a move on, people! We don't have all night."

The man shuffles back toward his work area and lifts his shovel. Another person stands, lifts one of the crates, and walks it to the mines, followed by another and another. They all follow the same slow succession to the opening, where they disappear into the mines to drop off their crates and then scuttle back toward their work area to resume digging.

I recognize Manuela's mama immediately—she has Manuela's dark hair and strong jaw. She stumbles when she gets close to the mine opening. The mayor reaches for her, steadying her with both of his hands.

Manuela's white tennis shoe swoop winks. She's no longer flat on her belly—she's sitting up. She looks like she's ready to run to her mama's side.

The mayor must have seen the movement out of the corner of his eye, or maybe he saw the flash of white. Because suddenly his head turns and sunglasses glint in our direction.

My palms are slick with sweat.

I drop to my stomach, but not before I catch sight of him walking straight toward Manuela.

## 26

*"Who's there?"* *the mayor's voice booms through the desert. I don't dare* raise my head. Instead, I press my stomach into the ground until I feel the dirt against my skin.

I can hear Mayor Warman's boots crunching, slow and steady like he's stalking prey.

"Don't try to hide, I saw you out there. Best you come on out where we can see you. Else I'll have to send Archie here to come get you."

*Archie.* Wasn't that the name of the handyman the mayor sent over to install the security alarm? And the same name Marco called the bearded man at the Pie Pantry.

I'm shaking so hard I can barely get my hands underneath me, but I manage to lift myself just enough to see what's happening.

The workers have stopped digging and lugging the crates, faces turned toward us. Manuela's mama is one of them, her mouth tight and worried. The mayor hovers a few yards away from Manuela, who's standing up in plain view of everyone now. Behind the mayor, the armed guard has his pistol raised.

Manuela raises her hand in a wave and smiles at the mayor. She looks like they just bumped into each other at the grocery store.

"Hi, Mr. Warman. Didn't mean to startle you. I was just looking for my mom."

"Manuela, what are you doing here?" Her mom looks as confused as the mayor. She shifts her weight, trying to steady the crate balanced between her arms.

"Manuela." The mayor draws her name out, almost like he's amused. "This is a closed work site. You know better than to be out here. Not to mention it's the middle of the night. It's not safe for a young lady to be wandering around the desert in the dark."

"I know, and I'm so sorry. It's just that my mom left her medication at the house. I couldn't sleep because I was worried she'd need it, so I thought I'd just swing by and give it to her. I was trying not to interrupt, but . . . well, I'm sorry. Would you mind if I gave it to her real quick? Then I'll be on my way and you guys can get back to work."

The mayor rubs at his beard and motions to the guard to lower his weapon.

Manuela steps forward, but he holds up a hand for her to stop.

"Hold it right there, Manuela. Like I said, this is a closed work site. Wouldn't want you getting injured or anything." A slow smile spreads across his face. "Rosa, why don't you come down here and get your medicine? Archie, go on over there and help her, won't you?"

The guard shoves the pistol into his waistband but keeps a

hand on it as he walks over to Manuela's mom. He takes the crate from her arms and sets it down carefully. Rosa marches toward her daughter, a confused grimace on her face.

When she reaches her, Manuela fumbles with something in her pocket, then wraps her mama in a tight hug and whispers into her ear. They stand like that for what seems like an eternity, and when they part Manuela dabs her eyes.

It's impossible to see through the sunglasses, but the mayor's face is trained on them the entire time, like he's analyzing every single move.

"I'll see you in the morning," Manuela says, her voice too bright. "And please don't forget your meds again. I was really, really worried."

"Okay."

The mayor claps his hands, startling Manuela's mom.

"Come on now, everyone back to work. Manuela, why don't you let me take you home? It's too late for you to be out here on your own. It's better to be safe, don't you agree?"

"That's so nice of you, thank you."

"Y'all keep going. Archie here's in charge until I get back."

He claps his hands again. Then I watch in horror as Manuela and the mayor walk side by side toward the parking lot.

Manuela glances back toward where I'm hiding, just once. Her face shines ghost-white in the moonlight, and I can see her lips form a single word.

*Go.*

# 27

*Minutes pass. I have no idea how many.*

Fear roots me to the ground, belly flat against the desert. I'm too afraid that movement will attract attention, or that the mayor will discover the second bike hidden in the parking lot shadows and come looking for me.

I start to crawl backward, slowly, keeping myself low and only daring short glances up at the worksite. The sound of metal against dirt fills the night as people continue digging.

Every thump or scurry of movement sends my heart into a maelstrom.

When I'm far enough away, I start to turn around, ready to quicken my pace and get the hell out of here, but my hand connects with something hard and slick sticking out of the dirt. Something that doesn't grow in the desert. Something manufactured.

It's too dark to see, so I explore the shape of it with my fingers. I feel the ridges of something metal and round—a lid—then skim the sides and feel the metal give way to something cool and smooth. I work my hands around the edges, trying to free it from the dirt while limiting my movements and keeping my body flat to the ground. It takes a painfully long time, but eventually I push away enough dirt to free it.

I realize all at once what it is, and I can't believe I didn't think of it until now.

It's a mason jar, just like the ones my dad uses to hold discarded memories. I knew he had people take them to the desert, but I never realized they were burying them out by the mines.

In the distance, I hear the rumble of a car engine. Headlights cut through the dark. Boots crunch against the dirt.

"We almost done here?"

My stomach clenches at the thick, gravelly voice. The mayor's back.

"Yes, sir. I think we've just about got them all."

"Good. I've got Charlie waiting in the trailer."

My mouth goes dry. *Charlie.*

Did the mayor bring him here? What if he picked him up before he dropped off Manuela? That would mean—

No. I squeeze my eyes closed, like somehow that will make it all go away. Like somehow that will mean Manuela's at her house, unharmed, with her memories still intact.

"People, I need you to move faster, ya hear? We don't have all night and I'm not paying you overtime to dawdle."

The crunch and scrape of digging speeds up. People scramble toward the mines, moving faster, crates held close to their chest. The mayor watches the scene like it's a late night rerun he's seen a hundred times before, drumming his fingers against his dusty pant leg.

Then Janice, a woman who works at the corner store part-time, stumbles just before she reaches the opening to the mines. For a moment it looks like she'll recover, but then she loses her balance and the crate falls from her hands. The lid flies off. There's a sound of glass breaking. Shards of broken jars litter the ground along with white Styrofoam pellets that must have been there to protect the glass.

For a moment, Janice is frozen in place, staring at the wreckage on the ground. Then she places a hand over her mouth and lets out a bark of laughter.

"Aw, Christ," says the mayor, jumping to his feet. "How many times do I have to tell you people to be careful with the crates, huh? How many times?"

The laughter gets louder and more hysterical. Janice laughs like she isn't standing in the middle of the desert with the mayor, the armed guards, and all the workers staring at her. She laughs like it's the only way she can get air into her lungs. She laughs until tears stream down her face and her cheeks are bright red from the effort. Then she spreads her arms out wide, tips her head back, and starts to spin in a circle.

"Archie, take her to Charlie. See if he can do something to calm her down. She broke at least two jars and they're full strength—haven't even been diluted yet. Who knows how long she'll be like this?"

Janice starts jumping up and down, clapping her hands like a little kid on Christmas morning. "What a perfect night!" she shouts to the sky. "What a perfect, perfect night! Isn't it so beautiful?"

When Archie takes hold of her wrist and starts tugging her toward the trailer she doesn't resist—her face is raised to the sky, her free hand over her mouth to stifle the giggles burbling from her chest.

*Full strength. Haven't even been diluted yet.*

I assume he's talking about the memories in the jars, except that doesn't make any sense. Janice seemed delirious with happiness. The burdens that get buried in the desert aren't good memories—they're made of the sorrow, regret, and guilt people leave behind at the Memory House. If anything, she should have reacted the way that Marco said Mr. Lewis did when they made him drink the black stuff.

Unless . . .

Does the mayor have some way to change the memories? Or—is there something else in the jars entirely?

"Nothing to see, folks. Best you get back to work." The mayor runs a frustrated hand across his face and examines the crowd. "But carefully, please—next person who drops a crate is going home without pay, you hear me?"

The people paused outside the mine opening start moving again, their white-knuckled hands clinging tightly to the boxes as they make their way inside. Someone moves forward to clean up the Styrofoam pieces and broken bits of glass splayed across the dirt.

If they're almost done, then I have to leave. Now.

*Move, Lucy. You have to move.*

With shaking hands, I pull myself up from the ground and start the slow crawl back toward the parking lot, the jar I unearthed tucked underneath my arm. I move in a sideways shuffle so that I can see the mines, but also make sure that nothing's behind me. Every few feet I dart behind the plants, checking to make sure no one is looking in my direction. It's slow and cumbersome, until eventually the mines disappear from view and the dim lights of the parking lot guide my way.

My bike is where I left it, hidden in shadows. Manuela's is gone, and I can only assume she took it with her when the mayor drove her home.

*Please let her be okay.*

The ride back is wobbly, the jar tucked under my arm making it harder to work the handlebars. I stick to the farthest edges of the roads, only turning my flashlight on for short bursts to make sure I'm going the right way. I can't risk being seen by anyone who might be out on the road, or by the workers at the mines when they finally head home for the evening. I listen for tires on gravel and watch for headlights, but no one comes.

By the time I finally walk through the front door of the Memory House, every muscle in my body aches. I'm thirsty, covered in grit, and in desperate need of sleep.

I don't bother being quiet as I take the stairs two at a time—Vivi won't be here for another few hours, and Dad's with the mayor.

The thought of him at the mines, ripping the truth from people without their consent, makes me sick. I push my bedroom door open with more force than I intended.

And nearly jump out of my skin and drop the jar when a light snaps on.

# 28

*"Where the hell have you been?" Manuela jumps off my bed. "Do you* have any idea how worried I've been? I thought you'd gotten caught!"

I'm so relieved to see her that I can't stop myself—I run straight at her and squeeze her in a hug.

"Ease up, you're choking me," she says, but she squeezes me back. I can hear the relief in her voice.

"What happened? You left with the mayor and I thought . . . when he came back without you and brought my dad—do you remember anything about tonight? Did they do something to you? Did my dad . . . ?"

"I'm fine. The mayor just took me home. I got here over an hour ago and figured you'd be right behind me. What the hell happened to you? You look like somebody tied you to their bumper and dragged you here. And what is that?"

She points to the jar. I set it on my nightstand and look down at myself. She's right, I'm filthy—every inch of me is covered in grime and grit. My arms are smeared with dust. My fingernails are so black it looks like I've dug my way out of a grave. I can only imagine what my face and hair must look like.

Manuela has her hand over her mouth, trying to hold in a laugh. Like this whole thing is *hilarious*. Like we didn't almost get held up at gunpoint in the middle of the night and forced to have our memories erased. Her hiccupping laugh reminds me of the woman who broke the jars.

"How are you laughing right now? I thought the mayor kidnapped you!"

Manuela's face turns bright red and she lets out a cackle that would have ripped Dad from sleep if he were here. "You look—your face—" She can barely get out words between chortles.

And then I don't know what happens—maybe it's the exhaustion or the adrenaline finally leaving my body—but suddenly I'm laughing, too. It starts as a giggle, but then the laughter explodes out of me until I can't catch my breath. I laugh until my throat is raw and my stomach aches. I laugh until tears stream down my dust-covered cheeks. I laugh until Manuela grabs my arm and steers me toward the shower, which only sends us into another fit of heaving, gasping laughter.

"You look grosser than Mayor Warman's beard after a chili-eating contest."

"Stop, I can't breathe!"

"We're gonna have to burn those clothes."

She shoves me into the shower and turns the knob until hot water spits onto my fully clothed body. Brown water pools at my feet. Bits of desert plant swirl with the dust down the drain. Manuela backs away, the door clicking closed behind her, and I slowly peel myself out of my wet clothes, scrubbing the desert with them as I tip my head up toward the spray. I turn the nozzle until the water is almost too hot to bear, ready to scald the secrets from my skin. To burn this whole night to the ground.

When I emerge, Manuela's staring out the window, her body angled toward Mama's park. I wonder if she's worrying about her own mother—if her mama will have any recollection that Manuela came to the mines, or if tonight will be just one more shadow of memory lost to the desert.

"What happened?" I sit down on the edge of my bed, careful not to let my wet hair drip onto the blankets. "How come the mayor didn't have your memory erased?"

She shrugs, like it's no big deal.

"I played innocent. People like Mayor Warman assume I'm just some silly girl who doesn't have enough sense to know a liar when she sees one—so I let him see what he wanted." She tugs at one of her braids and bats her lashes, raising her voice an octave until she sounds like something best listened to while chewing bubble gum and eating cotton candy.

"Oh, Mr. Warman, I'm *so* sorry I interrupted. I hope I didn't cause any trouble for my mom. She really needs the job and the overtime. It's *so* thoughtful of you to watch out for all the night workers. I won't be worried about her working late now that I know *you're* helping. Thank you *so* much for the ride home. Please tell Marco I said hi and that I hope he's feeling better, won't you?" She pushes her bottom lip out for effect, then just as quickly she drops the facade and gives me a wry smile. "I'd feel bad for him if it weren't so obvious that he's no better than a rattlesnake."

"You're kidding. He actually bought that?"

"Yup. It probably helps that he already thinks I'm just a giggling girl with a crush on his nephew. Who am I to contradict? He quizzed me a bit about what I saw, how long I was there before he saw me, why my mom forgot her medication in the first place, et cetera. But at some point, I guess he decided I was harmless because he dropped me off at my house. Easy peasy."

She gives me a smug smile. I sit back on the bed, impressed. I don't want to admit that I made similar assumptions about her. But something tells me she wouldn't be surprised to hear it.

"What about your mom's medication? I saw you give her something when you hugged her."

"I gave her my EpiPen—I'm allergic to bees, so I always carry it. Then I told her to act relieved, told her not to drink anything they gave her, and promised I'd explain everything in the morning. Do you think she'll be okay?"

"I don't know," I answer honestly. "My dad was there."

She nods. "I saw him leaving. I was pulling into your driveway when he was pulling out. I don't think he saw me, though. If he had, I'm sure he would have stopped."

Manuela is quiet for a minute. When she looks back at me her eyes are dark and her lips are pressed into a thin, white line.

"What do you think they're doing down there?"

I stand up and walk over to the window. The front yard is one giant stretch of shadow reaching into the night. Somewhere out there, Dad is probably taking people's memories against their will. Maybe a guard is pointing a gun at Dad, or maybe Dad's doing it by choice. What I can't figure out is *why*. People come from all over to have their memories taken—if my dad wanted to make more money, all he'd have to do is charge more for his services. Instead, he gives discounts in exchange for their secondhand crap because he wants to help people. So why is he involved in all of this?

Mama's ring is heavy against my finger. I reach for it, twisting the cold metal in a circle. Somehow, I can't shake the feeling that Mama's accident is connected to all of this, too. I can feel it in my bones, like Mama's calling out to me from her grave, asking me to find the truth.

"They aren't copper mines anymore," I finally say. Manuela gives me a look that says she figured that part out about a century ago. "I mean, I think the mines must have closed just like that article said. Which means they probably haven't been operating for a long time."

"So what, then?"

"You know Janice from the corner store? She was working there tonight and she dropped one of the crates." I tell Manuela about the laughing fit she had after the jars broke. Manuela's brows knit together. "I think they're digging up the memories from the Memory House. We've always buried them out in the desert so that folks don't accidentally find them and open them. I just didn't realize we were burying them out by the mines."

"What happens if someone opens them?"

I shrug. "They'd let the memory out and then they'd have to feel everything that person felt—all of their sadness and pain. It would be pretty awful."

"But you said Janice acted like she was happy after the jar broke, so that doesn't make any sense." Manuela frowns. "And anyway, what does the mayor want with people's sadness?"

"I don't know, but I found this when I was leaving." I walk over to my nightstand to show her the jar I pulled out of the desert. Except when I hold it up to the light, I notice something strange.

Normally, the memories look like a swirling silver fog with a dark cloud of sadness at the center. But now, the shimmering fog is hovering at the top of the jar. At the bottom, there's something black and sludge-like. It's like the memory separated into two parts, with the lightest portion floating up to the top and the darkest part sinking to the bottom.

It hits me like a slap.

I've always thought that we took people's sadness away. But it's not just that, is it? Memories aren't made of just one feeling. For a heart to break, it first has to love. Before someone fails, they first have to believe in the possibility they can succeed. The bad comes with the good, like two sides of the same coin. And in order to remove their burdens completely, the people who come to Tumble Tree to forget have to leave behind the good with the bad.

But somehow, the two pieces have been pulled apart.

I hold the jar back up to the light, marveling at the shimmering silver that hovers just below the lid, tendrils curling upward like it's begging to be let out. When I look closer, I can see that the black sludge is moving, too, but barely. As if it's weighed down by its own sadness, too heavy to move.

I think back to the jars I found in Dad's room and the one with the bright yellow label and old-timey text:

*Miracle Happiness Elixir*
*A cure for what ails your heart!*

My throat is tight; the realization slams into me like a fist.

"I know what the mayor is doing at the mines."

## 29

*Vivi's voice slices through my sleep.*

"Time to get up! You girls can't sleep the entire day away. Lucy, I need your help with the guests."

Manuela groans. I reach up to pull a pillow over my head, but Vivi snatches it away.

"Enough of that. I made you girls breakfast. Get up before I drag you downstairs myself."

Once Vivi leaves, Manuela rolls over to look at me. "She's a monster."

"You don't know the half of it. It's better to just do what she wants. Come on."

We clamber downstairs, the smell of eggs and bacon pulling us forward.

"How was your sleepover?" Vivi sets a plate of bacon on the table and motions for us to sit. She's smiling when she says it, but it doesn't quite reach her eyes and there's an edge to her voice I recognize all too well. She's mad about something.

"Great," we both answer in unison, and exchange an exhausted look. Vivi narrows her eyes.

"What did you do last night?"

I quickly stuff a piece of bacon in my mouth to delay having to answer.

"Oh, you know," says Manuela, "the usual stuff."

"No, I don't know. Enlighten me." Vivi walks a plate of scrambled eggs and a pitcher of sweet tea to the table. Her eyes are on me as she sets them down.

"Girl talk. Magazine quizzes. Pedicures. Basically your standard sleepover activities." Manuela reaches for the tea, smiling up at Vivi with a beatific grin.

"Pedicures? That sounds fun. Why aren't Lucy's toes painted?"

Manuela quickly darts her eyes to my bare feet, and I register the briefest flash of panic before she hides it behind an eye roll.

"I tried, but you know Lucy. I only brought blue polish and she refused, acting like blue toenails are right up there with face tattoos."

"I see." Vivi pulls out the chair across from me and sits down. "Was that before or after you snuck out of the house?"

Manuela chokes on a piece of bacon. I open my mouth. Close it. Cold fingers of panic creep down my neck. How does she know? Did Mayor Warman tell her?

Vivi holds up her hand to cut us off as we exchange a look. "Don't even try to deny it. I know for a fact that I set the alarm when I went home last night. And then this morning when I arrived it was conveniently disarmed. Care to explain how that happened?"

*Shit.* I completely forgot to reset the alarm.

It occurs to me then that the alarm was never really intended to keep people from breaking in, but rather to keep me from getting out.

Manuela kicks me under the table, and I realize it's my turn to respond. I quickly shove more food into my mouth.

"How do you know it wasn't Dad?" I say between bites, careful not to make eye contact.

Manuela sighs and sets down her glass of tea. Her face changes and I wonder if I'm getting an encore of the performance she gave the mayor last night.

"It was me," she says, her eyes round and innocent. "I'm sorry. My mom was working the late shift at the mines and she forgot her medicine. I was worried. I know it sounds silly, but I went down there to give it her. I didn't want to worry Lucy, so I left after she fell asleep. I didn't think anyone would notice."

Vivi flicks her eyes back and forth between us like she's trying to figure out if Manuela's lying. I can't decide if Manuela's a genius or a fool. Maybe both, but at least her little excursion can be confirmed in the event that Vivi hears something from her brother.

"And how exactly did you know the code to get out?"

"I didn't. It wasn't armed. I didn't even realize you had an alarm until just now. I think I heard Lucy's dad leave a little before I did. Maybe he went out and forgot to reset it? I'm sorry, Ms. Warman. Please don't be mad. Lucy had nothing to do with it."

Vivi watches Manuela, looking for flaws in her tale. But Dad's not down here—he must still be asleep. And Vivi has to know that means he had a late night with her brother.

"Where is Dad, anyway?" I ask, to reinforce the logic behind Manuela's story.

"Resting." Vivi sighs and walks over to the stove.

Manuela gives me a triumphant smile. For someone Marco claims isn't a liar, she's disturbingly good at it.

"I have to run some errands again, so I need you to look after things for a while, Lucy. Your dad said he'd see a few people this afternoon. I put a sign up that says we open at noon today. Can you make sure to take it down beforehand and see to the guests?"

I roll my eyes but nod my assent. Of course she'd find a way to tie me to the house all day. But at least if she's back to bossing me around, it must mean she's buying Manuela's story.

"I should go check on my mom. Thanks for breakfast, Ms. Warman. And thanks for having me over last night, Lucy. I hope we can do it again soon."

"Definitely." I stand and walk her to the door. "Maybe next time I'll let you paint my toes blue."

We exchange a conspiring look. When we're out of earshot, Manuela whispers, "I'll check on Marco this afternoon and see if I can get him away from the house. Will you be here in case I can get him to come with me?"

I nod.

Manuela surprises me by giving me a tight hug. "Stay safe," she whispers. Then she raises her voice so that Vivi can hear: "Thank you again!"

"You stay safe, too," I whisper, and I mean it. Then I close the door and walk back into the kitchen, avoiding Vivi's glare.

# 30

*It's a little before noon and Dad still hasn't emerged from his bedroom.*

Car windows are down and I can hear the burdened getting restless—there's a line of cars gathered just past the chain to our driveway, engines humming with the afternoon cicadas. I get the feeling that if I'm not down there at exactly twelve to take the chain down, they'll bust on through anyway.

As if to make the point, a horn honks. Do they think I can't see them down there? I roll my eyes and step back from the window, then head to the kitchen to get the sign-in ledger. I'm about to go into Dad's bedroom and rip the covers off him when there's a soft rap on the door.

*Great.* I really hate when the guests get restless like this.

I open the door, ready to stand my ground since the chain at the driveway *clearly* says we aren't open yet, but I stop when I see who's standing on the welcome mat.

It's the Oklahoma woman.

She looks thinner. The space under her eyes has hollowed out and her once-round cheeks look gaunt and sickly, like she's sucked them in one too many times and the skin decided to stay that way.

"Good afternoon," she says, looking past me into the house. She hugs her purse to her chest, fingers clutching the leather so tightly it's a miracle they don't burst through to the other side. "I'm so sorry to bother you, but there's something I'm hoping you can help me with. Um. I was wondering, have I . . . been here before?"

Her lower lip wobbles with the last word and immediately I understand why she has that untethered look in her blue eyes. She's an Echo.

Echoes always have a sad, withered look about them, like they've just been wandering, trying to grab on to memories that have been just out of reach ever since they left the Memory House.

"Ma'am, why don't you have a seat for a minute? Where'd you drive in from? Can I get you some water?"

I motion to a chair in our sitting room. Normally we don't let the guests come inside until their turn, but Dad always makes an exception for Echoes. They don't quite have their wits about them, he says, so the best thing to do is show them a little kindness until he can remove the memory fragments.

"Water would be wonderful, thank you. I drove down from Oklahoma. I just got in my car and started driving and then suddenly I was here. It's like my body knew where to take me even though my brain didn't. Isn't that strange?" She sits, her eyes tracing the fireplace mantel at the front of the sitting room like she's looking for something familiar. They settle on a picture of Mama and Dad with a one-year-old version of me squirming in their laps. "Have I been here before?"

"Yes, ma'am. You were here less than a week ago."

She turns to study me, her brow creasing with confusion. "I don't remember being here. Not exactly. But I can't get rid of this feeling that I'm missing something I lost. Do you know if I lost something the last time I was here?"

She twists a diamond ring on her finger, and I narrow my eyes, wondering if the ring is the culprit—if she didn't dispose of it like she was supposed to.

I swallow and look behind me, praying Dad's awake and will come out here soon. The woman looks like she might burst into tears any second. I'm too exhausted to spend the rest of the morning talking her down from this confused state.

"How about I go get you that water?"

I turn toward the kitchen, but Oklahoma's hand reaches out and grabs mine. Her fingers are sweaty and cold.

"Please," she says. Her nails dig into my palm. I can feel them trembling. "I can't sleep. I can't eat. I just have this feeling like something's missing from inside of me. And I keep having flashes of me in my car, driving here. Please, you have to help me. Why can't I remember?"

Of course we'd have an Echo today. Like I don't have a million other things I need to deal with. For maybe the first time ever I find myself wishing Vivi was here—she's always so good with the Echoes. She knows exactly what to say to calm them down, even if they have to wait for hours because Dad's in the middle of an unburdening. It's like there's nothing she can't cure with a glass of sweet tea and the right line of questioning.

I take a deep breath and steel myself for what will clearly be a long afternoon. This woman looks like she hasn't slept since she left the Memory House—her wide blue eyes are rimmed with red, and deep purple crescents circle the hollow space underneath. There's a grayish-yellow hint to her cheeks, and I wonder when she last had a solid meal.

Keep them talking, that's what Dad always says. Echoes aren't dangerous, they're just confused, but they spook easy if you don't keep them calm. Best thing to do is let them talk and think out loud until Dad can fish out the memory shards.

I offer her a sympathetic smile, squeeze her hand, and look directly into her eyes.

"Why don't you tell me what you remember?"

Her nails are suddenly sharp on my palm. I hear her words as if through a fog and feel something inside of me lurch forward, like the house is tipping on its axis and I'm about to tumble down with it, and then *snap*—there's a catch inside my head and suddenly I'm not seeing the sitting room inside my home anymore.

I'm standing next to a casket in a funeral parlor. There's a man inside of it wearing a gray suit, white satin surrounding him. I know him, but I don't know him. It's me standing next to him, but it's not me. I feel my hand touch the man, but it's not *my* hand. The fingernails are too long and the backs are dotted with age spots, but I can feel it as if it was my own. My heart feels like there's an anvil attached to it. My throat is thick with tears.

There's a flash of color, and suddenly everything around me turns blue.

Dad's words slice through me like a hot knife in butter. *There are really only three types of memories most people want to get rid of—memories colored by grief, regret, or guilt.*

*Grief is blue,* I realize. And then the rest of it clicks into place and I understand what's happened—I'm inside the Oklahoma woman's memories.

The scene rushes past. I see the man from the casket in a hospital bed. Pale white lids cover closed eyes. A monitor beeps in the background. I'm holding his hand. It feels strong and yet too fragile, and the anguish raging inside me is hotter than a stovetop. He won't make it through the night.

More scenes swim past me, some of them clear, others smeared fragments.

*Flash.* The man with his arm around me as someone snaps our picture. The image is bright gold with love. *Flash.* Forks scraping against plates as the two of us don't speak over an angry dinner—tinted dark gray with annoyance. *Flash.* My head in his lap, the television flickering, the scene flashing pale yellow with contentment. *Flash.* A kiss, bright gold. *Flash.* His warmth next to me as I sleep, pink with comfort. *Flash.* A Christmas tree. A turkey dinner. Him in a tux as our pastor tells him to kiss the bride. Gold. Purple. Orange. Silver. *Flash. Flash. Flash. Flash.*

An entire lifetime blinks past me in seconds and snippets, most of them unfurling so quickly I barely register what's happening. But in all of it, I feel the sorrow. The loss. The love. The pain. The happiness. The grief. The grief is the worst part, so heavy it's like the sky has heft to it. But there are so many other emotions—a rainbow of feelings, each one connected to the next, each one threatening to drown me.

The Oklahoma woman lets go of my hand and I fall backward, landing hard on the floor. The sitting room swims back into view—first the mantel, then the faded couch and chair, and finally the Oklahoma woman's face.

"Oh my goodness." The woman heaves great breaths and looks at me.

I have no words.

"How could I have ever wanted to forget him? He was my everything. How could I have done that?" She sobs, her body rocking side to side like she can barely keep herself upright. Tears travel down her frown lines and drop from her chin. She leans forward and cups her hands around her mouth to cover the low moans trying to escape her throat. "I'm so sorry," she whispers. "I'm so, so sorry. I missed him so much, but I should never have done that."

I pull myself off the ground, still a little wobbly from whatever just happened.

"Ma'am, are you okay?" I reach out to touch her, then jerk my hand back. What the heck just happened? What *was* that?

She keeps her hands cupped around her mouth for a few more seconds until the sobs turn to quiet gasps.

"I'm sorry. Oh my." More tears slide down her face, but she smiles at me. Her skin looks pinker than it did when she first arrived, her eyes clearer. "I think I'm okay now. I just missed him so much it hurt. I didn't think I could keep missing him like that and still go on. You understand, don't you?"

There's a low buzzing at the base of my skull as what she's saying starts to click into place.

"Thank you, dear. Thank you for giving me my Patrick back. I thought I couldn't live without him, but it turns out that I can't live without the memories of him—he's too much a part of me, even if he's gone. I'm only half a person without him, and now you've made me whole again. Thank you for bringing him home."

The buzzing in my head gets louder, like the cicadas from outside have swarmed the interior of the house. The last few practice sessions with Dad rush at me in a frenzy of red, green, and blue.

The first time I tried to take the memory of his tuna fish sandwich, I thought I'd failed. But I'd seen the memory, green with regret and unmistakably real, hadn't I? And afterward Dad had said, *I can still see the whole thing in my brain, plain as day. Sharp as a tack, actually.*

When I saw him the second time he'd been staring at a picture of Mama, trying to remember what joke he'd told her to make her smile. I hadn't made him forget the sandwich that day, either, but he'd remembered the joke after our session. *I just remembered what I said to your mom to make her laugh that day! What's a pirate's favorite letter?*

I thought I'd failed. I thought I wasn't able to take memories away. But that wasn't it at all, was it?

I clear my throat, afraid to ask the question, but desperate to hear the answer out loud.

"What exactly do you mean, 'I gave him back to you'?" The words barely break through the buzzing in my head. "What is it that you think I did?"

She wipes at her cheeks with the back of her hands and looks me square in the eyes, like I'm the one who's gone mental. "Is this part of what you people do? Am I supposed to admit it out loud as part of the brain therapy or something?" She looks at something behind me and stands, shrugging. "Fine, okay. I came here to have my husband erased after he passed because I'm a coward. It hurt too much to remember him." She snaps her eyes back to mine and raises her chin, like she has something to prove. "Then you made me remember him again and helped me realize what a mistake I made trying to have him erased in the first place. Thank you."

"Lucy did *what*?"

I spin around. Dad is standing at the end of the hallway, his hair sticking up in tufts around his head. His mouth hangs open, eyes wide. I have no idea how long he's been standing there, but the expression on his face tells me he heard enough. He knows.

Dad was wrong. The reason I can't make people forget isn't because I need more practice. It's because I *can't* make people forget.

I can make them remember.

I take one more look at my father's stricken face and do the only thing I can think of.

I run.

## 31

*I rip my bike from its resting place against the side of the house and take* a running leap onto it.

"Lucy, please! You have to listen to me. Come back!"

Dad's behind me, yelling so loud the whole town can probably hear. His footsteps pound against the porch and onto the gravel walkway, but I don't look behind me. I can't. I don't want to see the terror on his face and have to try to figure out what it means.

I zip past the chain blocking the driveway, past the row of cars waiting to be let inside. Someone yells for me to open the gate, but I keep pedaling. Past the mailbox, past Mama's park, past the cacti lining the road.

I can't take the main roads in case Dad decides to look for me. Instead, I take the back roads Manuela insisted on the other day. It's the safest option. Many of them are too narrow for a car to even drive down.

My heart pounds so hard it feels like it might catch fire. The sun is a blister in the sky, bright and glaring against the dusty road.

I make people remember. I can reverse everything the mayor's done. Everything my dad's done.

The realization is a firework inside my chest.

I follow the same path from yesterday, weaving in between potholes and plants blocking the way. By the time Marco's house comes into view, my thighs are aching from the effort of pedaling at top speed.

I lay my bike near a cluster of plants, then take a few seconds to catch my breath. I would kill for a sip of water or a towel to wipe the sweat stinging my eyes, but there's no time for any of that.

Dad was afraid when he heard what I could do. He was definitely afraid. But was he afraid for me, or for himself?

Marco's Yukon is parked in the same place as yesterday. I don't see any other cars, though that doesn't mean there isn't one in the garage. That doesn't mean he's alone. But it doesn't matter; I have to find a way to see him.

*I can make Marco remember.*

It's enough to get me moving. I take a deep breath and then I'm running toward his house.

I run from the side versus approaching head-on, but still. Anyone looking out the window will see me coming. When I get to the front yard I slow down, searching the windows for signs that someone's watching.

The curtains on the middle window are open—Marco's window. I pick up a woodchip from the landscaping and throw it. There's a sharp tap against the glass.

I step closer, my head craning to see inside the darkened room.

After a few seconds of no movement, I pick up a handful of woodchips and start pelting them one after the next at the window. The sharp *tap, tap, tap* of wood on glass sounds like gunfire.

A shadow appears. The window slides open. My heartbeat moves to my ears.

Marco leans out, his crooked-road smile falling into a confused frown.

"Lucy? What are you doing here? My mom's not here if you're looking for her."

I let out a breath. Thank God he's home. Thank God Vivi's not.

I put a finger to my lips. *Shh.*

"Let me in the back and I'll explain."

"Okay," he says, his voice thick with uncertainty. The window slides closed.

The back door is open when I come around the side of the house. Marco leans against it.

He studies me with a mix of confusion and curiosity. I can feel the ghost of something between us—like a hand reaching up from the hole in my memories, trying to grab hold. His eyes are dark as a midnight road. His crooked mouth quirks and I feel myself stepping closer to him, gravity pulling us together. I want so badly to reach for him.

"What's going on, Luce?" The sound of my nickname fills me with relief. Maybe I haven't been completely taken from him.

Maybe there's still a piece of me tucked away inside, even if only a small scrap.

"Is anyone else home?" I peer into the house behind him. The back door leads to a kitchen. The walls are painted a warm, buttery yellow. Lace curtains cover a window above a wide sink. Stools circle a large marble island in the center of the space. It looks familiar.

"It's just me. What's up? Is everything okay?"

I clear my throat. I already know the answer, but I need to ask anyway. Just to be sure.

"Do you remember meeting me a few nights ago at Miracle Lake? Do you remember what we talked about?"

Marco's brow furrows. "I haven't been to Miracle Lake in almost a week."

"What about the park near my house? Or Patty's Pie Pantry? Do you remember being at any of those places with me? Do you remember what happened at the mines?"

He shakes his head and steps back, squinting at me. I notice a tiny tremor in his fingers.

"The mines?" It's a question, but I can see the war on his face. I can see him trying to latch onto something.

"Can I come in?" I ask, barely able to keep myself from pushing inside.

He nods and moves so I can fit through the doorframe. My arm brushes his as I pass, and a shiver runs the length of my spine. The scent of his soap fills my nose; the familiarity of it makes my head swim. I've been in this kitchen before. I can feel it the same way I can feel the bones inside my body.

He leads me into the living room and motions for me to sit on the large leather sectional, but I shake my head. My eyes are on the ornate chandelier hanging from the center of the room, the intricate area rug covering the floor, the large oil paintings hanging from every wall.

"Wow," I finally say, unable to hide the shock in my voice. This is not what I would have expected from Marco's home. Or Vivi's, for that matter.

Marco shrugs. "My uncle likes nice things. It's a bit much, if you ask me, but he's proud of it."

Is this what the money he's making from the memories has bought him? A big house and a bunch of artwork?

Marco shrugs again and rubs his thumb across his lower lip. "My mom and I have the upstairs. We stay up there mostly."

He's searching my face. I wonder what he sees. A stranger, or something more?

"Why did you ask me about the mines?" he asks, then reaches into his back pocket and pulls out a torn strip of notebook paper. "Does it have something to do with this?"

I take the paper. What's left of the page is wrinkled and there's a spot of something that looks like tea or coffee smearing most of the blue ink into an unreadable blob. But two sentences are still legible.

*The mines are a lie.*

*Find Lucy.*

He told me to write everything down. He must have been doing the same.

"Yes," I answer, handing the slip of paper back to him.

Marco runs a hand through his hair like he's searching inside his mind for the shards of me tucked away in corners and nooks for safekeeping. "What's going on? That's my handwriting, but . . ."

"You don't remember writing it," I finish for him.

He nods, and it's all the reassurance I need. I don't wait for him to say anything else. I close the distance between us and grab his hands before my nerve leaves me. It only took a second for it to happen with the Oklahoma woman. I hope it works the same way with Marco.

I look straight into his confused eyes and try to feign confidence, making my voice bigger than I feel. Then I say the same thing to him that I said to the Oklahoma woman when I grabbed her hands.

"Tell me what you remember."

# 32

*I feel the moment it clicks, like a lock sliding into place. The living room* fades; his voice recedes. Marco disappears, and another face—the face from a memory—swirls into view. *My* face.

I'm laughing. My head is tipped back and my cheeks are flushed with what I can only describe as pure happiness. I can feel Marco's joy like it's my own, the warmth of it spreading inside me like honey over hot toast. We're sitting on the edge of Marco's bed, our legs touching. My hand feels warm and small inside Marco's—it's a strange sensation to experience someone's touch from their vantage point. He flips my hand over so he can study my palm. His thumb traces the path of my lifeline down to my wrist, and I feel my skin under Marco's fingers, feel my pulse start to quicken. Everything is tinged with gold.

"That tickles," I hear myself tell him, still laughing, but my face has gone serious like I know what's about to happen.

Marco leans toward me, eyes on my mouth, and then he presses his lips against mine. Or *I* press my lips against mine as Marco did that day.

Everything inside me bursts with the color and the light of a raucous city. We are the hustle of the New York City skyline; the endless crag of the Grand Canyon; the burn and bust of a Las Vegas casino; the trill of jazz exploding onto a New Orleans street. Every road leads to this moment. Every path begins and ends with this one perfect kiss.

*Our first kiss.*

I want to stay here forever, with this golden warmth inside me, but the image shifts.

Marco's memories begin to soar past me, some so fast I can't make sense of them, others in pieces slow enough for me to pull the fragments together and arrange them into a complete picture. My face is in almost all of them.

*Flash.* My face as Marco bends down to kiss me. *Flash.* My face as Marco reaches across the front seat of the Yukon to take my hand. *Flash.* My face looking up at Marco as we sway side to side on a twinkle-lit dance floor. *Flash.* My face as Marco spins me on Mama's tire swing, my hair fanning out around my smiling face.

In every snippet, I can feel the emotions swimming between us, darting through the pulses of memory and unfurling in a symphony of colors and love. And there's *so* much love. It grows louder and brighter with every thought. Our love is not just a flash of gold or a whisper of silver. Our love is the tangerine burn of a desert sunset. It is the endless aquamarine of Miracle Lake in the summer. Our love is a cerulean sky twirling above a tire swing. The fierce red of a star on a map, pointing the way home.

There are other memories, too. I see flashes of the mines. Flashes of the mayor. My dad. Most of them whip by too quickly to understand, but I feel the amber pulse of anger. The watery gray of confusion. The smoky black of deceit.

Then just as quickly, Marco steps back, breaking the connection. The living room swirls into view. Afternoon sunlight streams through the curtains. Somewhere upstairs I can hear a TV burbling.

I stumble when he releases my hands. My breath comes out in halting gasps.

Marco drops his head into his hands so I can't see his face. He's taken several steps away from me. A soft groan escapes his lips.

"Are you okay? Marco?"

When he looks up, I see his eyes are wet. His face has softened. His gaze seems clearer than before. There's something different about the way he's holding himself, like he's grown taller.

I've always wondered at the lightness of a person after their burdens have been lifted—the way they float out of the Memory House like the weight of the world's been lifted from their shoulders. I thought it was a gift to be able to take away the things that weighed people down, but looking at Marco, I realize how wrong I've been. Our memories are part of our fabric, each one a piece of a patchwork history that shapes us into the people we are. When the unburdened leave the Memory House, they aren't *lighter.* They're *different.* They've changed. They trust us, and we take something away from them that's made them who they are.

That's not helpful. That's *betrayal.*

How did I not see it before?

"Luce."

Marco's voice snaps back me to the present. The way he says my name sounds the way the colors in his memories felt. I want to drown in that sound. I want to dive in and never surface.

He closes the distance between us so quickly that it makes me jump. This time when our hands connect the grip is different—he touches me like he knows all the roads and pathways to reach me. Like we were never lost from each other to begin with.

"Luce." His fingers slide between mine, his thumb tracing my lifeline down to the thin skin of my wrist the same way he did in his memory. His eyes are shining with tears. "How could I have forgotten? How could I let them take you from me?"

He steps closer, shrinking the air between us to a hot, breathy inch. So close I can see the tremble in his lower lip; feel the warm push of his breath; see the lighter brown flecks swimming between the dark brown of his irises.

When he kisses me, I can feel that he remembers. He kisses me like we've done this a hundred times. Maybe a thousand times. Kissing him feels like coming home, like every highway leads back to him.

"I'm sorry," he whispers between breaths. "I'm so sorry I forgot you."

"It's not your fault," I whisper back, wishing so badly I could have my own memories of him. He gets to remember what we were like *before* instead of just remembering me gone. All I'm left with is the *after.*

When he finally steps back, his dark eyes are serious. I'm glad for the break because I need a moment to catch my breath.

"How did you do that?"

"I'm not sure, exactly. This woman came to the house this afternoon—an Echo. Vivi or Dad usually take care of them by talking and listening until they calm down, but it was just me today. I didn't know what else to do, so I grabbed her hands and asked her to tell me what she remembered and then—boom. I could see the memories my dad took from her, as if I *was* her, and somehow, gave them all back. It's like what my dad does for people, but I guess I can do it in reverse. I came straight here as soon as I realized. I was afraid they'd taken your memories again. That you'd forgotten me."

"They did. Archie—one of my uncle's men—saw us at Patty's and got suspicious. My uncle didn't want to risk it, so he made your dad take away my memories again. Then my uncle told me I'd been sick—that I had this really high fever and that's why I was feeling foggy and couldn't remember the last few days. He basically locked me inside the house with my mom standing guard, saying that I was still contagious." He hooks his pinkie finger with mine.

"Well, while you've been trapped at home, I've been doing a lot of digging." I take a deep breath and the words tumble out of me, one on top of the other in rapid, staccato fire.

"After we saw Missy acting strange at Patty's and figured something must be going on at the mines, I knew we had to be on to something when you didn't show up at my house. So I went to the library. Turns out the mines aren't mines—they closed down years ago. Manuela and I think the mayor is selling the memories from the Memory House—he figured out that the happy and sad parts separate after they've been buried in the desert. So he has people from town digging them up and siphoning off the good parts. Then he waters it down and makes an elixir that he sells. And we think the dark liquid you saw Mr. Lewis drink at the mines is made from the sad parts of the memories—it's like this sludge. He's been using it to control people, but it must have some strange side effects because people like Missy and Manuela's grandma are forgetting themselves entirely and—"

"Wait, slow down. You and *Manuela* figured this out?" Marco's eyebrows shoot up.

"It's a long story." I hold back a smile. "She's . . . not so bad."

I can see him processing this new tidbit along with everything else I just dumped on him.

"So, what do we do now?" Marco asks.

"I'm not sure yet. We can't risk being caught at the mines again. Last time they took my memories, but what if the next time they make me drink that sadness sludge? I don't want to end up like Missy or Mr. Lewis. I don't want to forget myself. It's bad enough that I can't remember so much of what has happened to me."

"Wait—why can't you make yourself remember? If you can

give other people back their memories, shouldn't you be able to recover your own?"

I open my mouth to tell him that's not how it works, but then I stop myself. Because actually, I don't know how it works. And he has a point; never in a million years did I imagine that I'd be able to give people back their burdens after they'd been taken. Why shouldn't I be able to do the same thing for myself?

"I don't know how," I say finally, but my mind is swimming with the possibilities, swimming with the smallest chance that I could get the missing pieces of my life back, too.

I think back to the few lessons I had with my dad.

*Eye contact is the most important part. It's what helps the memory find you.*

The idea comes to me like a lightning bolt.

"Where's the closest mirror?"

# 33

*Marco leads me down a hallway where a giant full-length mirror covers* most of the wall.

"Is this okay?" he asks, studying my reflection. I smirk at the size of it. If it's ever gonna work, this is the mirror that will do it.

The girl staring back from my reflection is hardly recognizable. Her lips are red and swollen from kissing, cheeks flushed. Her eyes are red-rimmed and tired from barely getting any sleep last night. Despite the tiredness, I see Mama in the lines of my face, the arch of my brow, the untamed hair. Same straight nose. Same gray eyes. Why didn't I notice before?

"Are you okay?" Marco gives my hand a reassuring squeeze. I have a million questions I want to ask him: how many times I've been inside his house; how many times we've held hands like this; how many times we've stared up at my ceiling map, talking about the places we'd go together. But if I can make myself remember, I don't have to ask him. I can get it all back—Mama, Marco—I can make myself remember every slice of my life that was taken from me.

My chest feels tight. My palms start to sweat. My fingers are trembling when I reach out to touch the glass. I keep my gaze steady on my eyes and take a deep breath.

*Tell me what you remember,* I think, staring into my reflection.

Hope is a balloon inside my chest. I wait for the catch inside my head.

Nothing happens.

Maybe I blinked. Or maybe Marco's not supposed to be in the frame.

"Do you mind stepping back over there?" I point to a space a few feet away, and Marco moves without question.

I make eye contact with my reflection again, careful to make sure I don't blink. I try saying the words out loud this time, just in case. "Tell me what you remember."

My reflection stares back at me, unmoving. Because . . . I don't know what I remember. I don't know what to say.

*No.*

This has to work. I deserve to remember, to know my past. I need to know what happened to Mama. What happened to me and Marco. I must be doing it wrong.

I try again. Nothing.

I try holding my own hand. I try pressing both hands to the mirror. Just my right hand. Just my left hand. I think the words. I say the words. Then I'm shouting at my reflection.

"Why won't you remember?"

I bang my palms against the glass. "Why?" Then I bang it

again, only my palm is a fist. The mirror swims in front of me, blurring with tears.

"Luce."

"I need to remember!" I scream, my throat turning raw. Warm hands grab me from behind. I shake them off. I step closer to the mirror. Maybe if I get closer. Bang harder. Shout louder.

I pound both of my fists against the glass, then pound again and again and again.

"Lucy, stop. Stop it!"

There's a loud crack. The glass spiderwebs outward. My reflection splinters into a hundred versions of me. Maybe one of them can remember. Maybe one of them can give me back my memories.

Marco pulls at my shoulders, trying to yank me back from the mirror, but I manage to *thwack* my palm against it one more time. There's a sharp pain and a splatter of red smears across the veins of glass. Marco yanks me back hard enough that I fall to the ground, blood spilling from the open gash on my hand. I'm sobbing so loudly I can barely catch my breath. The words coming out of my mouth don't make sense.

"I just . . . remember . . . why . . . want to remember."

Marco drops down to the ground next to me and pulls my head into his chest. I grab on to his arm.

"It's okay, Luce. Just calm down. Breathe, okay? You need to breathe."

I let out another sob and squeeze my eyes shut. Why can't I remember?

I'm not sure how long we sit like that. Limbs entwined. Huddled together.

But at some point my breathing steadies.

At some point the sobs turn to whimpers, then cease altogether.

At some point the tears dry on my cheeks, and I register the throbbing in my palm.

At some point reality slams into me.

My memories aren't coming back. I can give them back to anyone else, but I can't give them back to myself.

"We need to bandage that." Marco pulls my hand away from my chest to examine it, and I realize that his shirt is covered in blood.

"Your shirt—I'm so sorry."

"It's okay, don't worry about it. We should get that cut cleaned up. Do you think you can stand?"

I nod, my cheeks heating at the realization of what just happened. Shards of glass litter the ground around us. Splatters of blood dot the floor.

Marco places a hand underneath my arm to help me up, but stops.

There are footsteps on the front porch. The jingling of keys in a lock.

My heart jumps into my throat.

Marco's eyes bulge.

The front door opens with a blast of hot air.

"Marco?" A familiar voice calls down the hallway. Footsteps head straight toward us. "Marco, are you—"

Then the voice stops.

We're trapped.

*No.*

# 34

*Vivi.*

I scramble to my feet, the cut on my hand throbbing. I have to get out of here.

If she finds out what I can do—if she tells her brother . . .

"Lucy, what are you doing here? You're bleeding. Why are you bleeding?" She looks around the room, and all the color drains from her face.

"It's just a small cut." I fold my hand and hide it behind my back, suppressing a wince.

"It looks like a lot more than that. What the hell happened to the mirror? What are you even doing here?" Vivi has one hand on the hip of a turquoise dress. Her hair is swept up into her usual tidy bun. Her eyes bounce between me and Marco.

"I was looking for you, Vivi," I say, trying to catch Marco's eyes in the broken mirror. "I thought you might be here. Marco was showing me around and I . . . slipped . . ." I motion to the mirror with my bleeding hand. It sounds like a thin lie, even to me, but it's the best I can do right now.

Vivi's eyes narrow, focusing in on Marco. She shakes her head. "Something's different. Something happened." She steps closer, her heels clicking on the floor. "What's going on?"

"I told you, I—"

Marco cuts me off. "I remember." He moves toward his mom. "I know everything."

"Marco, stop," I hiss. What is he *doing*?

He ignores me, walking closer to his mom. Vivi's eyes widen.

"I don't know what you think you know, but—"

Marco's hands clench into fists and for a moment I think he's going to lash out, but then he steps forward and wraps Vivi in a tight hug.

"I'm sorry," he says. "I'm sorry I let him do that to you. I'm sorry I got you into this mess. I'm so sorry . . ."

Vivi's wide eyes well with tears. "What is it you think you know?"

"Everything. The mines. How my uncle's been stealing memories and selling them. About the last time we tried to escape. I know about all of it."

Vivi steps back to look at her son and touches the cast on her arm.

"That's not possible," she says, but she must have heard something in Marco's voice because she's looking at us with a mix of fear and wonder. "How? Who have you been talking to?"

"No one. It's Lucy. She can make people reme—"

"Marco, don't!" I shout. What is he doing? Vivi's *working* with the mayor. He's her brother. She's on his side.

Vivi turns to me, her brow creased in confusion. "Who told you? I need you to tell me how you know. If my brother finds out—he said the next time—if we tried to defy him again . . . This is bad. This is very, very bad. Tell me who told you."

She touches her casted arm again, fingers trembling, and a thought hits me like a slap. I think of the way Vivi looked when the mayor came to our house. The way her voice went up an octave, like she was putting on a performance, and the way her shoulders relaxed once he finally left the room.

"Did *he* do that to you?" I ask.

Vivi looks down at the cast. Marco clenches his jaw. It's all the confirmation I need.

"Why are you helping him?"

"Because I don't have a choice," she answers after a beat of silence. "Because he'll take Marco away if I don't. Because I've been trying to keep you both safe." She turns to Marco. "You say you know everything, but if you knew what he did when we escaped last time . . ." She trails off.

"I know," Marco says, reaching for her hand. "and I won't let him do that again."

"Do *what* again?" I ask, unable to hide the anger from my voice. "And what do you mean you're trying to keep us safe? You had our memories *erased*. You made us forget each other. How is that keeping us safe?"

"Because what you don't know can't hurt you!" She throws her arms into the air in exasperation. "Every single time, no matter what he did, you two always managed to figure out what he was up to. I thought maybe this time, if I watched you both more closely, if I kept you busy at the Memory House, Lucy—I thought maybe I could stop it from happening again. But then you showed up at the mines, and Marco started sneaking out—it was happening all over again. You don't understand what my brother will do. How far he'll go—"

"So you thought making us forget everything—including *each other*—was the solution?" My voice raises to a shout. "In what sick, twisted world is stealing someone's memories without their consent considered helping?"

"He didn't give us a choice! My brother will do whatever it takes to get what he wants. He said he'd . . ." Vivi swallows and wipes at a tear. It leaves a black smudge of mascara on her cheek. "He said he'd take Marco away from me if it happened again. That he'd make Marco forget that I ever existed . . ." Vivi lets out a sob and covers her mouth. "He doesn't need me or you, Lucy. We're expendable. He needs your father. And he needs Marco if there's going to be someone in the family to carry on the Warman legacy. But beyond that, he'll do whatever it takes to stop anyone from getting in his way."

The cut on my hand throbs.

"Don't you understand? All we've ever done has been to keep you both safe."

Marco squeezes his mother's hand, his mouth puckered into a frown. "She's telling the truth, Lucy. I know it doesn't look like it, but it's true."

I shake my head, trying to make sense of my tangled thoughts.

The jars. There must have been thousands of them buried in the desert. How many memories does the mayor need? How long has he been selling them?

But then something else Vivi said catches inside of me, and my mouth goes dry.

"Wait a minute. You said he would do whatever it takes. That he'd make Marco forget you ever existed. The only way he could do that is if my dad . . ." I can't even bring myself to finish the sentence, the thought is so disgusting. I look at Vivi. Black trails of mascara slide down her face. Her eyes are red-rimmed and pleading.

"It's true, then."

Oh my God.

*My* dad.

My throat is thick with tears. My heart feels heavy.

All this time, I wanted so badly to believe there was something *else* that could explain why my dad was doing what he was—that he was still a good man.

But that's not true, is it?

"Your father loves you very much, Lucy." Vivi takes a step toward me. "He doesn't want to help the mayor. He's doing what he has to to keep you safe. Everything he does, he does for you."

My chin quivers. I open my mouth. Close it.

*My father is a bad guy.*

*My father is working for the mayor.*

*My father is a liar.*

**275**

*And a memory thief.*

Vivi takes another step toward me, her casted arm clutched to her chest. I take a step back.

"Lucy, listen to me. We were trying to get you and Marco out of here. We had to be careful, because the last time we tried to escape, his men ran us down outside of El Paso. This time we were going to do it right and make sure there wasn't a paper trail. Your dad and I started skimming off the top and hiding money in places my brother doesn't know about. Your dad started planting more junk around the house to make it look like more people weren't paying him. And we were using you working at the Memory House as a way to get you a car—to make it look like you were just saving up so you could finally go on one of those road trips you've always daydreamed about. But then you showed up at the mines. And my brother started to get suspicious. He's been having Charlie watched day and night. It's been getting harder and harder—"

"Why couldn't we just get in Marco's car and leave?"

"He's got people everywhere, Luce." It's Marco who speaks this time. "And everyone knows my car. That's how they caught us the last time we tried to escape. Plus he has people regularly watching the exits out of town. He tracks when we come and go, and if we leave Tumble Tree he has one of his guards follow us. We're basically prisoners here."

I shiver at the thought. There's only one main road leading in and out of town. It wouldn't be that hard to monitor who's coming and going. And with no cell service around town—this place really *is* like a prison. All this time I thought it was because we were so far out in the middle of nowhere that the cell companies didn't want to bother with us. But what if it's on purpose? What if it's part of the mayor's plan to control the town?

"Why is Dad helping him? How could he take people's memories without their consent? And what about Missy, Mr. Lewis, and Manuela's grandmother? People are *forgetting* themselves because of what they're doing. Because of that horrible sludge and the sadness they're forcing people to drink. How can my dad just let the mayor get away with that?"

"Lucy, you have to listen to me—"

I shake my head and cover my ears.

Something still doesn't add up. Something isn't right. My dad wouldn't hurt me to protect me.

I look down at the shards of mirror littering the ground. At the eyes reflected back at me in the glass—Mama's eyes.

I think back to that night with Marco in the car—when he asked me what kind of accident Mama was in and I kept repeating the same words over and over again because I couldn't remember. Because the truth had been taken from me.

And now I deserve to know.

"What happened to Mama?"

Vivi blinks and takes a step back. She looks back and forth between Marco and me, like she's trying to measure the secrets, trying to figure out which ones we know and which ones are still hidden.

"Mayor Warman did something to her, didn't he? She wasn't in an accident." I try to make my voice confident so she won't question whether or not I know the truth. "Did she figure out what he was doing? Is that it?"

Vivi shakes her head, confusion replacing her usually stern features. "I don't know what you're talking about, Lucy. Your mama was in an accident."

The way she says it—flat and robotic—sends shivers down my spine. She doesn't know. One look at Marco's face tells me he doesn't know, either. Whatever the mayor did to Mama, he's done a good job of keeping it buried.

"She wasn't in an accident," I say. "He did something to her. I'm sure of it."

Vivi opens her mouth to respond, but her head snaps up, looking toward the road.

That's when I hear it—the rumble of a truck, the crunch of tires on the gravel road.

"It's my brother," Vivi says, her eyes round with fear. "You have to get out of here. Now!"

Marco doesn't hesitate—he grabs my good hand and yanks me toward the back door.

# 35

*Marco wrenches open the passenger side of the Yukon.* "*Get in!*" *he calls,* then runs to the other side.

I barely have the door closed before he punches the car into reverse and screeches out of the driveway onto the main road.

I spin in my seat, looking backward at Marco's receding house. Mayor Warman runs to the end of the front yard, shouting something at us. His sunglasses glint in the afternoon sun. He knows we're together.

Marco guns the engine and takes a sharp right, then a sharp left.

"Where are we going?" I grab on to the seat to keep myself from sliding all over the cabin, hastily reaching for the seat belt. I wince when my damaged hand makes contact. The bleeding has stopped, but the throbbing has gotten worse.

"I don't know yet. But we need to make sure he can't follow us. We can figure out where to go once we're safe. We need to get to the highway."

The engine roars. If the mayor has any sense, he'll know that's where we're headed. Which means we need to get there first.

"I thought you said he has people watching all the exits out of town?"

"I know, but we have to try. Maybe he hasn't had enough time to alert them yet?"

Marco makes another sharp turn onto a back road and my body snaps against the seat belt. I grab onto the side door handle for support.

Up ahead, there's a girl on a bike riding toward us. Dark hair. Red lips. Unnecessarily short shorts.

"Pull over!" I shout, pointing. "It's Manuela."

"I can't. There's no time."

"You have to! She's headed to your house to check on you. What if the mayor does something to her? You can't let her walk into a trap. Pull over. It will only take a second."

I try to say it confidently even though I'm not sure. I just know I can't risk something happening to Manuela after last night. I can't leave her behind.

Marco lets out a growl of frustration but jerks the Yukon to the side of the road.

"Get in," I shout to Manuela, shoving the door open.

She squeezes the brakes on her handlebars, bringing the bike to a stop.

"Um, how about a hello first?"

I roll my eyes and motion her to hurry. "I'll explain on the way, just get in *now*. Hide your bike behind those plants."

She flicks her eyes between me and Marco, then walks her bike to the far edge of the road behind a cluster of prickly pear. Marco keeps looking in the rearview mirror, his fingers twitching against the steering wheel.

"If someone steals it you're buying me a new one." Manuela climbs into the back of the Yukon. She hasn't even shut the door when Marco hits the gas pedal, lurching us forward.

"What the hell!" Manuela shouts, slamming against the front seat.

"Hold on to something."

The car fishtails as Marco takes another sharp turn.

"Are you trying to kill us? What the hell is going on?" Manuela eyes me through the rearview mirror.

I open my mouth to tell her when we hit a pothole in the road. The seat belt yanks my chest back against the seat as the momentum hurls me toward the dashboard. Manuela grabs on to the headrest with a yelp.

"Seriously, slow down! You're gonna make me sick."

"Just hold on. We'll explain when we're safe."

Marco hits the gas again and tires squeal as we turn onto the main strip. We only have about a mile left until we reach the highway entrance, but there's only one road that leads there and it's right through the center of town—in plain view of anyone who might be watching for Marco's car. How many people does the mayor have working for him? How many people could he send after us?

Marco doesn't slow down despite the thirty-mile speed limit.

his fingers tremble against the steering wheel. My heart pounds in my chest. Manuela must sense the tension, because she keeps her mouth shut, her eyes meeting mine every few seconds in the rearview mirror.

We pass the Dairy Queen. Patty's Pie Pantry. The Dollar General. The laundromat. The gazebo at the main square. The road leading to Miracle Lake. There's a line of kids snaking behind Mr. Whitcome's Snow Cone Stand waiting to get their multicolored piles of ice, oblivious to the secrets hiding in the Tumble Tree desert. How many of them have parents who spend their nights at the mines, only to come home with no recollection of what happened? How many of them are on their way to becoming like Missy and Mr. Lewis, empty shells of who they once were? How many of my classmates will grow up to one day work at the mines, too, and lose themselves in the process?

The highway on-ramp looms ahead. My fingers dig into my seat to keep my hands from shaking. I keep glancing out the window, expecting to see the black glint of Mayor Warman's truck roaring up behind us.

The Yukon eases onto the highway and picks up speed. In the rearview mirror, Tumble Tree shrinks. No one follows. Marco reaches across the seat and takes my hand.

We made it.

I let out a relieved breath. It almost seems too good to be true.

Marco grins and cracks the window open, letting warm air rush into the cabin. My hand is throbbing again—I'd almost forgotten about it, but now the pain is back, a sharp reminder of everything that's been taken from me, everything that I'll never get back.

Manuela sticks her head between the seats. "Is someone gonna tell me what this dramatic getaway is about or do I have to guess? And what happened to your hand?" She wrinkles her nose at the dried smears of blood.

"I think I have a first aid kit in the glove box." Marco reaches across me and opens it, rummaging around. He retrieves a stack of napkins and hands them to me. "Damn, it must be in the trunk. Press these against the wound for now. We'll get it cleaned up as soon as we stop. Does it hurt?"

"Not really," I lie.

Manuela clears her throat. "Hello? Explanation, please?"

I spin around to look at her. Despite the snark in her voice, I can see the fear in her wide eyes.

"I can't make people forget like my dad can," I blurt. I press the napkins against my throbbing palm, using it as a reason not to have to look at Manuela as I explain everything that happened since she left this morning. I gloss over the part where I destroyed Marco's mirror, skipping to Vivi, the mayor's arrival, and our too-close escape.

"So you can give me my memories back if they've been taken? And my mom's?"

I shrug, nodding. "Yeah, I think so. I mean, it worked on Marco and the woman from Oklahoma. No reason it shouldn't work on you, too."

**283**

*It just doesn't work for me.*

"What about my abuela? Do you think you can fix whatever the mayor did to her?"

"I don't know. Maybe." Hope swells in my chest. Can I undo what's been done to Mr. Lewis and Missy, too?

"How does it work? Can you do it now?"

"Why don't you wait until we stop?" Marco says, flicking on his blinker to signal a lane change. "I want to get a little farther away, but I'll need gas soon. Plus, we need to clean that cut."

I glance at the dash. The gas tank needle hovers just above empty. I have no idea what kind of gas mileage the Yukon gets, but judging by the size of it we don't have long before we'll need to pull over. I think back to what Vivi said about the last time we tried to escape—did they catch us before we left town, or after? How far does the mayor's influence reach?

The highway ahead stretches wide and black, heat wafting off it in steaming tufts. How many times have I imagined leaving, driving away on a road just like this one, on a day just like this one, and finally leaving Tumble Tree to the dust and the lizards, just like Mama always said?

*Mama.* My heart seizes.

"So . . . you remember everything, Marco?" Manuela's head pops back in between the seats. "You know what's going on?"

Marco nods solemnly. His Adam's apple bobs up and down. He glances into the rearview mirror, like he's checking the road, but I can tell he's stalling.

There's a sharp pain deep in my chest. He gets to know the truth; he doesn't have to wait for someone else to explain it to him.

"Lucy, there's something I need to tell you. Something you and I figured out before they erased our memories—about this town and what my uncle is doing."

He looks at me to make sure I'm listening. I am, but my mouth is suddenly too dry to speak. So I nod.

"Okay, so you know how the mines used to hold copper? It's what brought a lot of people to Tumble Tree in the first place, decades ago. Well, when the mines closed eight years back . . . I think a lot of people were gonna have to leave town because there wasn't enough work. But my uncle wasn't having it—he kept talking all this nonsense about how it was our family's legacy to keep the town safe and how he couldn't be the mayor that let the town fall to ruin after so many generations of Warman men helped it thrive.

"He started disappearing for days on end, sleeping in the desert and talking all this nonsense about Tumble Tree being the last bastion to simpler times and how it was his job to save it. But then one day he came back and said he'd found something out by the mines, that he had an idea for how he could keep the people in Tumble Tree employed while capitalizing on the town's number one attraction: the Memory House. He said he was going to save the town."

"He must have dug up the jars of memories," I say. "He must have discovered that the desert can separate the good memories from the bad."

"Wait, I thought your dad only took away bad memories?"

"I thought so, too. But then I realized, every bad memory is tied to a good one in some way. My dad can't erase the bad memories without erasing the good ones as well. He has to take all of them."

"So then how do the memories separate?" Manuela pokes her head between the seats again.

Marco shrugs, staring straight ahead at the black ribbon of road. "Both my mom and Lucy's dad think it might have something to do with the Tumble Tree heat. That, and something about what drew your family here in the first place, Luce."

Marco glances at me, like he's checking to make sure I haven't spontaneously combusted from this overwhelming info dump that of course I have no memory of ever knowing.

"The strangest thing is that when my uncle tried to take the memories out of Tumble Tree, they started to merge back together—the light with the dark. There's something about this place, something magic that allows the happiness and the sadness to separate."

I think of the picture of Great-Great-Great-Grandpa Miller hanging in Dad's office above his desk. Growing up, Dad told me stories about the Memory House being built all those years ago. Brick by brick, my great-great-great-grandpa found a way to restart in Tumble Tree, as if everything he'd done in his life led him to this small desert hideaway. Brick by brick, my family's legacy was formed.

He'd been running from his own burdens left behind by the war—lots of people were back then. But his burdens chased him clear across the country, to a place so far from civilization that it was nearly forgotten until he found it and brought it to life. He was drawn to Tumble Tree, like the desert itself had called him. It was the perfect place for a man ready to start fresh, the perfect place for someone looking to forget their burdens. And there must have been something magic out here in the desert, something that let him do more than just listen to people's problems, but make them go away completely. And once he discovered he could draw the sadness out of people, well—he wondered if maybe that's why the desert had been calling to him in the first place. So he started inviting folks to come to the Memory House to have their burdens lifted. And then, as word of the Memory House and the Miller family spread, people came from everywhere to forget.

I close my eyes.

This couldn't have been what he wanted. This couldn't have been what he'd intended when he built the Memory House. We come from a line of empaths, a line of people looking to help. What's happening in Tumble Tree isn't helping people. Not anymore.

"Wait." Manuela's eyes flash in the rearview mirror. "If your dad takes people's memories, puts them in jars, and buries them in the desert, how is it that you can restore them for people? Wouldn't you need to get the jars before you could return any memories?"

I chew on my lip and look out the window. The desert whips past; tangles of bushes, prickly pear, and yucca blur together into a dusty green smear beneath the wide blue sky. It reminds me of the colors I saw when I made Marco and the woman from Oklahoma remember. I felt their emotions as if they were water pouring from a faucet—as if they were a kaleidoscope of hopes and fears filling me until I might burst. Maybe the memories never got erased. Maybe they just lay dormant because they were untethered from the emotions that made them important enough to remember in the first place. Maybe I don't actually make people *remember*—maybe I bring their emotions back to them so they can feel their memories again.

I swallow, feeling the truth of it inside me. Seeing the different-colored emotions swirling past when I saw inside Dad's, Marco's, and the Oklahoma woman's thoughts.

"I think maybe we've had it wrong all this time," I say, still staring at the desert landscape sliding past. "I don't think my dad is actually taking away people's memories. I think maybe he finds the emotions tied to the memories—the good and the bad—and *that's* what he pulls out of people and puts into the jars. And without the feelings that made them matter in the first place, what good is a memory anyway?"

"So then the mayor is literally selling people's happiness."

"People will pay a lot of money to feel happy." Marco's eyes are locked on the road. "And there are a lot of sad people in the world."

I grit my teeth.

Thousands of people have trusted my family over the decades with their hurt and their pain. The people who come to the Memory House trust us with their deepest, darkest secrets. Even if these are memories they don't want anymore, that doesn't mean they want other people to have them. That doesn't mean they want them being sold to the highest bidder.

"And the black sludge—that's people's sadness, right? It's the sad parts of the memories that weigh them down when they come to the Memory House?" My throat is tight as I ask, because I already know the answer; I just need someone who can remember to confirm. "That's what the mayor uses to get people to do what he wants. Isn't it?"

"Yes." Marco swallows. "It doesn't just make people sad. It makes them sort of . . . pliable, if that makes sense. Like they're more susceptible to suggestions. They're more willing to do what they're told because they just want the sadness to go away. But if someone has too much or drinks it too often, it starts to eat away at them. Until eventually . . ."

"They forget themselves entirely," I finish for him, the reality of it making my stomach clench. "The mayor must know what he's doing to people at the mines. That by making folks absorb other people's pain and sadness . . . that it's making people act like they don't even know who they are. Like Missy and—"

"My abuela." Manuela's voice is venom. "She can barely remember herself. He did that to her, didn't he? He made her drink that stuff and now she's just a shell. What kind of monster would do that to the people he says he's sworn to protect?"

I reach behind the seat and give Manuela's hand a sympathetic squeeze. I don't want to promise her anything, but maybe—if I can help recover Marco's memories—maybe I can do the same thing for her abuela. But Manuela's right—the mayor clearly knows the side effects of drinking the sludge, so why does he keep making people drink it? There has to be something we don't see.

What is it that he's so desperate to hide that he would risk the very townspeople he claims he's trying to help?

"What about the happiness elixir?" I start, sitting up straighter as the idea starts to take shape in my head. I'm almost afraid to ask.

Marco glances over at me. Outside the window, trees rush past. Manuela's foot softly taps the back of the seat.

"If you take too much of the sadness, it makes people forget themselves, right?"

Marco's nod is solemn.

"So what about the happiness elixir? What happens if people keep taking that?"

I think of all the jars—the thousands that must have been buried in the desert from the decades of burdened people that have been coming to the Memory House. How many people has the mayor sold the elixir to, claiming to "help"? And how many of them become repeat customers?

Marco shrugs. "That," he says, "is what we were close to figuring out when our memories were taken the last time."

## 36

*The Memory House is a lie. It's not a place of kindness or reprieve. It's* not a place where people come to get a fresh new start after a life of pain. It's a mask. My whole life has been nothing but a mask.

I jam my fists into my eyes, trying to block the hot tears from welling up.

All this time.

How could Dad help the mayor do that to those poor people?

"Luce, are you okay?"

"Fine," I say. But I know my voice sounds anything but.

"So let me get this straight," Manuela says, her voice too loud for the small space. "People come to the Memory House to have their unhappy memories taken away. Lucy's family has been burying the memories, or emotions, or whatever, in the desert because they don't want people to accidentally find them and let the sadness out. But then the mayor started digging them up because he figured out how to siphon off just the good memories and he's selling those as some kind of happiness elixir that people pay top dollar for. Meanwhile, the mayor also has Lucy's dad wiping the memories of the people who work at the mines so that they don't know what he's up to. Does that about sum it up?"

Marco bites his lip and stares straight ahead, like he's trying not to look at me when he answers. "Yeah. I mean, mostly. They don't erase all of the mine workers' memories. Just the ones from people who unearth the jars and siphon off the good memories from the bad. My uncle doesn't want anyone to know what the key ingredient is."

"So Lucy's dad only takes memories from people on the nights when they're digging up the old memories. And in between—if someone gets too close or starts asking too many questions—the mayor uses the sadness they're unearthing against them."

"Pretty much."

"I don't get it," I whisper, my voice catching. "Why would my dad do that? It must have something to do with Mama, right? The mayor did something to Mama and he's threatening to do the same thing to me—is that it?"

Marco's dark eyes are too serious for the bright afternoon. He reaches across the seat for my uninjured hand. "I wish I knew, Luce. But I do know that your dad would do anything to keep you safe. And my uncle knows that. He must be using you against your dad. I don't know what happened to your mom, Luce, but I know your dad isn't doing this by choice."

"Of course he has a choice! People always have a choice. He could have said no. He could have told me what was going on. He could have called the police. He could have—"

There's a loud *whoop whoop* behind us as a siren cuts through the afternoon. Blue and red lights flash. A cop car slides onto the road behind us, emerging from a cluster of trees at the side of the highway.

"Were you speeding?" I ask, turning to look behind us.

"No, I don't think so. What do I do? What if it's somebody that works for my uncle?"

"Pull over," Manuela says. "You have to. He's a *cop.*" She spins in her seat to look at the black-and-white car. "I don't think it's from Tumble Tree."

Marco's white-knuckled hands grip the steering wheel as he squints into the mirror, weighing his options. The police car behind us seems to accelerate.

So does Marco.

"What are you doing? Slow down!" Manuela shouts.

"You don't understand, my uncle has people all over the place. If they catch us again—"

"What if he's not working for your uncle?" I say. "Maybe he could help us."

It's possible. We're far enough outside of Tumble Tree that it could be a cop from another town, completely oblivious to what lies hidden in the desert a few towns over. Maybe he's just pulling us over because Marco was driving too fast.

"Yeah, maybe. Unless my uncle called them. Unless they're looking for us."

The sirens seem to grow louder, like the cop's sending out a warning.

"Manuela's right. You have to pull over." I fight to keep my voice calm. "What are we gonna do, outrun him? You're almost out of gas."

Marco's hands are still tight on the wheel, but the car starts to slow. He curses and flicks on his blinker, then slowly pulls to a stop along the side of the highway.

Behind us, a uniformed officer climbs out of his vehicle. Aviators cover his eyes . . .

Because of the sun.

Because it's just a coincidence.

But somehow, my pounding heart doesn't believe me.

# 37

*The passenger door on the police car opens, and a second uniformed cop* emerges from the car. He says something into the walkie-talkie mounted to his chest. A hat is slung low over his face so that it's hard to tell from this distance, but he looks familiar.

The first cop walks toward us languidly, which gives me a smidgen of hope. Maybe it's just a routine stop. But is it standard protocol for both officers to get out of the car?

"Act cool," Manuela says. "Don't give them a reason to be suspicious."

Marco slowly rolls down the driver's side window. The first officer leans down to have a look inside and his eyes rest on both our faces for a beat too long, then he flicks his gaze to the back seat.

"Everything okay, officer?" Somehow Marco manages to keep his voice even. The officer ignores him and looks back toward his partner.

"There's three of them." he says.

"Three? Hang on."

I turn to see the second officer lifting a walkie-talkie to his lips. There's a crackle of static and jumbled words, then he steps to the back of the Yukon to look at the license plate. Says something else into the speaker.

My blood goes cold. There's no reason for him to check the license plate and report the number of people in the car unless someone's looking for us.

"Out of the car. All of you." The first officer's voice has a hard edge. The second one begins to circle the perimeter of the Yukon, peering inside the windows as if looking for something.

"What seems to be the problem, officer?" Manuela's voice goes up an octave. She tugs at one of her braids and bats her lashes, ready to perform. "We weren't speeding, were we?"

"Out of the car. *Now.*"

"I'm sure there's been some kind of—"

"Now, or I will rip off this door and make you get out." He places his hand on his hip, where his gun is holstered.

I look at Marco. His forehead is covered in a sheen of sweat. "Do what he says," he tells us, then to me he whispers: "They don't know what you can do. No one knows but us. It'll be okay. Whatever happens, they can't keep us apart. Not anymore."

A wan smile flashes on his face. I nod once, then yank open the door and slide out onto the dusty highway shoulder. The sun screams from the sky and I shield my eyes to cover the glare.

"This all seems very unnecessary, officer." Manuela tugs at her shorts as she climbs out of the back seat. She's smiling at them, but the color's gone from her cheeks. "We were just headed out of town to do some shopping. I'm sure there's—"

The first officer grabs Manuela's wrists and pulls them behind her back. She lets out a sharp gasp, almost falling forward.

"What the hell are you doing? That hurts!"

"Best if you don't struggle. You'll only make it worse." Then to the second officer he says, "I'll take this one. You get the other two." He tugs Manuela toward the waiting cop car.

The second officer lifts his hat to wipe the sweat from his forehead, and I finally get a good look at his face. It's Mr. Lewis's son.

Marco's hands are wrenched behind his back. He lets out a grunt. Officer Lewis fastens them together with a zip tie, then steps toward me.

I lock eyes with Marco, all hope whooshing out of me. When my hands are pulled behind my back I grit my teeth against the shooting pain that screams from the cut in my hand. The napkins I'd been holding flutter in a crumpled pile on the side of the highway.

Then we're marched to the waiting police car, Marco's Yukon forgotten on the side of the road.

# 38

*They shove us into the back seat next to Manuela.*

"I demand a lawyer! You didn't even read me my Miranda rights. This is totally illegal! We didn't do anything wrong!"

The officers ignore her pleas and slam the door, trapping the three of us inside.

"We're on our way," says the first cop into the walkie-talkie. "Should be there in about twenty minutes."

They don't turn on the sirens, but it feels like we're going well above the speed limit. They exit and loop around so that we're headed back in the direction of Tumble Tree. It's hard to stay upright with our hands bound behind us, so we keep knocking into each other like bowling pins.

"Where do you think they're taking us?" I whisper, though I'm not sure why I'm keeping my voice down, or why I'm asking in the first place. It's clear they're taking us back the way we came. Maybe if we hadn't stopped to pick up Manuela, if we'd exited sooner, if we'd headed the other direction . . . maybe then we could have made it somewhere safe. Somewhere where we could have figured out what to do next.

Or maybe there is no way out. Maybe we're doomed to live in this vicious cycle of forgetting and rediscovering for as long as we live in Tumble Tree.

"I don't know," answers Marco. "Wherever it is, I bet my uncle's there."

"And my dad," I add, trying to fight the rising nausea. My hands are shaking so hard I can barely make a fist. "So that's it, then? They're gonna wipe our memories clean and we go back to the way things were? There has to be something else we can do. There has to be a way to stop them."

Manuela kicks the barrier separating us from the front of the car, then kicks it again. "This is kidnapping. You hear me? Kidnapping! You can't get away with this."

The officers either don't hear her or choose to ignore her. There's another loud *thwack* as Manuela kicks the seat again. I see the moment she gives up—her face falls and her body slumps against the seat, like the air's been sucked out of her.

"We'll figure something out," I tell her, even though I have no idea how or what. She turns her face toward the window.

Too soon we're back on the main road, passing the Snow Cone Stand. The turnoff to Miracle Lake. The laundromat. The Dollar General. The Dairy Queen. People come and go like nothing's changed—as if Tumble Tree's just another town on a map with regular people living their regular lives. They don't know that everything here is a lie—that it's all being orchestrated so they see only what Mayor Warman wants them to see.

A few minutes later we pull into the Tumble Tree Police Station parking lot. It's eerily empty, and I'm not sure if that's a good thing or a bad thing.

The car drives around back. Officer Lewis climbs out and opens the door. He grabs Manuela's arm, and without saying a word, yanks her from the car and marches her toward the station. They disappear inside. He returns a few minutes later and pulls Marco out, leaving me alone in the back seat with the first officer up front.

"What are you going to do to us?"

Silence.

"You know what they're doing isn't right, don't you?"

A muscle in the officer's neck twitches, but beyond that there's no sign he's even heard me.

I should be scared for whatever's about to happen, but I feel oddly calm. Like my body and my subconscious know this is just part of the cycle. Forget. Remember. Repeat. Forget. Remember. Repeat. How many times will we do this?

The backs of my legs are sweating and I slip against the seat, fighting to stay upright. My fingers have started to lose feeling from the zip tie holding my wrists, and my injured hand throbs to the rhythm of my heartbeat. Worse yet, I have to pee.

Officer Lewis emerges from the building and makes his way to the car. He shields his eyes from the sun, and that's when I realize that he's not wearing sunglasses like the officer in the front seat. I could swear he had them on when I first saw him, but maybe he took them off?

We make eye contact through the window, and suddenly I know what to do.

My pulse speeds up, but I force myself to sit up as straight as I can, to give nothing away.

He opens the car door and reaches for me. My legs squeak against the seat. I tip sideways slightly, and he catches me.

"Come on," he says, tugging me out. "Don't make this harder than it needs to be."

My feet connect with the black asphalt. Heat wafts up like a stovetop. I squint into the glare of the sun and smile at him.

"Sure is hot out," I say. His fingers dig into my arm as he drags me forward.

There's an accessibility ramp leading to the entrance, and he yanks me toward it instead of the main steps. Our feet creak against the rickety paneling. A blast of stuffy air greets us when he opens the door. It smells like mildew and burnt toast inside the station. The back door leads to a small kitchen and beyond that, a hallway. Manuela and Marco must be somewhere deeper in the building.

I'm sure I've been here plenty of times before, but I don't *remember* being in the station. I do recall Dad mentioning it was small, though. Which makes sense since Tumble Tree doesn't really have much need for policing. Or at least, I didn't think it had much need for policing until now.

"I have to go to the bathroom," I announce, pulling back against his grip.

"You'll have to hold it."

"I've been holding it. I can't anymore." I pull a card from *Manuela's Guide to Manipulation* and do a little shimmy, like I'm a five-year-old struggling to hold it in. It's not too hard to pretend since I really do have to go. "Please. I'm gonna wet my pants if I don't go soon. I'll only be a minute. I really have to go."

I do the shimmy thing again. He rolls his eyes and shakes his head but grabs my arm and tugs me toward a closed door off the side of the kitchenette.

"Fine, but you better be quick about it."

He opens a door and flicks on a light, revealing a small white bathroom. I take a step inside, then turn back to look at him.

"Um, sir?"

"What?" His voice is impatient. He turns back to look at the entryway, like he's expecting someone. Maybe the other officer is coming. Or maybe whoever he spoke to on the radio is on the way.

"I, um—I can't unbutton my shorts with my hands behind my back." I shrug, like there's nothing I can do about it.

He stares at me for a second, weighing his options. The badge on his chest catches the light, reflecting like the mayor's sunglasses.

Officer Lewis glances over his shoulder again, then back to me. I shimmy, bite my lip, and try my best to look like my bladder is gonna explode any second.

"No funny business, you hear me?" His hand goes to his gun holster and I nod, not needing to fake my fear. "Turn around."

I do as he says. There's a tug on the zip tie, followed by a *snap* as the plastic breaks. I rub my wrists and smile at him gratefully.

"Be quick about it," he says, then pulls the door shut.

I pee quickly, trying to ignore the sound of the officer's shoe tapping impatiently on the other side of the door. The water stings my cut when I wash my hands, but I grit my teeth and force myself to rinse the dried blood away. The girl in my reflection looks red-faced and wild-eyed.

"You can do this," I tell her, and force myself to stand up a little straighter.

"Hurry up!" Officer Lewis calls with a swift rap on the door, making me jump.

I take a deep breath and push the door open. Then I hold my hands in front of me, like I'm offering them up to be zip-tied.

"Thanks so much." I step forward and keep my eyes on his, smiling like I'm truly grateful. Like this is no big deal at all.

He doesn't return my smile. When he grabs my right wrist, I close my fingers around his thumb so that we're holding hands.

My gaze is steady. And Officer Lewis doesn't look away when I say the words.

"Tell me what you remember."

# 39

*For a second I worry that I'm wrong—that his memories haven't been* tampered with and there's nothing for me to give back to him. But then he sways in my grip and his words come out slow and robotic, as if he's in a trance. I feel the familiar catch as my mind takes hold, and his stolen emotions and the memories connected to them begin to take shape around me.

Most of them are fuzzy and zip by too quickly for me to piece together, but I see enough to know that he's been working for the mayor for a while now. Sometimes as a guard. Sometimes driving delivery vans carrying the elixir to and from the mines to their various drop-off locations. Some of the things he's done seem harmless, but other memories are tinged bright red with guilt.

*Flash.* The sound his fist makes as it connects with one of the mine workers. *Flash.* His hand wrapping around a jar of black liquid as he forces someone to drink it. *Flash.* He sits on the side of his father's bed, worry creasing his face as he feeds him a spoonful of soup. *Flash.* My own father's face looming above him just before his memories are stolen. *Flash.* The mayor screaming at him to hurry up and do it, do it, do it.

For Officer Lewis, there was relief in forgetting because it meant he didn't have to face up to the things he'd done. It meant he didn't have to live with the knowing. Especially when his father started forgetting himself, and he realized just how high a price he had to pay.

Until now.

Officer Lewis releases my hand and steps back. Wet eyes meet mine. In that moment he looks too young to be a policeman, too young to be caught up in the middle of all this. There's a cut on his chin, like he nicked himself shaving, but his face is so smooth and boyish that it's hard to imagine him with facial hair. I think of Mr. Lewis's pride when he told me about his son and feel a pang of sympathy and a flash of anger at what the mayor's done to this town.

"Are you okay?" I take a few steps toward him, then stop myself. A trembling hand covers his mouth and looks away from me, backing up until he hits the wall.

"How did you—" His voice is thick and raspy when he clears his throat. "Oh my God."

His eyes jump around the small space, looking everywhere but at my face. I wonder if he's seeing the things I just saw, if the memories are rushing past him in zips and flashes as everything that was taken from him comes crashing back.

"It's okay, Officer Lewis."

Outside, a car door slams.

Officer Lewis turns to look behind him, like he can see through the wall outside to the parking lot. He presses his fists against his eyes. Shakes his head.

Through the window I can make out the low rumble of someone talking. Then heavy work boots start to stomp up the ramp, followed by a second set of footsteps.

"You need to come with me. Now." Officer Lewis doesn't wait for me to answer. He grabs my arm and tugs me down the hallway, toward the front of the station.

The back door creaks open. Light spills into the hallway as we turn a corner. Voices grow louder.

"This way." He tugs me so sharply I trip over my feet, nearly falling. Then he rips open a door and shoves me inside, slamming it quickly behind me before I can ask what's going on. Keys jingle in the lock. I twist the handle and press against the wood, but it's no use. He's locked me inside.

"Lucy!"

I spin around to see Marco and Manuela seated a few feet apart with their backs against the far wall. There's a small table in the center of the room with four chairs. A filing cabinet. Shelves with a few dusty books stacked in a corner. A whiteboard with faded red and green marker streaks hangs on the wall next to a map of Tumble Tree. Greenish light spills from the overhead fluorescent light, along with a dull electric hum.

Marco tries to stand, but his arms are still bound behind his back and he can't get his balance. I run to his side and wrap him in a tight hug. He smells like sweat and desert, and I never want to let go.

Manuela clears her throat.

"What the hell took you so long? And how'd you get your hands free?"

I reluctantly pull away from Marco and explain everything that just happened, ending with the footsteps I heard outside.

"So is that cop gonna help us or what?" Manuela asks. "And can you get these things off us?" She turns to show me her bound hands, like I'd somehow forgotten.

"He seemed like he wanted to help, but then he threw me in here with you guys. So I don't know. Let me see your hands."

I examine the plastic bindings on Manuela's wrists. The plastic is too thick to break with my hands, never mind that one of them is injured.

"Do you have anything sharp on you? Like a pocketknife or maybe even a set of keys?"

"I left them in the car," Marco says.

"Same." Manuela shrugs, and I recall seeing her small pink backpack in a heap in the back of the Yukon.

I yank open one of the drawers on the filing cabinet. Then another and another, but all I find is files and papers—nothing that I can use to get the zip ties off their wrists. There's not even so much as a pencil.

"Check over there." Manuela nods her head toward the set of dust-covered shelves.

Just one glance at them tells me there won't be anything useful, but I humor Manuela and walk over to inspect them anyway. Books. An instruction manual. A binder with faded yellow papers. Then I spot a box on the top shelf, and next to it, a silver letter opener. The edges are dull, but the tip has enough point to potentially be dangerous.

"Maybe this will work?" I hold up the letter opener for them to see.

That's when I hear voices on the other side of the door. That same low, familiar rumble. A dry laugh.

". . . be over soon . . . last time . . . shouldn't worry."

The hairs on my arms stand at attention despite the stuffiness of the room, because I'd recognize that smarmy drawl anywhere.

# 40

*I run to an empty spot on the wall and sit with my hands behind my back,* the letter opener clutched in my uninjured hand. I need to buy myself time so that we can figure out what to do.

The voices grow louder. Keys scrape against the lock.

Officer Lewis leads the way into the room, stopping just inside the threshold. He catches my eye, then quickly looks away. Did I make a mistake giving him back his memories?

The mayor strolls into the room, a slow smile stretching across his face as he surveys us. There's a toothpick between his lips, and he rolls it from one side of his mouth to the other with his tongue. The aviators slip down lower on the bridge of his nose, revealing the tips of his dark eyelashes. The diamond ring on his right hand flashes.

"Well, well." He takes the toothpick out and pushes the sunglasses back up his nose. "I guess I shouldn't be so surprised, but I really thought we were done doing this."

He has the same dark hair as Marco, curling slightly above his ears. It looks damp, like he recently took a shower. His usually dusty beard is clean and neatly trimmed around the edges. My blood boils at the notion that Mayor Warman took a leisurely afternoon shower while his nephew was getting run down by the police. A glance at Marco's dark expression tells me he's thinking something along the same lines.

The mayor takes a few more steps into the room and faces Manuela. "I'm disappointed in you, Manuela. I thought I could trust you. I thought you would be good for Marco." He sighs and pops the toothpick back in his mouth. "Just goes to show that you can't really trust anyone in this town, can you? You can bet I won't make that mistake again."

Manuela bites her lip and looks away.

When the mayor turns to me, I don't need to see his eyes to know they narrow. "Somehow, you're always in the middle of this, aren't you? You just can't seem to mind your own business."

"Leave her alone." Marco shifts his weight like he's trying to stand, his hands jerking uselessly behind his back as he thumps against the wall.

"Come on, Marco, don't be like that. I'm not going to *hurt* her. I just want to have a little chat, that's all." The smile on the mayor's face is slow and crawling. "What is it with you and Lucy Miller, anyway? You get to live in the biggest house. You're next in line to continue our family legacy of running this town. You can have your pick of any girl you want. And yet you keep going back to her, no matter what I do. I just don't get it." He shakes his head, rolling the toothpick back and forth between his lips. "We're just going to have to figure something else out this time. Your mother begged me not to, but I reckon it's about time I took a closer look at some of those boarding schools on the East Coast. Maybe make her a little less familiar to you by skimming some of your memories of her off the top." He sighs. "I shouldn't have let your mom's tears sway me so much last time. I can be such a softy."

"So that's it? You're just gonna wipe my memories and ship me off? You're a real asshole, you know that?"

The mayor crosses the room in three quick steps. The back of his hand sounds like a thunderclap when it strikes Marco's cheek.

Marco's head snaps to the side. His cheek flares red. I squeeze the letter opener as hard as I can to keep myself from rushing to him.

"You have no idea what I've done for you. For this entire town." The mayor points a sharp finger at Marco's face. "If it wasn't for me, this place would be nothing but a worthless dust bowl with a gas station. *I* made Tumble Tree a place people can prosper in. *I* made sure people had work so they could pay their bills and feed their families. So that you could continue going to school with your friends." Mayor Warman grabs Marco's chin, forcing him to meet his gaze. "I'm your uncle, and I'm the mayor of this town. You will show me respect, do you understand?"

Marco grits his teeth and pulls his chin free from the mayor's grip.

"Whatever you say, *Uncle*." He practically spits the last word. "But you're delusional if you think I'd want to follow in your footsteps." There's a long silence as the two study each other. Marco's jaw is tense with the words he's holding back. The mayor's smirk is unnerving, like he's imagining all the ways he has of making Marco do what he wants.

"Enough with this nonsense." The mayor backs away from Marco and turns to the door where Officer Lewis is standing. "Charlie, Otis, get on in here. Best we get this whole mess over with."

Officer Lewis walks the rest of the way into the room, his face pale and waxy-looking. Then my dad follows behind him, and it's like the air has been sucked from the room the second his foot breaks the threshold.

His head hangs so low his chin is almost flush with his chest. His hair sticks up in wild tufts around his head, like he couldn't be bothered to comb it. The blue checked shirt he wears is badly rumpled. In fact, I'm pretty sure it's the same thing he had on yesterday. He looks like something that rolled in with the dust and tumbleweeds.

What happened to the man I used to admire? To the man who cared so much about helping others that he'd spend entire days trying to clear them of their burdens, willing to take whatever form of payment they could offer? I don't know this broken puppet of a man who follows the mayor around like a dog. He may as well be a ghost.

When Dad's eyes meet mine, a scream starts to build in my chest. My body hums with hot rage until it threatens to burn me from the inside out. Lies—that's all I see when I look at him.

My dad knows exactly what kind of man the mayor is, and yet when Mayor Warman says jump, Dad's right there at his side, ready to do the unthinkable. Because of my dad, I'll never remember what my life was like before Marco was taken from me. I'll never get back the years we spent together. I'll spend the rest of my life with this sense of *missingness* inside of me, unable to piece together my true history. How many other unknowable things have been ripped from my head without my permission?

Like Mama and the truth about what happened to her.

"How could you?" I finally growl, barely recognizing the sound of my voice. "How could you do this to me? How could you *keep* doing it? And how could you do it to the whole *entire town*?"

Dad looks down, ashamed. But I can't stop.

"My whole life, I thought what you could do was so special. I thought you were a good person. I wanted to be just like you! But you're no better than the mayor." My chin quivers as I struggle to get the words out. Hot tears stream down my cheeks, blurring Dad's face. "No, you're worse than the mayor. Because you're a liar *and* a thief. How can you live with what you've done?"

"Lucy, please." His fingers reach for me, then fall back to the side. His eyes brim. "You don't understand. I had to keep you safe."

I almost laugh at the phrase that everyone keeps using to describe what he's been doing. As if my safety is a crutch he can lean on to justify his actions.

"*Keep me safe?* The only thing in this town I needed to be kept safe from is you!" My body trembles with fury. "You took everything from me. Everything! And don't you dare try to deny it. I know about the mines. The memories you guys are unearthing and selling. I know about the sadness the mayor is using to control the townspeople and the side effects. I know about me and Marco. I know about"—my throat closes around the next word—"Mama."

Something in Dad's face shifts. His mouth forms a small *O*. He takes a step back, like he's trying to put distance between us.

"Now, Charlie," drawls the mayor, placing his hand on Dad's shoulder. "She's just talking nonsense. She doesn't know anything. How about we just get this over with, okay? Just finish it up and we can all go home and put this whole nasty mess behind us."

Dad hesitates, his eyes darting between me and the mayor. It's all the confirmation I need.

I stand and hold the letter opener in front of me in defense, my rage blazing hotter than the desert sun. My fingers shake but I do my best to hold them steady.

"Tell me what you did to my mother," I say to the mayor. "I know it was you. Tell me what you did to her. Did she find out what you were doing? Did she try to stop you, and you took things into your own hands?"

"I have no idea what you're talking about." The mayor raises both hands in the air and steps toward me, the toothpick sliding from one side of his mouth to the other. His voice is irritatingly calm. "Now put that down before you hurt yourself. Really, there's no need for all these theatrics."

Blood roars in my ears. I say the words slower now. "What did you do to my mother?" I force myself to stand straighter when I look at the twin mirrors covering his eyes.

"Sweetheart, I told you I don't know what you're talking about, but I suggest you drop that thing before someone gets hurt. You don't want Officer Lewis to have to step in, do you?"

Behind him, Officer Lewis puts a hand to his gun holster. How could he still be on the mayor's side after I showed him what the mayor stole from him? But his fingers are shaking. A bead of sweat slides from his temple to his jawline, curving under his chin toward his shirt collar. He may be on the mayor's side, but I know he doesn't want to hurt me.

I squeeze the handle of the letter opener and raise it higher.

"I know she wasn't in an accident. I know my memory of what happened to her's been erased. Did she get in your way? Did she try to stop you? Tell me what you did to her!" I can't stop my lower lip from quivering when I speak. "You killed her, didn't you? It was you!"

The mayor's laugh is a cruel thing. I want to rip the smile from his face.

"Oh, you poor girl. You have it all wrong." He closes the distance between us until there's barely an inch between him and the letter opener trembling in my outstretched hand. Then he wraps his hand around the dull blade and pushes it aside. It makes me realize how foolish I was to think it could be used as a weapon in the first place.

He smiles around the toothpick and releases his grip on the letter opener. "I didn't kill your mama, Lucy. No one did. Your mama's still alive."

# 41

*Ladybug, I love you bigger than Texas. Bigger than all the stars in the sky.*

*Ladybug, one day we'll fly away from here.*

When I squeeze my eyes shut, Mama's there, her dark hair spilling out behind her as she spins in our tire swing.

*Let's leave this town to the dust and the lizards.*

When I open my eyes, Mayor Warman's standing there with an expectant smirk on his face. The letter opener shakes in my hand, the dull tip glinting under the fluorescent lights like a joke. I let it drop to the ground with a sharp clatter.

"You're lying." My words are just above a whisper. The room starts to tilt, like everything's balanced on the edge of a razor. "Mama's dead." A fresh wave of hot tears spring to my eyes.

"You sure about that, Lucy? Why don't you think real hard on it?"

"Stop it." Dad's hand is on his heart, like he's trying to keep it from beating out of his chest. "Stop it right now."

"Or what?" Mayor Warman steps back and looks at my dad, his

head cocking to the side. "Maybe if I tell her the truth you'll stop dragging your feet. We had a deal, Charlie. I'd keep your secrets if you kept mine. But lately it seems you ain't doing such a good job of keeping my secrets, doesn't it? Maybe I ought to just tell Lucy the whole truth. Maybe that will motivate you to make her forget again."

Dad squeezes his eyes shut.

"Please don't," he begs.

"What's he talking about?" I whisper.

At the same time Marco shouts, "Stop it! Leave her alone."

*Ladybug, let's never look back.*

The room shifts again, and I have to dig my nails into my palm to keep the tunnel vision at bay. Mama's ring seems to pulse against my finger.

*Taillights disappearing down a dark road.*

*Someone yelling, repeating the same words over and over again.*

*Hands at my back, pulling me away.*

A sharp pain shoots through my brain, like a balloon's inflating inside of my skull. I press my fingers to my temples and squeeze. Am I imagining it, or has her ring gotten hotter? It's flashing like a beacon, pushing the Echoes forward.

"Stop it!" I shout, but I'm not sure who I'm saying it to. I blink and see my mother. I blink and the room comes back into focus. I hug my arms to my chest. The walls seem too close. When I close my eyes, Mama's there, two hands on the wheel of her Buick.

"Your mama always thought she was too good for this town."

The mayor's voice is a low growl. "She always threatened to leave. So it shouldn't have been a surprise when she finally did."

"What are you talking about?" I ask.

"There was no accident, Lucy. Your dad just made you think there was so you wouldn't know the truth—your mama left you."

"Stop it," Dad moans, and I don't have to look at him to know that he's crying.

"You're lying," I say again. "She wouldn't do that."

I squeeze my eyes shut. I see her face as she spins me on the tire swing. See her mouth moving as she says the words she used to say to me all the time. I hear her voice.

*Ladybug, someday we'll see the world. We'll leave this place to the dust and the lizards.*

"No. You're wrong," I say. "She didn't want to leave us. She didn't want to leave *me*."

The mayor looks at me with a mix of pity and pure triumph. "Are you absolutely sure about that?"

His words reach inside me, and slowly, they brush away a layer of dirt from the secrets buried there.

When I close my eyes I can see it . . . I can feel it, the same way I feel the hot metal of her ring against my finger.

*My bare feet pound on the dirt-packed road. My nightgown tangles around my legs, almost tripping me. Taillights flash red against the darkness. My raw voice screams into the blackness.*

"Someone called the station," drawls the mayor. "Said there was a girl screaming bloody murder down at the Memory House.

They thought someone was trying to kill you by the way you were carrying on. So I came to the house to see what all the fuss was about."

I open my eyes and see black spots. Dad's head is in his hands. He looks like he's lived a thousand lives, like the weight of everything he's taken from the world is written in each crease marking the time that's passed.

"Stop it," he moans. "You promised you wouldn't tell her. You said if I helped you—"

"When I pulled up the road I saw your dad holding on to you like you were a spooked horse about to make a break for it. You were a mess. Hair flying out every which way. Face bright red from crying. Nightgown torn. And you just kept screaming the same thing over and over again." He raises his voice an octave to mimic me. "Come back, Mama! Mama, come back!" He shakes his head and feigns a sympathetic frown. "Saddest damn thing I've ever seen."

I squeeze my eyes shut, feeling the words inside of my mouth. They fit neatly—soft and familiar.

Mama's ring is tight against my finger. I touch it, feeling the warmth of her there. Feeling the truth. And suddenly the smoke around the image clears, finally breaking free.

"She was driving away." I close my eyes again. The taillights. "And I was screaming for her to come back."

"That's right. You screamed yourself hoarse."

I want so badly for it to be a lie, but I know it's not. Every detail slides neatly into the hollow place inside me that once kept Mama close.

When I close my eyes, I can see Mama's old Buick pulling away from the house. I can feel the dirt on my feet as I run after the car, shouting for her not to go. I can feel Dad's hands on my shoulders, holding me back. The Echo has been there all along, on the edge of my memories, waiting for me to claim it. I just needed someone to tell me the truth, needed something to shake it loose.

I hate that it's the mayor who finally pulled it out of me.

When I look up, Dad's face is blurred behind a wall of tears.

"I'm so sorry," he sobs, the hand over his mouth muffling the words. "I'm so, so sorry, Ladybug."

"You made me think she was in an accident. You made me believe she was—that she—" I can't even say it, can't get the words out. It's too horrible to comprehend.

Mama's alive. She's *alive.*

"How could you?" I whisper. "How could you take her from me? And *keep* her away, all this time?"

Something between a moan and a scream escapes Dad's mouth. "I thought—you were so upset, Ladybug. So, so upset. You wouldn't eat. Wouldn't speak. For weeks. I didn't know what else to do. I was afraid you'd end up like her—"

"And you thought it was better to make me believe she was dead?!? What kind of man—you stole her from me!" I'm shouting now, strings of spit flying out with my words. I march toward him, fingers curling into fists. Everything inside me is fire and rage. "Where is she? Tell me where she is! Tell me how to find her!"

Tears spill from Dad's eyes. "I don't know. She didn't tell me where she was going. She didn't tell either of us—"

"You're lying. She wouldn't have left me! She said we were going to see the world together—she said we—she said—"

Dad's voice quavers. "I never meant for this to happen. I thought if I loved her enough, she'd stay. I tried so hard. And when she finally left . . . you were so upset. You were despondent. I didn't want you to hurt. Can you understand a dad not wanting his daughter to hurt like that? I thought if you believed she didn't leave by choice—if you thought it was an accident—that maybe you could find happiness again. I just wanted you to be happy. Can you understand that? A father so desperate to see his daughter happy again, that he'd do whatever it took?"

I'm sobbing now, too. "But . . . why? Why would she leave? She said she loved me—"

"She did love you, Ladybug. Bigger than Texas, she used to say. But she started to get sad—really sad. She stopped getting out of bed. She wouldn't let me help her. Kept saying we were better off without her. I tried to tell her she was wrong—I tried so hard to make her stay. But . . ." He shakes his head at me, like the words have left him. Or maybe there are no words to explain how someone can love you and still leave you behind. "I was afraid if you knew the truth, you'd try to leave me, too. Or that I'd lose you anyway to the despair and pain your mother brought on. I couldn't bear the thought of you disappearing into your sadness, the way she did. You're so much like her. You both deserve better." He swallows and wipes at his eyes with his fists. "And I've made such an awful mess of things."

"You can make it all go away, Charlie." Suddenly Mayor Warman's hands are on my arms and he's dragging me toward my dad. His hands feel like ice against my skin. "You can go on about your lives like none of this ever happened. All you have to do is make her forget. Just say the words and be done with it and we can go back to the way things were."

"No." Dad shakes his head. "I can't do this anymore."

"You can and you will. Unless you want Lucy to lose more than just her memories. Unless you want it to be just you all by yourself in that big old house. You don't want that, do you? Now get up." The mayor shoves me, closing the distance between me and Dad. Then he grabs Dad by the arm and forces him to stand. "Do it, Charlie!"

All the words have left my body. The pain in my head is too big. The room feels too small. The mayor's fingers dig into the flesh of my arms. Behind me, Marco and Manuela shout, their words a jumble of noise and fury. I can feel the afternoon heat pressing against the windows, hear the buzzing of the overhead lights, smell the thickness in the air, and it's all too much. There's not enough air in the room to breathe.

"Give him your hand," the mayor says, wrenching one of my arms from my sides. I don't have the strength to pull it back.

Dad's wet eyes jump back and forth between me and the mayor. "Do it!" Mayor Warman's voice is a cannon.

Dad sways slightly on his feet. The mayor jerks my hand by the wrist at the same time he reaches for Dad. Then suddenly our hands are forced together, the mayor pressing down on the back of my hand so I can't break away.

"Ask her what she wants to forget, Charlie. Ask her!"

*Please don't do this,* I want to say. But my lungs have stopped working. My heart is beating so hard I can feel it in my head. My vision swims.

Officer Lewis pulls the gun from his holster, and I almost laugh because what's the point? The mayor wins. *Always.* I don't need a gun pointed at me to figure that out anymore.

Maybe it won't be so bad, forgetting. At least then this pain will stop. At least then I won't have to look at my father and know what he did. At least then I won't have to look in the mirror and wonder what it is about me that made it so easy to walk away.

Out of the corner of my eye, I see the gun coming closer. I see Officer Lewis, taking a step toward us.

Then—

"Let them go."

I look back at the officer, and that's when I realize that the gun isn't pointed at me or Dad.

It's pointed at the mayor.

# 42

*"I said let them go." Officer Lewis's grip is steady on the gun and leveled* right at the mayor's head.

"What exactly do you think you're doing?" Mayor Warman squeezes my arm harder, making it clear that he has no intention of letting me go anywhere.

"What I should have done a long time ago."

"Now, Otis." The mayor's tone changes, like he's talking to a small child. "What's gotten into you? Put that gun down. Or at least point it at someone useful."

"Don't talk to me like I'm one of your idiot sheep. I know all about you and the things you made me do, and the things you stole from me. I'm done helping you." There's a click as Officer Lewis cocks the gun. Then he squeezes one eye shut, like he's taking aim. "Release the girl and back up against the wall."

"Otis, stop this nonsense—"

"Now!"

Mayor Warman drops his hands from my arm and steps back toward the wall. His brow creases in confusion.

"Put your hands in the air where I can see them." Officer Lewis grips the gun so tightly his knuckles turn white.

The mayor does as he says. He's no longer wearing a cocky smile, and the toothpick that had been in his mouth a second ago has fallen to the floor, forgotten. I realize then that the mayor's not armed. But I guess why would he need to be when he thinks he's got the whole town in his pocket? He lets everyone else do his dirty work.

"You mind at least telling me what the hell is going on?" the mayor asks. His sunglasses glint in the dim light of the room.

"What's going on," Otis says, "is that I know the truth now. And I'm done playing your games. We all are. It's time you told Charlie the truth about what happened to Lucy's mama. It's time you tell him why she really left."

"What do you mean?" says Dad.

"I have no idea what you're talking about." The mayor's voice sounds confident, but there's a slight tremble in the hand with the diamond ring on it.

"Like hell you don't. I know what you did to that poor woman. It's the same thing you did to my dad. People get too close to figuring out what you're up to, and you use that black drink to mess with their heads—to control them."

Dad's eyes flick between Otis and the mayor. My heart is a fist pounding against my chest.

"What're you talking about?" Dad asks, eyes fixed on Otis and the gun he has pointed at the mayor's head.

"You sad old fool." Officer Lewis shakes his head. The muscles in his jaw tense. "The mayor's been playing you this whole time. Just like he plays everyone in this town."

"He's lying," the mayor growls. "He's just trying to make me look bad. He's had his eyes on my operation for years now. Probably wants it all for himself."

"I don't want anything to do with you and your operations." Otis keeps the gun trained on Mayor Warman as he looks at Dad. "Amelia was planning to take you and Lucy far away from here. She was planning to get you out, but the mayor couldn't have that. He *needed* you to—"

"He's lying. I'm telling you, Charlie, he wants to take over!" The mayor starts to lower his hands, but Otis shakes the gun at him in warning.

"Mayor Warman was selling the memories for years before he started using your help, Charlie. After the mines closed, people were all too willing to help him dig up and bottle the unwanted memories because they needed the work and the pay. Except when they realized how little he was paying them relative to what he was making . . . well, folks got mad. And rightfully so. They threatened to take over the operations and to tell you what was happening. That's when he started using the sadness on folks. He'd experimented with it a bit before and discovered that it weakened people's resolve and made them susceptible to his commands. It was the perfect solution to his problem—the perfect way to get the townsfolk to do what he wanted again."

The mayor opens his mouth to object, but Otis walks toward him until the gun and the mayor are practically nose to nose.

"He started making house calls around town. Checking up on all his employees. And while he was there, he'd slip a little of the sadness concoction into their drinks. Tell them they needed to get back to work or he'd make it even worse for them. But about five years ago, the mayor ran into a problem. A big problem, wouldn't you say?"

The mayor swallows.

"The desert was nearly empty of memories. He'd sold just about every last one of them. And here was Amelia, talking all this non-sense about leaving Tumble Tree and taking Charlie and Lucy with her. If you left, the whole operation would fall apart, wouldn't it? And what would our dear mayor do then?" Officer Lewis says.

He keeps his gun trained on the mayor's face. "He needed the Memory House to keep running. He needed you, Charlie, to keep filling the desert with people's burdens so he could keep things going. Ain't that right, Mayor Warman?"

Dad's lower lip quivers. The room blurs around me. I think of the way Missy looked at the Pie Pantry. Of Manuela's abuela sitting in that faded yellow chair, her eyes staring off into nothing. Is that what happened to Mama? Is she out there somewhere, with no memory of me or Dad or how she got to wherever she is?

I lean down and pick up the letter opener. Maybe it's not sharp enough to do much damage, but I need to feel its weight in my hand. I need to do something other than stand here, helpless.

I walk forward and press the letter opener to the mayor's cheek. I smile when he winces.

"What did you do to her?"

"He drugged her is what he did," Otis says, shaking his head. "He'd come round your house under the guise of checking in on your family, and he'd slip a little of the sadness into Amelia's tea. And when she was good and sad, he'd whisper things in her ear. Horrible things about how she wasn't good enough for Charlie. How y'all would be better off without her. How she should do y'all a favor and just leave."

I squeeze my eyes shut. Mama never did like the sweet tea everyone else drank. She liked hers black, and always kept a separate pitcher of it in the back of our fridge, just for her. It would have been so easy for the mayor to slip the sadness into her tea without any of us knowing.

Dad's voice quivers when he speaks. "All this time—I thought it was something inside of her that was making her sad, just like the people who come to the Memory House. But it was you. You made her like that."

Dad stands up straighter and his eyes flash. He looks like he's about ready to launch himself at the mayor.

"The night she left—when Lucy was inconsolable—*you* were the one who suggested I make her think that Amelia had been in an accident. You told me that if I didn't, Lucy might end up just like her mother. That sadness like Amelia's is the kind that runs deep in the blood, and the best thing to do was to take away Lucy's pain before she had time to let the sadness seep in the way it had seeped into her mom." A tear slides down Dad's cheek at the same time his fingers curl into fists. "All this time I thought it was me. I thought it was something *I* did that brought out the sadness that lived inside her. That I did something to make her leave, but it was you, wasn't it? You drove her away."

Mayor Warman looks like he's about to try to deny it, but Otis cuts him off.

"The mayor had you exactly where he wanted you, Charlie," Otis continues. "And once he convinced you to make Lucy forget, he had the leverage he needed. He could use what you did to Lucy against you. He could get you to make the townsfolk who dug up the memories forget, too, so that he didn't have to rely so much on the sadness drink. Because he knew that if too many people drank it, and started acting like my dad, other people in town might get suspicious."

Officer Lewis looks at me then. "Which is exactly what happened."

"You knew it was making people forget themselves," I add, staring into the twin mirrors covering the mayor's eyes. His mouth twitches. "You knew about the side effects, and you didn't care, did you?"

The mayor clears his throat. "It's my job to keep the town running." His voice is a low growl. "I just did what my family has done for generations. Any one of you would have done the same thing in my position."

"Where is she?" Suddenly Dad's at my side. He rips the letter opener from my hand and presses it against the mayor's throat. "Where is my wife! Tell me where she went!"

A string of spittle flies from Dad's mouth when he yells. With the hand not holding the letter opener, he shoves the mayor backward. Mayor Warman falls back against the wall, his aviators bouncing against the bridge of his nose.

He lets out a laugh. "You're all just going to take him at his word?" He nods at Officer Lewis.

"He's telling the truth," I say. "I know he is, because I made him remember."

"She made me remember, too." Marco smiles his crooked-road smile. "She can make everyone in town remember what you've done to them. You're as good as finished around here."

"That's not possible," says the mayor. But his voice quivers when he says it.

Dad's eyes go wide and he looks back and forth between me and Officer Lewis, like he's working it all out. He saw me with the Oklahoma woman, so he knows what I can do. Maybe he's piecing together that I did the same thing for Otis Lewis. He lowers the hand with the letter opener. His eyes are filled with an expression I can't quite identify.

"So it's true," he whispers. A sad smile stretches across his face. "I should have put it together that day in my office when you helped me remember your mama. I just didn't think it was possible." His smile widens. "You're a miracle."

"That's not possible. She makes people forget," the mayor says, like he's seen me do it before. "I thought you said she could make people forget?"

Dad shrugs, his eyes filled with something akin to wonder. "Looks like I had it backward. I said all the Miller *men* made people forget. It never occurred to me that Lucy might be different. That she'd be the best of all of us."

The mayor turns to look at Marco, and something he sees there must finally connect, because all the color drains from Mayor Warman's face.

"That's not possible," he says again.

Marco gives him a wry smile. "It is. I know everything. *Everything.*"

"Turn around and put your hands behind your back." When the mayor hesitates, Officer Lewis grabs him by his shoulder and slams him against the wall. "I said put your hands behind your back!" Then he pulls a set of handcuffs from his waistband. They make a satisfying *click* when they close around the mayor's wrists.

"Excuse me," Manuela shouts, sounding all at once relieved and annoyed that everyone seems to have forgotten her. "Can you cut these things off me already? I can't feel my fingers."

Officer Lewis walks over to her and pulls a pocketknife from his belt. "Dangerous runaways, huh?" He glares at the mayor.

Manuela's eyebrows shoot up to her hairline, then she rolls her eyes. "Hardly. My hands, please?"

Marco glares at his uncle from under a furrowed brow. "That's what you told the police to get them to pull us over?"

The mayor's silence is answer enough. He's slumped forward at an awkward angle, and I wonder how tight Officer Lewis made the handcuffs.

Manuela stands, rubbing the red grooves on her wrists. Officer Lewis moves to Marco next.

"I'm sorry," Otis tells him, releasing the bindings with a *snap*. "I thought I was doing the right thing pulling you over before you could get too far outside of Tumble Tree. The mayor said it was for your own good."

"He's a good liar." Marco's barely loose before he's crossed the room and pulled me into his arms. "Are you okay? Did he hurt you?"

I bury my face in his shoulder and breathe him in. I don't know that I'll ever be okay, but I'm not hurt, so I nod.

"So now what?" Mayor Warman bellows, his voice edged with the threat of a laugh. He looks at me. "Are you going to go *save the town*? Make them all remember so they know about the awful things they've done?"

"Someone has to fix the mess you've made," says Marco.

"The *mess* I've made?" The mayor snorts out a laugh. "There would be no town if it weren't for me!"

"We were doing just fine before you came along," Officer Lewis says.

"That was before the mines closed, Otis." Mayor Warman shakes his head at us like we just don't get it. "You know as well as I do that when the mines closed, there wasn't enough work. Without work, people didn't have money to spend. Don't you remember what it was like around here? Stores started to close. Jobs started to disappear. You need money to run a town. I found a way to bring in money. I found a way to protect this place."

The mayor's sunglasses slip down the bridge of his nose, and with his hands behind his back he has no way to push them back into place. For the first time I can remember, I see the mayor's eyes. They're the same rich brown as Marco's.

"Your granddaddy built the house you grew up in, didn't he, Otis?"

Officer Lewis hesitates. "Yeah, what of it?"

"Things got so bad after the mines closed that your daddy was planning to move, just like everybody else. It just about broke his heart, the idea of leaving the house his daddy built. Can you imagine your family having to abandon your childhood home? This whole town was on the brink of collapse. Tumble Tree would have become a forgotten town on the side of an empty stretch of highway.

"So I created a way for people to keep working. I brought money into this town so that we could keep things running. Your daddy got a job as a mailman. Patty Cohen got to keep the Pie Pantry open. Anthony Whitcome opened his snow cone stand. Then the Dollar General moved into town. And so on and so on down the line. We became a thriving community again. A safe place where people could stay and raise their families. We just needed to make sure it stayed a secret."

The smile on his face is smug as he looks around the room.

"Don't you see? My family built this town. Keeping it safe is our legacy. You need me."

"You're not keeping this town safe, you're brainwashing people," I say. "Good, honest people. And for what? So you can be some hotshot in a small town? So you can have a big house and snakeskin boots?"

The mayor shrugs. "What are a few people's memories in exchange for a whole town's survival? Do you know what it's like out there?" He jerks his chin toward the window, as if *out there* is just beyond the glass. "There's a reason people are willing to pay so much for a little piece of happiness. Haven't you ever wondered why more and more people keep showing up at the Memory House year after year? It's because things outside of Tumble Tree aren't as great as your mama would have had you believe. The rest of the world is plagued by greed, sadness, and loneliness. You see it all the time, Lucy, in the people standing on your front porch begging for your dad to save them. It weighs them down. Makes their hearts heavy with burden. Do you want Tumble Tree to become like the rest of the sad, lonely world? Or do you want it to stay the way it is—a place on the edge of the country that offers a reprieve from all the fast-pacedness of the rest of the world? Where you can forget your troubles and return to life better than when you left? Tumble Tree needs me to keep it that way. *You* need me, Lucy, like it or not."

"If we needed you so badly, you wouldn't have gone so far to keep what you were doing a secret. Seems to me like *you're* the one who needs *us*."

A thought occurs to me then. I think back to the conversation in Marco's car.

"What about the happiness elixir?" I ask, studying the mayor's face. "What happens if people keep taking it?"

The mayor looks away and lets out an exasperated breath. "I'd imagine it keeps making them happy, the way it was intended to do. It's a sad world out there. Don't you think people deserve a little happiness?"

I shake my head. The mayor keeps his face angled away, still not looking at me. He's lying.

"No, that doesn't make sense. If people take too much of the *sadness*, it makes them depressed and susceptible to negative thoughts, and they eventually start to lose themselves. What happens when people take too much of the happiness elixir?"

The mayor starts to shake his head, like he's going to deny knowing, but Marco speaks up.

"We were close to figuring that out last time, weren't we?" he says. "That's why you worked so hard to keep us apart. There's something wrong with the elixir, too, isn't there? It makes people act wild and lose control of their emotions if they take too much of it. Right?"

I watch the mayor for a reaction and remember Janice that night at the mines, the giddy elation on her face when she was exposed to the happiness jars. She couldn't stop laughing or get control of herself.

"What happened to Janice that night after she went home from the mines?" I ask the mayor.

Only it's Otis that answers.

"Janice?" he asks. There's a strange look on his face. "Um, she wasn't working at the corner store this morning. Jim said she showed up for work like normal, but started acting all strange, saying she didn't know where she was or how she got there. So he sent her home, said she's taking some time off."

My stomach clenches.

I think back to the other morning at Patty's Pie Pantry. I think about Missy—who's always *so happy and giggly*, as if nothing fazes her. How she couldn't remember my regular order, and wasn't chatty like usual. She seemed . . . different, and then out of nowhere, it was like she'd lost herself. She was just suddenly . . . gone. The confusion in her eyes when she looked at Patty—a person she'd known just about her whole life—and asked who she was.

And now Janice . . .

Oh my God.

"It doesn't matter, does it?"

All eyes turn to me.

"If people keep taking the happiness elixir, it doesn't just make them lose control of their emotions. It strips them of themselves entirely, just like with the sludge. It doesn't matter which elixir you drink. It's all just a scam. Isn't it? You never intended to 'help' anyone."

The mayor's eyes dart around the room, avoiding my face, and I know I'm right.

"How could you?" I say. "You're not just hurting the town by selling that elixir. You're hurting *everyone*. You're making people— *decent* people, here in Tumble Tree and all over—believe you've found some cure-all for what ails them knowing full well that it's dangerous to absorb someone else's happiness whether you dilute it or not. Because eventually, it'll make people forget themselves completely. And if people knew the truth, they'd stop buying it. They'd shut you down once and for all. And you couldn't have that, could you?"

The mayor's silence is all the confirmation I need.

But I'm not finished.

"As long as no one in town knew your secret, you were safe. Because the people who'd already lost themselves to the elixir—like Missy—couldn't remember what happened to them, so they weren't a threat. But me, Marco, and anyone else who figured out what you were up to—*we* could speak up. We could get you in trouble. So you had to keep us all quiet."

The mayor swallows. "I was helping the town," he says, but his voice is barely a whisper. Because when you get right down to it, the only person he was really helping was himself.

"You know what I think?" Manuela flips her hair to the side and narrows her eyes. "I think it's time we gave the mayor a taste of his own medicine. Literally. We should make him drink that black stuff and see how he likes it."

"Yeah." Marco's voice is flat when he lets go of my hand.

"I agree. It's about time you got a taste of what you've given to the rest of us." Officer Lewis grabs the mayor by the shoulders. "We should have Charlie steal *your* memories for a change. That seems like a fair trade to me."

He gives Mayor Warman a sharp shove and he stumbles toward Dad. The force knocks the sunglasses from his face, and they fall to the ground with a clatter. The room goes quiet.

Without the sunglasses, the mayor somehow seems smaller. His shoulders don't look as broad. His jaw doesn't seem as confident. His stance doesn't seem as strong. Without them, Mayor Warman looks like an ordinary man.

Marco's breath is uneven, like he's trying to hold his emotions in check. I can only imagine what he must be feeling—maybe it's not too different from how I feel about my father right now: split down the middle by memories of the man I know and love, and the man who's done unspeakable things.

"We should make him forget that he was ever the Mayor of Tumble Tree," says Otis Lewis.

"We should make him forget he was ever born," Manuela says, half joking, but her hands are clenched into fists.

"Go on, Charlie," the mayor says with a resigned sigh. "Let's get this over with." He steps toward Dad, offering up a wan smile that's so much like Marco's crooked grin it almost hurts.

Dad pinches the skin at the bridge of his nose. When he looks at me with red-rimmed eyes, I know that he's asking for permission—he wants me to be the one to decide.

I think of the Oklahoma woman after I helped her remember.

Maybe she left the Memory House the first time feeling lighter because she didn't have to deal with the pain of losing her husband, but she came back because the pain of not remembering him fully was worse.

And then there's Mama. All this time my dad thought he was protecting me from a truth I wasn't strong enough to handle. But if he'd let me keep the truth—no matter how much it hurt—maybe none of this would have happened. Maybe Dad and I would have left Tumble Tree to the dust and the lizards a long time ago, the way Mama always said we would. Maybe we would have learned the truth about her long before now, and we could have been looking for her.

How many of the burdened people who've come to the Memory House went on to repeat the same mistakes over and over again because they never learned the right lesson the first time around? Maybe we need our burdens so we don't keep repeating the same mistakes. Maybe we need to let our wounds heal, rather than trying to pretend they never existed in the first place.

"No." I move to stand by Dad and take hold of the trembling hand that he was about to use to unburden the mayor. "No more forgetting. It's time we let people live with the mistakes they've made. Especially the mayor."

Dad nods once in agreement, but the finality in the gesture tells me all I need to know.

He's through taking people's burdens. For good.

# 43

*The Tumble Tree Police Station has only one jail cell, typically reserved* for nights when someone in town gets a little too drunk and rowdy. This is where we decide to put Mayor Warman.

"I'll give Vivi a call," Dad says, hands in his pockets. "She can help bring meals and such. Plus, she knows how to handle the mayor. She'll know what to do."

I have so many questions, but now's not the time. There'll be plenty of time for answers later.

Marco's quiet when Officer Lewis marches Mayor Warman out of the room and down the hall to his cell. Surprisingly, so is the mayor, like he's resigned to his permanent fall from grace.

It's my idea to call the town meeting.

"I feel like we should all get a vote in what we decide to do," I say. "Plus, if we gather everyone together, we can give people the option to have me call back the things they were made to forget."

They nod and Manuela gives me a grateful smile. It makes sense, and even if it didn't, we're all too tired to debate. Tomorrow night, we'll gather the town and tell them the truth.

We'll give them a choice.

Officer Lewis drops Manuela at her house and takes Marco back to his car, which is still parked along the side of the road where we got pulled over. Back at Marco's house, Vivi will be waiting. I wonder how it will feel to finally be out from under her brother's controlling thumb. I wonder if the house will still feel like a home, or if it will hold too much of Mayor Warman and the things he's done.

I climb into the passenger seat of Dad's car, the silence stretching between us. I don't know how we'll find a way through, but for now, the quiet feels like a good place to start. At least he's stopped saying that he's sorry every five seconds, and the tears seem to have dried up along with the words. Forgiveness will be a long road, but I see now that he really believed he was doing what was best for me. Even if he was horribly wrong, he's lost as much as I have. Maybe more, because he has to live with the choices he's made.

We're about to make the turnoff toward our house when I realize I can't go home. Not yet. Not without seeing for myself.

"Wait," I tell Dad. "I want to go to the mines."

I can see the hesitation on his face, but he doesn't have a reason to say no. Not really. So we keep driving until we hit the unmarked, unpaved road that leads to the mines.

The parking lot is vacant. In the bright afternoon, the emptiness feels wrong—forgotten, like a dust-filled room in an abandoned house, with sheets covering the furniture and empty squares where pictures once hung.

The desert crunches beneath our feet. The mine shaft yawns wide. I step inside.

It's cooler once we're out of the sun's glare. The afternoon light quickly thins from sepia to black once we're inside the tunnel.

"Hang on," Dad says, disappearing into the shadows. A few seconds later the narrow space fills with light and an electric hum. Dim bulbs are strung along the ceiling, filling the tunnel with a grayish-white glow. Stacks of crates and other supplies line the wall.

"They're empty," Dad says from behind me. "The memories are kept further in the back, behind a rock wall. It looks like a dead end, but the right side of the wall is a hidden door. I can take you if you'd like."

"No." The string of lights winds toward the back of the cave, where I assume they lead to the fake dead end. "I'll go by myself."

The air is dusty. I fight back a cough as I walk farther into the dimly lit tunnel, past craggy rock walls and more stacks of supplies. The lights let off a dull buzz. I try to imagine people working—stacking boxes filled with the swirling memories, siphoning off the good from the bad, making the elixir. I wonder if they worked in silence, listening to their feet slide against the gritty floor, or if they talked as they worked. Maybe listened to music. There's no way they mistook what they were doing for mining. Nothing about the tunnel suggests this place is an operating mine shaft.

Finally, I come to what looks like a dead end. Rocks are piled to the ceiling, completely blocking the way. I touch the right side of the wall the way Dad instructed. It feels unnaturally smooth, like it was only manufactured to look like rock. I feel along the space until my hands find a groove. And I pull.

The hidden door is surprisingly easy to open. I step into the narrow opening and squint against the darkness. I can just make out a thin cord hanging from the rocky ceiling. When I give it a tug, the small space fills with light.

There are rows and rows of jars lining the wall. The light catches on the glass, making them shine. They glitter like promises. They glitter with stolen hope. They glitter the way a father loves a daughter—enough to lie and steal and bury secrets in the desert so that his daughter can hold on to her mama's promises.

If I didn't know enough to look closer, I might think they're empty, but when I lean in, I can make out wisps of grayish-silver fog dancing at the top of each jar. There's no darkness pulsing at the center—these memories have been emptied of the sadness that brought people to the Memory House in the first place. What's left now is the happiness that once made the memories whole. Happiness people never intended to give away. Happiness that, when taken too often by someone it doesn't belong to, makes a person lose themselves.

I have to undo this.

• • •

The next night, all of Tumble Tree shows up for the town meeting, filling the metal folding chairs Vivi and Marco carefully arranged inside the high school gymnasium. She hands out sweet tea and pecan pie brought over from Patty's Pie Pantry. I offer to take charge since the meeting was my idea, but Dad steps forward instead.

"I'm the one who helped him. I should be the one to explain."

He tells them everything that's happened, his head bobbing up and down in agreement when people shout their frustrations at him. There are hugs and tears and shouts of disbelief. There is anger. There is pain. There is acceptance. Then, one by one, people come up to the stage to meet with me, and I take their hands and call back the emotions that will restore their memories.

I start with Manuela's abuela. I'm not sure it will work since it was the sadness that made her forget and not my dad, but I take her hands anyway, hoping against hope that I can undo the damage. One moment, her eyes are blank, staring off in the distance at something she can't see. Then all at once the light comes back, filling with the colors I see inside of her as one by one, her memories reform.

Images and emotions hit me in a kaleidoscope of color: red guilt, green regret, golden love, turquoise forgiveness, orange happiness. By the time I get to the last person, my head's so full I might topple over from the weight of it all. It turns out just about every person in town had some role in what happened down at the mines. Almost everyone in Tumble Tree, it seems, had a secret they buried—something taken from them they never intended to give away.

And everyone has questions.

"What are we gonna do now?"

"I need that job to keep food on the table. What are we supposed to do without the mines?"

"I've got an uncle that manages a factory outside El Paso and he's looking for good, honest workers. I'm sure if I gave him a call he'd be willing to give some of y'all work."

"Does this mean we'll have to move?"

"What about my house? I can't just abandon it. My grandpa built it. Tumble Tree is my home."

"What's gonna happen to the Memory House? And all the memories Charlie takes from now on?"

"Nothing's gonna happen," Dad says. "Because I'm done taking memories. I know I haven't done much to earn your trust, but I promise you all that's over now. You have my word. I did what I did to protect my daughter, but it seems to me Lucy doesn't need my protection. She probably never did."

"We should get rid of the mines. Make sure it never happens again." Mr. Lewis removes his baseball cap and rubs at his balding head.

"Dad's right," Otis Lewis adds, placing a hand on his father's shoulder. "I know a guy who runs a construction site about an hour outside of town who can get us some dynamite. I bet we could close the opening to make sure no one else can get to the memories being stored there. Bury the whole place once and for all."

A murmur ripples through the crowd. A few people clap. Others shout their objections.

The room fills with noise. In the end, we decide to put it to a vote.

All but five people vote to permanently shut down the mines. I realize with a sinking feeling that this probably means one thing—most of the people in Tumble Tree will have to leave.

I've spent my entire life tracing the pathways leading out of Tumble Tree and dreaming of the road that would finally lead me far from the squelching heat of my desert home. I've read travel journals, magazines, road atlases, and everything in between to plan my escape, but never once did I imagine there wouldn't be a Tumble Tree to come back to. In my heart, all the roads that lead me away could just as easily bring me back; back to Mama's park and the tire swing where my memories of her are as bright as a cloudless Tumble Tree sky; back to the winding dirt road that leads to the endless pool of Miracle Lake; back to the front yard where Mama and I counted license plates and daydreamed of a morning when Hawaii or Alaska would rumble over the pothole in the driveway. No matter where I go, Tumble Tree will always be my home. I couldn't change that even if I wanted to. I squeeze the star charm between my fingers and finally understand why Marco gave it to me—I'm the girl from his story with the compass for a heart, and this is the star that leads the way home.

So there needs to be a home that I can always come back to.

I take in the faces of my friends and neighbors.

Missy from the Pie Pantry, who always gives me an extra pancake when I sit in her section. She's smiling now, back to her usual boisterous self.

Manuela's mom and abuela, who raised a girl with enough fight and grit to topple any would-be mayor.

Mrs. Gomez, who sets aside the new travel books that come into the library just to make sure my hands are the first ones that get to hold them.

Mr. Lewis, who always greets me with a smile and a comment on the never-changing weather; who was brave enough to stand up to the mayor even in the face of threats and guns.

Manuela, who turned out to be so much more than I expected, and perhaps, if I'm lucky, the kind of friend who'll keep coming over for sleepovers and bike rides and whatever else the future holds for us.

And Marco—the boy another version of me fell in love with. The boy who made me fall for him all over again.

Where will they go when the mines close? And what will I be without them? Tumble Tree is our home, the red star on our map. The mayor was right about one thing: we can't let this place become just another forgotten town on the side of an empty stretch of highway.

"I have an idea," I say. I step into the center of the room and feel the weight of everyone's eyes on me when I tell them what I've been thinking about. It might not be a permanent solution, but for those who are willing to stay, it will be a good, honest start.

# 44

*People come from everywhere to remember.*

Ever since Dad fixed the pothole in our driveway, it's hard to tell when a new guest arrives at the Memory House—the noise from all the construction down the road doesn't help much either—but Vivi has ears like a bat. She always seems to know when someone new pulls up.

"It's a bus," she shouts, sticking her head inside the house. The pitcher she's carrying sloshes water onto the welcome mat. "I think it's from one of the colleges upstate. I don't know where we'll put them all."

"Downtown's already crowded enough. We're gonna need another stoplight if the traffic keeps up like it is." Dad wipes his brow and sets his toolbox on the ground so that he can look outside. He's been a one-man repair shop the last few months, dead set on getting our house back into shape. It's nice to see him busy. Busy is good. It keeps him from thinking too much about the past.

I walk to the front room and look out the window. Sure enough, there's a coach bus full of college-age kids parked along the far edge of the lot. A few of them climb out onto the dirt-packed parking lot, shielding their eyes from the sun while dabbing at the sweat already beaded at their hairlines. It rained most of last week, but you wouldn't know it—the sun's already soaked up the moisture from the ground, returning Tumble Tree to its standard state of hot, dry, and thirsty.

Vivi marches toward the bus with her clipboard in hand. Manuela's mom is behind her along with the rest of the staff assigned to greet new arrivals. They're all wearing matching shirts with the new logo for the Memory House that Manuela designed.

"Five more people showed up this morning about the letters and one person came in response to the ad," I say, shielding my eyes against the glaring sun. "Seems like we're getting a half dozen or so a day now. That's not too bad, but I was expecting we'd have more by now."

Dad looks out at the packed lot. "Vivi and I chatted and we're going to hire a few more folks to help write letters. And we got folks looking into expanding the number of ads we placed, too. That should help, but it's still going to take a long time, Luce. I've unburdened a lot of people over the years. Same for your grandpa and his grandpa before that. May take years before we find them all. And even once we do, some people may not want to remember—some folks will want to leave their burdens here."

"I know. But what matters is that we give them a choice."

I don't care how long it takes, I want every burdened guest who's ever walked through the doors of the Memory House to have a chance to recover the things they lost. It only feels right that we give them an explanation for the holes in their memories and the sense of missingness that may have plagued them since they left. And as for the people who took the mayor's elixir—we'll search as long as it takes to find everyone who took it. The mayor may have been the one who made this mess, but I'm not going to quit until it's cleaned up once and for all.

Dad's quiet for a second, his eyes on the front yard.

"I'm proud of you," he finally says, keeping his back to me.

I can tell he wants to say more, but I don't press. These days we're giving each other the space we need to work through our feelings. I don't know that we'll ever get back to the way things were, but Dad's trying his best. And he's trying hard to forgive himself for letting the mayor worm his way into his life and use him the way that he did. I'm working hard to forgive him, too. It helps that we spend time talking about Mama and the weeks leading up to her departure.

He tells me how the sadness crept over her slowly. So slowly that he didn't notice it at first, until one day his wife—once full of laughter and adventure—no longer had much interest in anything, let alone the things she used to love. He tells me about the days when her sadness kept her in bed, and how no matter how much he begged she wouldn't let him help her, wouldn't let him lift her burdens. It was as if something had slithered inside of her and made her believe she didn't deserve help.

He tells me how on Mama's really bad days I would climb into bed with her, dragging her old travel scrapbook with me, and recount the stories and memories she'd shared over the years to try to bring her back. And some days it worked—some days Mama would perk up at the sound of my voice, and once or twice even got out of bed because of it. But then the mayor would come, and Mama would slip back into her sad state, until eventually even her own daughter couldn't help.

It wasn't unusual for the mayor to make house calls. Back then, he was Dad's closest friend, and Dad never gave it a second thought when Mayor Warman offered to sit with Mama and bring her a glass of tea, black just the way she liked it.

Now that we've got the benefit of hindsight, it's hard for Dad not to blame himself for missing the signs of what the mayor was doing—like how Mama always seemed more despondent after one of Mayor Warman's visits, or how one day she started mumbling all this nonsense about us being better off without her in this slow and drawn-out way that sounded a lot like the mayor's smarmy drawl.

Dad doesn't like to talk about the night she left, but he does it for me. He does it because it helps me piece together the memories I can't recover. He shows me the note she left behind—the three short sentences that now read so clearly like ideas someone else placed inside her head: *I'm a burden. You and Lucy will be better off without me. I'm sorry.*

Dad didn't just make me forget that last night when Mama left me standing in the dirt, begging for her to come back. He took away all the bad stuff in between, leaving me with only the best memories of her. Which is as good as leaving me with only half a mother. In some ways, this perfect version of Mama I've been coveting all these years is a lie. Because Mama wasn't perfect—no one is. She ached. She cried. And ultimately, she left, even if it wasn't her fault.

But she's out there somewhere, maybe still believing all of the mayor's horrible words. Or maybe she went the way of Missy and Manuela's abuela, forgetting herself entirely. But like all the people Mayor Warman hurt over the years, I'm going to find her. I'm going to fix it. I'm going to get my mama back.

"Are you going to see any guests today?" I ask Dad, trying to keep my voice light. I know better than to pressure him.

"Maybe." He bites his lip. "I'll talk to them for a bit. See if that helps. Did Vivi send them into town?"

I nod. "I think a few of them are staying down at the Tumble Inn. Vivi can have someone check on them once she's done checking in this latest crop of guests."

Dad hasn't taken away any burdens since we reopened, even though people still come to see him. He brings them into his office to talk, where he listens to their stories with a sympathetic ear, but ultimately ends up telling them that they need more time to heal. Time, he agrees, is the ultimate healer, and he doesn't want to shortchange it by taking something from someone who can heal all on their own. Maybe one day there'll be someone he decides needs his help, or maybe listening is the only service he'll offer from now on. It's not my choice to make, but I trust he'll know what's right when the time comes.

"All right, I'll be up in my office. Tell Vivi to send them on in when she's ready."

Outside, Vivi takes down the names and phone numbers of the newest arrivals, handing each person an instruction sheet explaining what to expect and a coupon for Patty's Pie Pantry.

"We'll call you when it's your turn with Lucy. In the meantime, you can head into town and enjoy yourselves for a while."

It was Vivi's idea to take the mayor's profits from the mines and invest them back into the town. It only made sense that we spread them around for everyone to benefit from. And there was plenty of fixing up to be done. But the first order of business was an easy one for folks to agree on—Tumble Tree's very first cell tower.

Despite the improvements to the town, after we destroyed the opening to the mines and shut down operations there once and for all, a lot of people still decided to leave. Even after I pitched the idea of turning Tumble Tree into a destination for remembering, and we started hiring people to write letters to the unburdened and to run front of house greeting the guests. Even after Manuela's family had the idea to open a souvenir store and turn the main drag downtown into a place where people can spend time shopping while they wait to have their memories sharpened. Some people just needed a change of scenery, others wanted an escape from everything that happened, and others still worried that the idea wouldn't work and they'd end up having to leave one way or another.

Those of us who stuck it out have been working hard to turn Tumble Tree into a town we can be proud of—putting it on the map, so to speak. It turns out it's not just the people Dad unburdened that I can fix—I can sharpen just about anyone's fading memories, like how I helped Dad remember Mama that day in the park. All I need to do is call back the emotions that start to fade with time, and the memories come back into focus. And it turns out people will pay a lot of money to sharpen the things they've forgotten, especially older folks and students heading into exam season. And they spend a lot of money in town while they're waiting to be seen, especially on the memory tchotchkes Manuela's abuela makes, like the hand-painted signs that say silly things like I'LL ALWAYS REMEMBER MY TRIP TO TUMBLE TREE.

Manuela has been a huge help, too; it was her brilliant idea to advertise "memory sharpening" to local colleges. Based on this week alone, we may have to start turning people away. It's not even lunch yet and the lot's nearly full. Some people in town converted their houses into bed-and-breakfasts to accommodate the overflow, but we've still had to send people to nearby towns because the motels keep filling up. Otis and his dad invested in a new hotel downtown, but construction won't be finished for at least another six months. Until then, we'll have to make do.

I can't promise the town forever. There are still maps to follow.

Cities at the end of highways begging to be explored. Roads that unwind like spools of ribbon. There's a whole world out there waiting for me. But for now, there's Tumble Tree. For now, there are wrongs I can right. And for now, at least, that's enough.

Marco's Yukon jerks into the last remaining parking spot at the back of the lot. My heart does its usual flutter-kick when I catch sight of his crooked half grin. I step out further onto the porch and wave.

His hair flops loosely around his ears. He's been letting it grow long; I think because it makes him look less like his uncle.

The town agreed to keep Mayor Warman in the local jail cell until we could figure out what to do with him. But it turned out we didn't have to look far for him to get the punishment he deserved. State and federal authorities had been tracking the happiness elixir for a while. There were growing reports of people drinking a strange concoction and doing ridiculous things like laughing for weeks on end, unable to stop to so much as eat or sleep. And there were also growing reports of people suddenly seeming to forget themselves for no apparent reason. All it took was an anonymous call to the state police before they swooped into Tumble Tree to collect the mayor.

Some folks worried that the town would be implicated in the mayor's scheme, but it's amazing what a group of people can accomplish when they stand together. As far as anyone outside of Tumble Tree is concerned, the mayor ran his operation in secret and used the black sadness drink to manipulate unsuspecting townsfolk. It's not a lie. Not exactly. We're just leaving out some of the details to protect the folks the mayor took advantage of. I suspect the authorities will be putting the mayor away for a long, long time. Maybe even for the rest of his life. Let *that* be his legacy.

Marco shoves open the Yukon door and nearly falls out onto the dirt. The car's still running, and he leaves the door hanging wide open as he weaves between the other cars in the lot, shouting as he runs.

"I found her!" he yells. "Tell Charlie to get out here! Hurry!"

He's waving a piece of paper over his head, like I'm supposed to have any idea what it is.

Dad comes out of the house, scratching his head at all the shouting. Even the people climbing out of the bus turn to stare as Marco takes the porch steps two at a time.

He bends down to catch his breath, half grin stretching into a full-wattage smile.

"I think we've found her," he says to my raised eyebrows. "Your mama. Someone called this morning and said there's a woman who's been staying with them who looks just like the picture in your ad."

My mouth goes dry. I take the paper from Marco's outstretched hands, fingers shaking.

There's an address scrawled on it in Marco's sideways handwriting.

"New Mexico?" I read, halfway between a sob and a laugh at the idea of Mama being holed up in another desert town this whole time.

"You sure it's her?" Dad asks, hand on his heart as he comes to look over my shoulder.

"I mean, I guess there's no way to know for sure without seeing her, but they said she looks just like her picture. And they said she doesn't have any memories of where she was before she got there. All she has is this picture of a man and a little girl who sound a lot like you two. She showed up a few years ago looking for work. It's some kind of commune or yoga retreat place—I guess a lot of people come there looking for help or looking to put their past behind them. Anyway, I mapped it out. It's just outside of Albuquerque, about a four-hour drive from here. You could get there before the sun sets if you leave now."

"Today?" My tongue feels too big for my mouth. "You're saying I could see her *today?*"

Marco nods. "If you want to. Or tomorrow. Or whenever. Doesn't sound like she's going anywhere."

Dad's arm slides around my shoulders, and then suddenly we're hugging each other and laughing and crying and my heart feels bigger than the sky—bigger than Texas. At some point, Vivi comes to the porch to find out what all the fuss is about, and as soon as Marco tells her what's happened, she's right there with us laugh-sobbing before she marches back out to the parking lot to put up the closed sign and send everyone home for the day.

"Why don't y'all go inside and get cleaned up, and I'll run into town and fill up your car. Keys in the bowl by the door?" Marco asks.

I nod, unable to find any more words. Unable to make myself

think of anything except the picture of Mama we put in all the newspapers—the one Dad took that day at the picnic when I was a baby, when he told Mama the pirate joke.

In the parking lot, license plates glint under the Tumble Tree sun. Oklahoma, Kentucky, Alabama, Louisiana, Texas—so many places in the world, and Mama's just one state over, not even a half day's drive away.

I tip my head back and laugh, and it's like Mama's standing right there beside me in her faded jeans with an expectant smile on her face, marking down the license plates in our notebook like no time has passed. I see her reach past the Oklahomas and Kentuckys to the space labeled *New Mexico*, where she scribbles down a tick mark. Her hair is dark and wild as a storm cloud. Her grin is white teeth and promises.

"I've been waiting for you," she says, reaching for my hand.

"I know," I tell her, and I close my eyes and picture the map on my ceiling, the red star that every memory and every road leads back to.

The star that points the way home.

# Acknowledgments

Thank you to the talented, generous, and kind humans who helped transform this story from a pile of words into a real live book. You will forever have my gratitude.

To my amazing agent, Joanna MacKenzie: thank you for pulling this story out of the slush pile and seeing it for what it could be. You are a tireless advocate, and I am so fortunate to have you in my corner. Thank you, thank you, thank you.

To my editor, Liza Kaplan: thank you a million times over for making my childhood dream come true and for taking this story to new heights. Not only is this book better than I could have imagined because of you, but I learned so much throughout the process. From the bottom of my heart, thank you.

A huge thank-you to everyone at Penguin and the Philomel Phamily for helping to make this dream a reality, including Talia Benamy, Jill Santopolo, Ken Wright, Elise Poston, Gaby Corzo, Marinda Valenti, Sola Akinlana, Ellice Lee, Lathea Mondesir, and Kara Brammer. Thank you also to Jess Jenkins for the beautiful cover artwork.

To Sally Engelfried, Rose Hayes, Lisa Ramee, Kath Rothschild, and Lydia Steinauer, also known as the Panama Math and Science Club, with a shout-out to Keely Parrack: Where do I even begin? I am so lucky to have you in my life. Thank you for being the best crit group a writer could hope for. I've learned so much from you throughout our years together, lost a few pounds from laughing, and then gained them back from wine and those tiny Trader Joe's cheese thingies. Thank you for your words of wisdom, spot-on critiques, brilliant brainstorm sessions, and endless laughs. I wouldn't be the writer I am today without you. You make this whole writing roller coaster a hands-in-the-air fun ride. Thank you.

Thank you to the SCBWI for creating a space for kid lit authors to learn and grow. Special shout-out to the SCBWI team that organizes the Green Gulch retreats. So much of this story was written there—thank you for organizing an amazing event in such a beautiful setting.

Thank you to the Dirty Thumbs, with a special shout-out to Selina, Gabe, and Robyn, for reading and providing input for an early draft of this story. I can't wait to grow old with you at a Wrinkle in Time. Thank you to Gabe and Melanie for the writing chats, brainstorm sessions, and mini retreats in Timber Cove. There's nothing like two hours of writing followed by six hours of rosé to get the creative juices flowing. I think we've got that ratio just about right. And thank you to Rocio for your thoughts on this story when it was just a seed of an idea.

Thank you to Leslie Schrock for the photo session. Is there anything you can't do?

Thank you to my parents and brother, Mike, for your love and support, and for reading to me when I was little. Who knew that *Happy Birthday Baby* read repeatedly would inspire a career? A special shout-out to my mom, Sharon, for leaving her Stephen King books sitting out on the table. Yes, I peeked. Yes, I was too young. No, I don't regret it.

To my husband, Jay, for his never-ending support, thank you. You never complain when I take off for a writing retreat or hole myself up in the office with my headphones on. Thank you for your support of this dream, and your willingness to pull off the highway during road trips so I can explore tiny towns and write about cacti. I love you.

And finally, to anyone who picks up this book and decides to read: thank you for spending time with the voices in my head. I hope you'll remember Lucy, Marco, and Manuela, and that you find your own red star on a map.